finally &
forever

Also by Robin Jones Gunn:

Katie Weldon Series

Peculiar Treasures

On a Whim

Coming Attractions

Christy Miller Series

Sierra Jensen Series

Christy & Todd: The College Years

www.robinjonesgunn.com

katie weldon series

finally & forever

BOOK FOUR

ROBIN JONES GUNN

ZONDERVAN®

ZONDERVAN.com/
AUTHORTRACKER
follow your favorite authors

*For all the Peculiar Treasures who wrote and encouraged me
to continue the tale of Katie and her adventures. Your comments on Facebook
are insightful and motivating. Keep 'em coming!*

With special thanks to Lexie Anders for suggesting the title of this book.

ZONDERVAN

Finally & Forever
Copyright © 2012 by Robin's Nest Productions, Inc.

This title is also available as a Zondervan ebook.
Visit www.zondervan.com/ebooks.

Requests for information should be addressed to:
Zondervan, Grand Rapids, Michigan 49530

Library of Congress Cataloging-in-Publication Data

CIP applied for: ISBN 978-0-310-72971-6

All Scripture quotations, unless otherwise indicated, are taken from the Holy Bible, *New International Version*®, *NIV*®. Copyright © 1973, 1978, 1984, 2011 by Biblica, Inc.™ Used by permission. All rights reserved worldwide.

Second Timothy 1:7 is taken from The New Testament in Modern English, revised edition — J. B. Phillips, translator. © 1958, 1960, 1972. Used by permission of Macmillan Publishing Co., Inc.

Any Internet addresses (websites, blogs, etc.) and telephone numbers in this book are offered as a resource. They are not intended in any way to be or imply an endorsement by Zondervan, nor does Zondervan vouch for the content of these sites and numbers for the life of this book.

Published in association with the Books & Such Literary Agency, 52 Mission Circle, Suite 122, PMB 170, Santa Rosa, CA 95409-5370, www.booksandsuch.com.

Cover design: Cindy Davis
Cover photography: Synergy
Interior design: Michelle Espinoza
Interior composition: Greg Johnson/Textbook Perfect

Printed in the United States of America

---

12 13 14 15 16 17 18 /DCI/ 20 19 18 17 16 15 14 13 12 11 10 9 8 7 6 5 4 3 2 1

K atie Weldon woke with a start.

She drew in a jagged breath and tried to focus. The list of credits for an in-flight movie was running on the small TV screen embedded in the seat in front of her. Her headset was in her lap, and a thin airline blanket covered her legs.

Katie's heart pounded as she slowly turned her head to see the familiar face of the passenger beside her. Eli met her gaze with a steadfast look and the same intensity that had unnerved her more than once during the past year.

I didn't dream this. It really happened. I am on a plane right now on my way to Africa with Eli Lorenzo.

"Am I insane?" The words were supposed to be only a thought, but they tumbled out of Katie's dry lips before she could catch them.

Eli removed his headset and leaned closer. "Did you say something?" His sun-streaked brown hair was mussed up just enough to make him look even more outdoorsy than he usually did. His warm expression seemed to be kept aflame by his coal-gray eyes. He had shaved his goatee at some point when Katie wasn't noticing a lot of details about him, and now rough stubble shadowed his jawline.

"No," Katie answered, "I didn't say anything. I mean, yes, I did, but I didn't mean to." Feeling claustrophobic, she unbuckled her seat belt. "I need to use the restroom."

Eli stepped into the aisle and offered his hand to Katie as she slid out of the row. She didn't accept the offer of assistance but looked away and hurried past rows of sleeping passengers. As soon as she reached the back of the plane, the click of the bathroom's lock served as a starting gun for her emotions. Her pent-up fears took off running as tears streaked down her face.

"What have I done?" Katie pulled a bunch of tissues from the box built into the wall.

What was I thinking? This is crazy!

She blew her nose and took a long look at her reflection in the hazy mirror.

"Come on, Katie Girl. Pull yourself together. You are on an adventure. That's what you were thinking. You wanted to take a risk and you wanted to be with Eli. This is what you wanted, remember?"

She wiped her tears and remembered the kiss, Eli's kiss, their first kiss, the one they had shared almost ten hours ago at the San Diego airport. It was like no other kiss she had ever experienced. Katie could vividly see the expression on Eli's face when he realized that she was at the airport because she had decided to travel to Kenya with him. He had taken her face in his strong hands, looked at her intensely, and asked, "Are you sure?"

Katie's answer was, "Yes, I'm sure."

To which Eli replied, "Then I'm going to kiss you." And he did. Oh, how he did!

Katie touched her lips, stared into the bathroom mirror, and wondered what it all meant. Jumping on a plane and flying off to Africa with Eli seemed to make sense in the middle of the night when her friends, Todd and Christy, helped her to book her flight and encouraged her to make this wild leap into the unknown. Now it seemed crazy. All of it.

It was Eli's African proverb that got to me.

Katie mumbled the words that had sunk deeply into her thoughts when Eli first said them to her in the cafeteria at Rancho Corona

University. "If you want to go fast, go alone. If you want to go far, go together."

And here she was going very far from all that was familiar, and she and Eli were going together.

Katie started to cry again. This was so unlike her.

Stop it. Get a grip.

Wetting a paper towel, Katie held her copper-colored hair up and pressed the towel to the back of her neck. The pulp scent from the damp towel reminded her of the dorm restrooms at Rancho Corona University, the place she had called home for the past few years. Dabbing her tears with the towel, she gave herself a pep talk.

You are a college graduate. You are a competent woman. You have been waiting for an adventure like this for a long time. God opened all the doors for you on this. You know he did. Don't turn into a doubting mush-head now. Go with it.

A whisper of peace settled over her. The stall somehow felt more spacious.

"Okay." She lightened her tone as she looked at her clear green eyes in the mirror and repeated, "This is what's next for my life. I am going to Africa. With Eli. This is a good thing." The words felt like a prayer of acceptance more than a rallying cheer. But it worked; the wave of panic receded.

Katie offered Eli a smile when he rose to let her back into her window seat.

"Are you feeling okay?" he asked once she was settled in.

Katie nodded. She leaned closer. "Would it terrify you if I told you I just came pretty close to freaking out?"

"No." He took her hand in his and wove his rough fingers between hers. "This is a big deal, Katie. You'll probably have a meltdown or two once we arrive in Nairobi. It's okay. It doesn't change anything. All it means is that you're adjusting to a huge upheaval in your life."

Katie rested her head on his shoulder. For the first six hours of the flight, the two of them had talked nonstop about what their expectations were of each other and what would happen once they arrived at Brockhurst, the conference center outside of Nairobi where Eli's parents lived.

Eli's steady, logical approach to this last-minute leap of faith for Katie made everything seem as if a plan was in place for both of them, and all they had to do was show up and do the next thing. Eli's dad worked for a mission organization that helped dig wells in Africa to provide clean water in villages where diseases were rampant. The health and welfare of the people were radically altered by the accessibility to clean water.

Katie was familiar with the work. She had helped to put together a fund-raiser that spring to gather money to dig more wells. Eli assured her that his parents would welcome her with open arms and that she would have plenty of work to do wherever she wanted to jump in, either at Brockhurst, or even in the villages with the well-digging projects.

"Are you having doubts about us?" Eli's lips were buried in her hair as she rested her head on his shoulder.

"I don't know." Katie pulled back and looked at him. "I mean, no. That's what I meant to say. I had a flash of uncertainty a few minutes ago, but I know that I have to remember what you said at the beginning of the flight. We have all the time and space we need to figure out where our friendship is headed. Kenya is just the backdrop for us as we take each day and see what happens."

"That's right. It has to be that way in Africa. Flexibility is the only way to survive in the culture we're going to."

Katie nodded. She understood the words, but the meaning had yet to be discovered. She had no doubt that everything was going to be radically different.

And it was.

From the moment they stepped off the plane in Nairobi, Katie knew she was in another world. The air felt humid and much cooler than she had expected, even though Eli told her they were arriving during the end of the rains. He had explained that, being south of the equator, Kenya had its hottest days from December to early March, and then the rains came until early June. The rest of the year was dry with temperatures in the upper seventies, with another round of short rains always hoped for in November.

Katie followed Eli through customs and on to baggage claim. She thought of how not only had they landed on the other side of the world, but the seasons also were in reverse order. Of course life was going to feel upside down and backwards. But she could deal with that. This was an adventure. She longed for adventure.

So why the anxiety attack on the plane?

Katie overheard someone next to them say "*Hakuna matata*" in a loud voice. She knew she'd heard that saying somewhere before.

"What does that mean?" she asked Eli.

"Relax. No worries."

"That's right. It was in *The Lion King*. Hakuna matata. I need to remember that."

Eli grinned at her.

"What?"

"You've only been here fifteen minutes and you're already speaking Swahili. I knew you'd fit right in."

Katie appreciated Eli's supportive words but she still didn't quite share his optimism.

Once they had pulled their luggage from the congested baggage claim carousel, the first thing Katie hunted for in her large duffel bag was her favorite Rancho Corona University hooded sweatshirt. She pulled it on and realized that when she lifted her arms, she didn't smell as fresh and friendly as she had when she started this journey almost thirty hours ago.

They stepped outside of the baggage claim area, and Katie was assaulted with a myriad of sounds and unpleasant fragrances from the smash of travelers and the log jam of vehicles. It was dark. She had no idea what the local time was. This didn't feel like any airport she had ever been in.

Eli stopped and looked around. Katie watched as a slight smile grew on his face. She knew that this was all familiar to him since he had spent his childhood in several different parts of Africa. For Eli this was home, and he was comfortable maneuvering his way through the throngs of people. It felt strange to watch Eli in these surroundings after having watched him try to fit in to the Southern California setting for the past year.

A man in a white shirt with ebony skin glistening with perspiration made eye contact with Katie and spoke to her with a British accent. "May I take your bag, miss?"

Assuming he was an airport porter of some sort who would carry her bag to the bus stop, Katie said, "Sure. Thanks."

Just as she was about to hand over her heavy bag, Eli grabbed the handle, and in a firm but friendly tone, he said, "I have it. *Asante sana.*"

Trading Katie one of his large, wheeled suitcases for her duffel bag, he creatively slid his arms through the two strap handles and carried the beast on his back. "Here. We need to go this direction."

Katie trotted along beside him. "I thought that guy was a porter."

"That's probably what he hoped you thought."

"Why else would he ask to carry my bag?"

Eli glanced at her and raised his eyebrows. He kept walking. "The question is, where would he have carried your bag off to?"

Katie caught on. "That was a scam? He saw that I was obviously not from around these parts, and he was trying to grab my bag and run?"

"It's possible. I always like to be cautious." Eli adjusted the bulky duffel bag on his back. "I'll tell you one thing. He might have gotten his hands on this bag, but I doubt he could have run very far. What did you bring with you, Katie? This thing is heavy."

"Pretty much everything I own. That's the extent of my worldly possessions. Right there. Thanks for carrying it for me." Katie realized that if she were completely honest with Eli, she would tell him that although he was carrying the extent of her worldly *physical* possessions, she did have another significant possession. She had a lot of money in the bank, thanks to an inheritance she'd received several months ago from a great-aunt she had never met.

During all the heart-to-heart conversations she and Eli had on the plane, Katie never felt quite right bringing up that detail. She wondered if Eli had any idea about her inheritance. One of these days, she knew she needed to tell him.

Eli picked up the pace as they wove through clusters of travelers gathered at the curbside. "Almost there," he called over his shoulder.

Katie knew his parents weren't picking them up. Eli had told her that they were going to take a shuttle bus to where his parents lived, which was about an hour and a half from the airport. He stopped at the end of a line of people and unstrapped the duffel bag, letting it fall to the ground with a thud.

"Careful. I might have something breakable in there."

"Like what?"

"Like ... I don't know. Something breakable." Katie knew the irritation in her voice was noticeable.

"Okay. I'll be more careful."

She tried to calm down by looking around. She saw an older couple with fair skin standing a little farther ahead of them in line. That's when she was struck with the realization of how "white" she and Eli were. She never had felt that way in California, even though she was always around a blend of ethnicities. In California she felt like part of the diverse mix, with her red hair and pale skin. Here she felt like an alien. A white-bread-and-mayonnaise sort of foreigner with noticeably red hair.

"You know what you said earlier about me fitting in? Well, I need you to retract that thought. People are looking at me."

"You'll get used to it." He moved forward, toting the duffel bag as the people ahead of them boarded a small shuttle the size of a large van by US standards.

Katie hung back, assuming that after a dozen or more people had entered with their luggage, the van would be full. The people behind her pressed her forward.

"Come on." Eli hoisted Katie's duffel bag in through the side door that slid open. He then reached for his two large, wheeled suitcases, and someone inside the van extended a hand out to help haul them inside.

"Are we going to fit?" Katie asked.

"Of course." Eli motioned for her to step up into the van.

As she did, she noticed that all the seats were taken. "Where am I supposed to go?"

"Right there is fine." Eli climbed in and stood smashed up against her and all their bags.

The guy behind him started to climb in but then seemed to assess the situation and withdrew. He closed the sliding door, and the van took off with a jerking motion.

Katie was standing facing the back of the van with her head bent down since she was too tall to stand up straight. Eli already had taken a seat on top of one of his suitcases. He patted the top of his knee, indicating that if she was going to have a seat on this shuttle, there it was.

She was sweltering in her hooded sweatshirt and wanted to take it off, but that simple task seemed challenging in the cramped conditions. Reaching out and bracing her hand against the closed window, Katie cautiously sat on Eli's lap, fully aware that a sea of dark faces was fixed on them. An unpleasant mixture of intense perspiration odor, thick dust, and diesel emissions filled Katie's nostrils as she wrapped her other arm around Eli's shoulders and tried to balance herself so she wouldn't be too heavy on his lap. She would have sat elsewhere, on her duffel bag or Eli's other suitcase, if that had been an option. But those had been shoved under the front bench seat, and at the moment a large woman balancing three plastic shopping bags on her lap was using Katie's duffel as a foot rest.

"We should have waited," Katie mumbled.

"Waited for what?"

"The next shuttle," she whispered. Since English was the language that had been taught in Kenyan schools for decades, Katie had a pretty good idea that everyone in the van could understand what she was saying.

Eli didn't seem to be concerned about keeping their conversation private. In a regular voice, he said, "The next shuttle van would probably have been just as crowded."

"At least we could have been the first ones on and gotten a seat."

"We'll get a seat eventually. Not everyone will be going as far as we are."

Eli's words about "going far" reminded Katie of the African proverb, and she couldn't help but swallow a grunt over the irony of it all.

"What?"

"Nothing."

"I heard you just now. You were trying hard not to react to what I said. Why? What was so funny?"

Katie gave in but kept her voice low. "You said not everyone is going as far as we are."

"They're not. They'll get off at the stops along the way, and we'll have a seat before we head up the mountain."

"Never mind."

"No, what was it you were thinking? Tell me."

Katie paused. She took inventory of the moment. Here she was, sitting on Eli's lap, whispering to him her deepest thoughts and riding in a bumpy shuttle bus with a dozen strangers watching her every move. If a school locker suddenly appeared and she was unable to remember the combination, then she would know for sure this was all a dream. A bizarre, surrealistic dream.

Katie looked down at her worn-out tennis shoes. She was in Africa with Eli, and only two other people in the world knew she was here: Todd and Christy. The reality was that Eli was all she had. If this relationship ended up not going very far, then where would she go? What would she do? All her eggs were in one basket, and in a setting like this, Katie was realizing how easily such a basket could be upset.

"What is it, Katie? What are you thinking?"

Katie paused. Eli wasn't like any other guy she had ever known. He didn't sidestep topics, no matter how intense they might be.

"I was thinking of the proverb you told me." She wished she wasn't telling him this. Her whispered words came out with an unwelcomed wobble. She tried to steady her voice. "The part about going far if you go together."

Eli leaned his head closer.

"You said these people aren't going as far as we are and ..."

"And you're wondering just how far our relationship is going to go." This time his voice was low and sounded tender. "Is that it?"

Katie hesitated. She wasn't sure if she liked the fact that he had the ability to read her and was willing anytime, anywhere, to address her deepest thoughts and fears. Turning to her usual defense mechanism, she tried to be humorous.

"Maybe that's what I was wondering. Or maybe I was wondering just how far this van is going to make it on this road."

"Are you saying you don't like getting a free African massage?"

"A what?"

"That's what my mom calls it when we're on roads like this. It's an African massage. No extra charge."

"That's not what I'd call it. It's more like shock therapy, if you ask me."

Just then, the van hit a deep rut in the road. Katie bounced off Eli's lap, lost her balance, and fell across the legs of the woman who was using Katie's duffel bag as a footrest. The woman's grocery bags went up in the air, showering Katie with an assortment of vegetables.

She felt Eli's firm hand grip her arm as the van bottomed out on another rut. A loud explosion sounded and she ducked.

"What was that? Is someone shooting at us?"

Before Eli could answer the van came to an abrupt halt. Suddenly Katie felt something sharp puncture the skin on her shoulder.

I've been hit!

2

"Katie, are you all right?" Eli reached over to help pull her up.

"It's my shoulder. I've been hit."

"It was only a yam and a couple of onions." Eli held up the suspected culprits and handed them back to the woman.

"No. It wasn't that. It was something sharp. I thought it was a bullet." Katie noticed that the driver had opened his door and gotten out. Two of the young men in the van were opening the sliding door on the side, climbing over Eli's suitcase as they exited. Everyone was calm and moving at an even pace as if nothing out of the ordinary had happened.

"What's going on?"

"It's a flat tire. We need to get out. Come on."

"But my shoulder ..." Still dazed, Katie followed Eli's lead and crawled out of the van. He had a hold of both his carry-on bag and hers, but he left their three large pieces of luggage in the van. Katie knew she wasn't imagining the injury. The sharp pain was still there.

"Eli, I'm serious. I think something hit me. I'm not making this up."

"Come around to this side. Stay close to me."

The van was precariously parked alongside of a busy road. They walked carefully into the darkness as cars zoomed by, seeming to take little notice of the wounded vehicle. Eli ushered Katie around the front of the van and over to the side of the road, where the driver

15

was shining a flashlight on the punctured tire. Two other guys stood beside him, taking a look at the damage.

"It's right below my shoulder blade," Katie told Eli. "It felt like a dart went into me." She stretched her arm across her stomach and reached under her sweatshirt and T-shirt. She felt a warm fluid trickling down her back. "Eli, I'm bleeding!"

"You are?" Eli pulled out his key chain and turned on the small attached flashlight. "Let me see. Where is it bleeding?"

Katie was aware that several of the men who had disembarked from the shuttle bus were staring at her. She lifted up the back of her sweatshirt and T-shirt, careful to keep the front pulled down. She would never feel comfortable exposing her back like this in normal situations, but nothing about this moment was normal.

"Can you see what it is? It feels like shrapnel."

"How would you know what shrapnel feels like? Oh, wait. I see why you'd say that. It's the metal thing on your ... on the strap of your ... It went through your skin."

If Katie weren't so uncomfortable at the moment, she would have teased Eli for being unable to say the word *bra* aloud. She immediately knew what the problem was. She had worn her oldest, most mangled bra and packed all her good ones. The small metal piece that adjusted the straps must have snapped in her tumble, and the sharp edge had dug into her back.

"Can you pull it out? It really hurts."

"Are you sure?"

"Yes, yank it out."

Eli gave a tug, and Katie could feel the blood flow down her back. "Where's my bag? I have some tissue in my shoulder bag."

Eli held out her carry-on bag, and Katie fished around in the dark. She found a small packet with two tissues and tried to somehow stick them under the wide part of her bra band to hold the tissues in place. It wasn't a feat she could pull off by herself. "Here. Can you try to put this on the spot where the blood is coming out?"

Katie held still while Eli attempted the sort of patch job that any one of Katie's girlfriends would have had no difficulty accomplishing. For Eli it seemed to be a challenge, making his way around unfamiliar straps, hooks, and strips of elastic.

"How's that? Is that better?" he asked.

"A little. Thanks." She lowered her shirt and noticed that none of the men were staring at her any longer. They all had gone on to the task at hand, which was changing the tire. The tissues didn't really feel good, but at least they would help to stop the bleeding. She realized that, with the strap now broken in two and with all the moving around she had done, the right side of her bra had drooped in the front. It didn't really matter, because she was wearing a baggy sweatshirt. But it felt odd to be held up on one side and set free on the other. Katie tried to fiddle with the strap, but it was pointless. Without a safety pin, she couldn't remedy the drooping.

"Wait right here," Eli said. He headed toward where the other men had gathered by the flat tire.

"Did you just tell me to wait right here?" Katie called after him. "Right. Like, where am I going to go?"

She lifted both of her hands and waited for him to turn around, but he kept going. Katie stood alone in the dark with their carry-on bags at her feet. Several of the people who had been in the van were now walking down the road, carrying their belongings.

"Hello! Hey. Hello? Where are you guys going? What do you know that we should know?"

No one answered her. Eli was beside the driver, holding his flashlight to provide a better view of the jack that was being inserted under the van. One of the men had gathered some large rocks and was trying to wedge them into the right position under the back tire. As Katie watched, Eli and another man pulled off the flat tire from the rim, and like an efficient roadside service team, they put the spare tire in place.

Cars and shuttle buses maneuvered past them and picked up speed once they got by. The air felt saturated with exhaust. Katie couldn't imagine it was safe for the people who had taken off and were walking alongside the road.

She noticed again how much Eli stuck out in the group of men beside the van. It was just as Katie had felt at the airport. His white skin made his the only face she could make out in the dark. He seemed tall. Taller than he had ever appeared to her at Rancho Corona. She knew he was at least four or five inches taller than she was, but when she met Eli, she was dating Rick Doyle, who was over six feet tall and had a commanding, large personality to match his appearance.

Rick would never help anybody change a tire. Especially in a situation like this. But then, Rick would never put himself in a situation like this. He would never come to Africa.

Two unexpected thoughts came to Katie. The first was that right now Eli was more of a man than Rick would ever be. And second was that Eli was the kind of man she wanted to spend the rest of her life with.

Whoa! Where did that come from? Slow down, Katie Girl. You're supposed to be taking this one step at a time—one day at a time, remember? After all the emotional ups and downs you went through with Rick for the past year, you weren't going to put any expectations or projections on your relationship with Eli.

Katie tried to focus on something else. She thought about how hungry she was, how tired she was, and how uncomfortable the puncture wound in her back was. Those elemental points of discontent turned her thoughts back to the present situation.

Before long the reduced group was back in the shuttle and were on the road again. Eli and Katie had a seat this time. Their luggage was now safely stowed in the back of the van, and they continued on the bumpy roads, jostling up and down and side to side on the middle seat. Eli closed his eyes and fell asleep while Katie kept a sharp watch on the road as the driver bobbed and swerved his way up a steep incline. She was surprised to see so much traffic at this late hour. They stopped three times, and all the passengers except for two others got off.

On one of the bumps in the road, Eli woke with a start and turned to Katie in the dim light.

"Hi," she said.

Eli blinked a few times before he seemed to recognize her. Remembering how she'd felt when she woke on the plane, she said, "And you thought this was all a dream, didn't you?"

"No." Eli reached for her hand and meshed his fingers with hers. "Living in California always felt like a dream. One long, surreal dream. But being here, Katie, and being here with you, this feels real. Very real. This is a dream come true sort of real for me."

Katie felt her heart warm at his words. She'd never been anyone's dream come true before. Yet something inside her still felt anxious and unsettled. She couldn't think of how to reply.

In response to her lack of equal enthusiasm, Eli gave her hand a squeeze and seemed content to sit with her in silence as he looked out the side window. Eli leaned forward as if trying to see the road ahead in the headlights' glow.

"We didn't miss our stop, did we?" He called to the driver, "Have we come to Lemuru yet?"

"Five kilometers," the driver called back. "You are for Brockhurst, are you?"

"Yes. Asante."

"What does that mean?" Katie asked.

"Asante? It's Swahili for 'thank you.'"

"How did he know we want to go to Brockhurst? Did you tell him earlier?"

"No, I told him Lemuru. It's logical that we would be going to Brockhurst since it's a center run by westerners for westerners."

"What does that mean?"

"It originally was built by a group from England to serve as a retreat center for missionaries from the US, Canada, and Great Britain. It's used for a variety of services now, like the headquarters for the clean water group my dad heads up. I thought I explained a lot of this on the plane."

"You probably did."

Eli leaned back. He seemed to be studying her expression in the dim light. "Are you okay? How's your back?"

"It's okay." Katie was aware of how gritty her teeth felt and was certain her breath was deadly. Turning her head slightly so she wouldn't blast Eli with her breath, she said, "Thanks, by the way, for not making fun of me when I said I'd been stabbed."

"That's something I never take lightly."

Katie remembered how Eli had told her several months ago that the L-shaped scar behind his left ear had been inflicted on him when he was eleven years old and had wrestled with a knife-wielding intruder.

The van turned onto a narrow road, and Katie could see that they were driving over a bridge. It was too dark to tell if a river was under the bridge or what kind of foliage grew along the roadside. They made another left turn and pulled up short in front of an imposing gate. A uniformed guard emerged from the booth next to the gate and waved to the driver before pressing the button that caused the gate to swing open.

"Is this it?" Katie wasn't sure what to expect, but this seemed much grander than she had pictured a retreat center.

Eli shifted in his seat like a little boy filled with anticipation. "Yes, this is it. We're here."

The van driver pulled up in front of a small building that had a turnaround space in front. A motion-sensitive security light turned on at the front of the stone building and lit up a patch of gorgeous blue flowers lining the front of the narrow porch.

"I'll grab the bags," Eli said. "Can you get the two carry-ons?"

"Sure." Katie snatched up the two smaller pieces of luggage.

As soon as Eli was out of the van with the suitcases, he went over to the driver's open window, and the two of them entered into what seemed like a calm debate. Eli held up some Kenyan shillings, but the driver refused to take them. He spoke in English, but his accent was so heavy, Katie couldn't tell what he was saying. In the headlights' reflected gleam, she could see his face. He was determined. Waving the handful of money at the driver once again, Eli spoke more force-fully. Katie heard him say he would not pay a "skin tax." Was the driver trying to charge them a higher fee because they were white?

Katie reminded herself that Eli was used to this. Such experiences were normal to him. She wasn't sure if it would ever become normal to her.

Glancing at the unlit windows of the building, she wondered if Eli's parents lived there. Were they inside right now, waiting for them? Or had they gone to bed long ago, knowing Eli would wake them when he arrived? What would they say when they saw her?

At the airport in San Diego when Katie surprised Eli by showing up, Eli had surprised her with something he said. He said his mom had a feeling Katie might come home with him. It was kind of cool and kind of freaky that Eli's mom had called this even before Katie knew she was going to Kenya. Eli had said his mother was a praying woman, and she had been praying for this.

Still, she felt jittery about the meeting that was about to take place. *What if Eli's parents don't like me? What if I don't fit in here? Then what am I going to do?*

Eli settled the bill and now the driver headed back toward the gate.

"How much did you end up paying?" Katie asked.

"The set amount. Plus a little more. Not the extra he wanted, but a little more. It's okay. It's how things are done here. Are you ready?"

Katie picked up her carry-on bag and felt a twinge in her shoulder, reminding her of the wound. She switched sides and asked, "Is this your parents' house?"

"No, this is the office. We have to go up the path to where my parents are staying. Are you okay with the shoulder bag?"

"Yes, I'm fine. I can take something else. What do you want me to take?"

"Are you sure?"

"Yes, I'm sure."

They divided the luggage between them as they had at the airport and trekked up a narrow path that was dimly lit by what Katie guessed were solar-powered lanterns wedged into the ground at precise intervals. The air was cool and smelled of green grass. It was still too dark to make out much of their surroundings, but Katie could tell they were strolling past individual cottages along the trail, each of them set off just far enough from each other to provide some privacy and a buffer for noise. Which was good, because the wheeled luggage was making clicking sounds as it rolled over the uneven walkway.

Katie felt out of breath by the time Eli turned down a side path and stopped in front of a cottage. "This is it," he said.

A lovely sight greeted them. In the front window was a single, tall candle that was lit and glowing.

"That is so beautiful," Katie said softly.

She turned to Eli and saw that his eyes were glistening with tears. His jaw was set, his shoulders were back. The expression on his face was one Katie didn't think she had ever seen on him. He looked content.

Katie felt a catch in her throat. She had never had the same sort of response when she went to her parents' home in Escondido. No one had ever lit a candle and placed it in the window for her. She could only imagine what Eli was experiencing right now after the horrendously long journey, to finally be on the doorstep of the place he wanted to be.

How could she describe what she was observing right now? Then she knew.

Eli was home.

Before either of them moved forward to put a foot on the narrow entry porch, the door handle clicked, and the front door began to open.

Katie drew in her breath. This was it. This was the moment she had anticipated and dreaded. She was about to meet Eli's parents.

3

The stone cottage's door opened, and lights snapped on inside and out. Eli's dad emerged, and the moment he saw his son, he shouted, "Elisha!" His arms were around him in an instant. They embraced each other with manly pats on the back, firm handshakes, and then another strong embrace.

Eli's mom appeared in the doorway and rushed to him with no words, only a gush of tears. She kissed his face, held him, and laughed softly as Eli's dad circled both of them with a big hug.

In the light flooding the entryway, Katie could see the expressions of pure delight on his parents' faces. She had never seen anyone greet a grown child with such spontaneous joy. What made the homecoming even more winsome was that both of them were in their pajamas and looked as if they quickly had flung on their robes in the race to the front door when they heard the luggage wheels clacking on the walkway.

Katie had been hanging back in the shadows, not wanting to interrupt this moment. She still wasn't sure how Eli's parents would react when they saw her. She didn't have to wait long to find out. Eli's mom looked up, and the instant she saw Katie, she broke into a huge smile.

"Katie." She spoke the name as if it were a statement. A discovery. She put her hand on her heart and drew in a short gasp. "You came." Her exclamation was barely above a whisper.

The moment Katie heard her name spoken with such an expression of acceptance and love, she felt her fears dissipate. She knew she was welcome in this place.

Eli's dad drew back and expressed much more surprise than his wife had at the sight of their unexpected guest. "Katie?"

"Yeah, this is Katie," Eli said casually. "She followed me home. May I keep her?"

Eli's unexpected joke sent Katie into a round of nervous laughter as she received hugs from Eli's mom and dad followed by a splash of her own tears.

"Come in, please." Eli's mom reached for Katie's carry-on and slipped her arm through Katie's, leading her across the doorstep into their small bungalow. Mrs. Lorenzo's short, silver-gray hair was sticking straight up in the back, as if she had fallen asleep with the back of her head smushed against a sofa cushion. Everything about her shape, haircut, and gait suggested quiet efficiency, as if she were a woman who didn't need a lot of fuss to get her up and going in the morning. Katie could relate to that sort of low-maintenance lifestyle.

In the flurry of all the hugs, the wound on Katie's lower shoulder had been bumped and was sore. She knew that if she took off her sweatshirt in the warm house, she would have an issue with the drooping right side of her busted bra and the bloodstained back of her T-shirt. Not to mention the odors her nervous body had mustered during all her travels. The scent would be obvious if she lifted her arms without the barrier the sweatshirt provided. Not a good way to make a first impression.

Eli and his dad brought in the rest of the luggage as his mom cleared a stack of papers and books from the worn couch that was more of a loveseat than a regular-sized sofa. "Have a seat, Katie. I'll bring some tea. Do you like tea?"

"I love tea."

"Good, that's very good." She disappeared around the corner into what Katie could see was a narrow kitchen. Katie could hear her making swift preparations.

"Do you need some help, Mrs. Lorenzo?" Katie called out.

"No, you just sit. This will only take a minute. And please, call me Cheryl."

Katie glanced around at the disheveled room. The space was small and cluttered with an abundance of stacked boxes and files.

"We're moving our offices," Eli's dad said.

Katie looked up and realized he had caught her scanning the orderly chaos.

"We take possession of our new space next week. You're here just in time to help us make the move." He smiled warmly.

"I would be glad to help."

What surprised Katie the most about Eli's dad was how white his short hair was. The photos Katie had seen on the clean water website must have been taken when he was younger and still had brown hair like Eli's. He had a trim moustache and goatee. Even in his pajamas and robe with the big side pockets and tie hanging all the way down on one side, he looked distinguished.

Eli left the luggage inside the door by a tall bookcase, and, making room on the couch, he settled in next to Katie, putting his arm across the back of the cushion. It felt just right. He seemed to be making it clear to his parents that the two of them were "together," while at the same time giving Katie room to breathe in her warm sweatshirt.

Eli's dad took a straight-backed chair from beside the table covered with lamps, books, and folders and positioned the seat across from the sofa. That left the best spot in the room, a fairly new-looking leather recliner, open for Eli's mom when she returned carrying a tray with stacked teacups, teaspoons, and a plate of shortbread cookies. She placed the tray on top of the nicked up steamer trunk that served as a coffee table.

"Go ahead and have a biscuit. I'll be right back with the chai."

Eli reached for the plate of cookies and politely offered them to Katie first. She took a nibble. His mom returned, and Katie watched as a surreal tea party unfolded in front of her. If Alice felt befuddled at the Mad Hatter's party, Katie felt equally off guard sitting in a stone cottage in Africa holding up a rose-rimmed china teacup and saucer. Eli's mother stood in front of her in a fuzzy, pale pink robe with one collar of her pajama top sticking out at the neck as she poured tea for Katie from a floral china teapot.

Katie thanked her and took a sip. It wasn't chai, or at least it wasn't what Katie called chai. This tasted like a sweet tea latte. Warm and soothing.

Eli's mom poured the other three cups of tea and settled into the recliner. "So, tell us." She looked relaxed and at the same time full of anticipation as she focused her attention on Eli and Katie.

Katie looked at Eli. Clearly his parents wanted to hear the story of how it happened that she was now sitting in their home beside their son. Since they appeared to be so unconcerned about their appearance, Katie felt as if she could be equally relaxed. Even though she didn't want to compare this moment to the first time she and Rick sat down to talk with his parents, the comparison was impossible for her to ignore. The differences between the two encounters were worlds apart. Literally.

Eli calmly sipped his tea. He dipped his chin to Katie in a nod, as if handing off the story to her.

"Well, as you know, I just graduated from Rancho with Eli, and I wasn't sure what to do next. I kept praying and thinking, and I don't know if I can explain how it all fell into place, but I decided to come. Here. To help. To work with you guys, wherever you need help."

"When?" Eli's mom asked.

"I can start tomorrow morning."

"No, I meant when did you decide to come?"

"Last night. Or, well, whatever day that was. Two nights ago, I guess. It was the night before Eli's flight. I was at the home of some friends—"

"Todd and Christy," Eli filled in. His mom and dad nodded, and Katie remembered that Todd and Eli had worked together on an outreach project a number of years ago in Spain.

"Yes, Todd and Christy. She's been my best friend since high school. They helped me think through the decision to come," Katie explained. "It was only a few hours before Eli's flight took off, and I knew this was an opportunity I needed to respond to, and so I did." Her mind felt mushed, and she knew her words weren't coming out as confidently and clearly as she wanted them to.

"She showed up at the airport, and it was a complete surprise," Eli said. "I was checking the board for my departure gate, and when I looked over, there she was. I knew the only reason Katie would be there was if she was coming to Africa with me."

"What did you do?" Eli's mom leaned forward.

Eli looked at Katie and then back at his parents. He said plainly, "I told her if she was sure, then I was going to kiss her."

Katie blushed. She could never talk this openly with her parents.

"And?" his mom prompted.

"She said she was sure. So I kissed her."

Eli's mom leaned back and smiled a closed-lip smile, as if she had just watched the end of her favorite movie and was about as content as she could be with the conclusion.

Katie could think of only a few people whom she felt this sort of acceptance from. Eli's parents weren't as she had expected them to be. She anticipated that they would be nice, innovative, and courageous since they had spent their married life in Africa. But she didn't expect to feel so instantly connected and welcomed into their family.

"It's true that I came because of Eli. But more than that, I came to serve. I want to help in any way I can. So put me to work."

Eli's mom balanced her teacup on her lap, nestling it in the folds of her robe. "There will be plenty for you to do and plenty of time to do it. We appreciate your willing spirit, Katie. And we will put you to work. But not right away. First you need to let your body and your spirit be reset to the African rhythm of life. It's different than in California. You need to settle in. Find your heartbeat. Then we'll put you to work."

"We're glad you're here, Katie," Eli's dad added. "Very glad."

"Thank you. I'm glad I'm here too." She stole a glance at Eli. He winked at her. Katie couldn't remember if she had ever seen him wink before. If she had, she had a feeling she would remember. It was adorable. She tried to wink back but had a feeling the gesture turned out looking more like a nervous tic, because she blinked twice, and both times she felt her lips involuntarily go up.

"I think it's too late to set up Katie in a room in Building A," Mr. Lorenzo said. "What do you think about giving her Eli's room?"

"Please don't go to any trouble. I can sleep on the couch," Katie said. Then she realized the couch was where she and Eli were seated at the moment, and it wasn't long enough to stretch out on. It didn't matter. She was so tired, she felt as if she could fall asleep sitting up.

"No, you take the bed, Katie. I'll sleep on a mat." Eli placed his emptied teacup on the top of the steamer trunk.

Within a quick twenty minutes, everything was arranged, and all of them were off to bed with wishes for good sleep for everyone and promises to catch up in the morning.

Katie was given a bath towel, a washcloth, and an invitation to take a shower if she wanted. She decided to wait until morning and crawled into bed still wearing what she had worn for the past two days, sweatshirt and all, although she did remove her broken bra.

The twin bed had a fitted sheet on the mattress but no top sheet and only a single blanket. The temperature in the room was cool because of the walls that looked as if they were some sort of rock or cement block. The room was packed with computer screens, file cabinets, and stacked boxes. All she had was a narrow trail to reach the bed, but that was all she needed. Everything else could wait until morning. Katie closed her eyes and smiled to herself as she repeated a line from a movie that had become a favorite of hers long ago, "I dreamed of Africa."

And she was pretty sure she would.

The birds woke her long before she was ready to wake up. The cry coming from outside the closed window was like no other birdcall she had ever heard before. It began with what sounded like *tee-oo*, *tee-oo*, *tee-oo*. The cry was repeated exactly three times and followed by a pause. Then, just when it seemed that peace and quiet had returned, the sharp cry sounded again, the same as before, exactly three times.

Katie tried to roll over, but when she did, a searing pain shot through her wounded shoulder. She realized she should have taken a shower last night or at least washed the wound.

Grabbing some clean clothes from her duffel bag that was balanced on top of a stack of boxes, she took her towel and washcloth and slipped into the bathroom. The shower handles worked differently than anything she had experienced before, and it took her a while to figure out the system. Once she did, she was surprised and happy to feel warm water coming out of the showerhead. What a luxury to wash her hair and let the tiny pellets of warm water minister to her back and clean her small wound. She tried to look at it in the mirror but only got a partial view. It didn't seem like much now that the dried blood was rinsed off. She dressed and tried to adjust her strap so that it didn't hit right on the place where the metal clasp had punctured her.

Exiting the bathroom with her hair wrapped up in a bath towel, Katie nearly ran into Eli's mom, who stood beside the door and seemed to be waiting patiently for her turn in the bathroom.

"Hope I wasn't in there too long."

"No, not at all. You're just fine." Her voice was low, and Katie guessed the guys might still be sleeping, which seemed impossible the way the sunlight was flooding through the windows and the birds were in full chorus mode outside.

"Are you ready for some coffee or chai? I haven't started any yet, but you're welcome to poke around in the kitchen and help yourself to anything you see that you would like."

"Thanks." Katie started to walk away and then asked, "What do you like in the morning? Should I make something for all of us?"

"That would be lovely, Katie. Jim is a coffee drinker in the morning. Eli used to be; I don't know if he still is. I prefer chai."

"Okay." Katie put away her clothes and padded on bare feet into the kitchen. It was the least cluttered room in the bungalow and had the least amount of appliances and kitchen kitsch of any apartment she had been in for a long time.

If I had moved into the apartment in the same complex as Christy and Todd, like I had planned, this is what my kitchen would look like. Bare bones basic.

She filled the teakettle on the two-burner stove and realized she needed a match to start the flame. The kitchen filled with the scent of propane, which she remembered smelling on some of the camping trips she had taken in the past with Christy, Todd, and the youth group they worked with. Katie made a mental note to email Christy to tell her she had arrived safely and all was well. She made another mental note that she really should call her parents or at least send them a letter telling them where she was. Not that she thought it would matter. But somebody should know what she had done, where she was. Somebody besides Todd and Christy.

Katie decided she also would send an email to Nicole, who had been a resident assistant with her in the dorms over the past year. It felt a little odd keeping Nicole near the top of her list of forever friends. She and Nicole got along great and had grown close over the past year, but then Nicole and Rick had started to date within what seemed like minutes after Katie had ended her relationship with Rick.

At the time, Rick and Nicole's relationship made sense and seemed to fit. Katie encouraged their getting together. This morning, though, standing alone in the kitchen of this little bungalow, Rick and Nicole and the entire universe that revolved around Rancho Corona University seemed far away.

The teakettle whistled, and Katie realized she hadn't yet found the coffee or chai. She opened cupboards and found an eclectic mix of plates, cups, and bowls. The assortment made her smile. That's how she would have outfitted her kitchen if she had stayed in California.

This was pretty much how she had equipped her dorm—with random bargains she picked up at garage sales and at her favorite clearance store, Bargain Barn.

"Morning." Eli entered the kitchen still wearing the clothes he had worn on the plane. "You look good, Katie."

"You don't," she quipped.

"Just waiting for my turn in the shower. The shower certainly did you some good. How's your back?"

"It's okay." She crossed her arm over the top of her shoulder and reached to give the affected area a pat. When she did, she flinched at the tenderness.

"Is it still sore?"

"A little."

"When you got your yellow fever and typhoid shots, did you also get a tetanus shot?"

Katie thought a moment. "I think so. Yes, I'm pretty sure. Don't they last for, like, ten years or something?"

"I think so. There might be a doctor staying here at Brockhurst in case you need someone to look at that for you."

"I'm sure it will be fine. I'll ask your mom if she has some ointment I can put on it."

Eli reached into one of the cupboards and pulled out a metal tin. When he opened it, the aroma of ground coffee filled the small space. He pulled out from the bottom cupboard an old-fashioned metal coffee percolator. Katie wasn't sure she knew how it worked, so Eli showed her how to fill it with drinking water and put the grounds into the round canister that was dotted with holes. The canister, with a slender cylinder running up through the middle of it, acted as the filter.

"When the water boils, it will go up through this tube in the middle and come out the top, pouring over the grounds in this canister." Eli snapped on the lid. "You have to watch it so that the water doesn't boil over, and you can't let it percolate too long or it makes the coffee too strong."

"Okay, can do." Katie wondered what was next. What sort of wonderful breakfast might they create together? She was so hungry. Scrambled eggs and bacon sounded divine. Or pancakes and sausages.

"Should I start to make breakfast?" she asked. "Or does your mom like to have the kitchen to herself when she cooks?"

"I'm sure she wouldn't mind if you started something. She might have been planning to just have *ugali*."

"Is that as in, 'Eww, golly, Miss Molly'?"

"No, that's as in ugali, the daily bread of Kenya. It comes from maize and looks like white cement, but it fills you up. And it's inexpensive."

"White cement for breakfast? Okay, now you're just making up stuff."

"Am I?" Eli grinned and walked away.

"What? Are you trying to tell me you're serious?"

"It's my turn in the shower," he called back to her. "Just relax. You'll like it. And I bet you'll like the *chapatti* too."

Katie stood alone in the kitchen and mumbled, "*Ugali? Chapatti? Seriously?* Those can't possibly be real words, let alone foods."

She went back to searching for a box of chai tea bags and thought about how she once told Christy that she would only eat foods from her four preferred food groups: sugar, fat, preservatives, and artificial flavoring. That was back in high school, right after she had broken up with Michael, the health food buff and exchange student who had come to their school in Escondido from Northern Ireland.

Katie smiled to herself remembering that season of her life. Oh, how much she had changed since then.

She thought about Mrs. Lorenzo's admonition to let her body and spirit settle into the rhythms of Africa. That process might take a little while. But she was excited to dive into the challenge of all the changes that were before her.

The thing Katie was discovering about Eli was that she couldn't always tell when he was serious and when he was teasing her. She liked that about him. She liked watching him come "home" and settle into his natural rhythm. It helped Katie to understand how challenging it must have been for him to make the adjustments to the culture and fast-paced lifestyle of Southern California.

Katie thought of all the times during the past year when Eli seemed to be staring. Perhaps it was his way of simply standing back and observing. Katie had tried to help him last fall by giving him a signal when he was doing the staring thing, but now she was beginning to understand how concentrated observing was a normal response in an unfamiliar situation.

For Eli this was familiar. Comfortable.

For Katie even the birds spoke a different language. And apparently chai didn't come in a box marked "chai," because she had no success finding it in any of the cupboards.

Leaning against the sink, she waited for someone to come in the kitchen and teach her the basics of how to prepare a Kenyan breakfast. She really hoped Eli was teasing about the ugali.

Before Katie put her head on a pillow at the end of her first full day in Kenya, she had compiled an extensive list of "Notes to Self." During college she came up with a variety of short reminders whenever she wanted to make sure she didn't step into the same awkward situation again or fumble and say the wrong thing a second time.

Here in Kenya the note-making seemed essential if she was going to find her rhythm, as Cheryl had suggested the night before. Even calling Eli's mom "Cheryl" was a different rhythm for Katie and therefore went on her list of notes. Other top reminders included:

- Don't make fun of any food offered to you. (Or at least wait until you're by yourself and can crack yourself up with silent jokes about both the names of local favorites as well as the fact that ugali does look like white cement and tastes about the same as one would expect dry cement to taste.)

- Just listen instead of trying to process everything aloud. For instance, attempting to mimic the early-morning birdcalls when you are being introduced to the director of the Brockhurst Conference Center is unnecessary and comes out as an odd little sound you can keep to yourself from now on.

- Slow down. Apparently it's normal to walk more slowly here and linger a little longer after a meal. You need to calm down and slow down.

Katie rolled on her back in bed and decided to stop with the notes to self for the moment and try to downshift. This first day had kept her in a state of constant surprise. She knew jet lag had to be part of the reason for that. But a bigger part was that nothing was as she had expected. And that was saying a lot, because she had very few expectations.

The family breakfast time included Eli's dad reading from the Bible and the family praying together. Katie loved it.

She also loved the tea, or "chai," Cheryl had prepared for them. It was as delicious as the chai she had served the night before and the preparation was an eye-opening experience. First Cheryl boiled two cups of water in a saucepan and added about four teaspoons of loose tea leaves. She then poured in two cups of cold milk and what looked like about an eighth of a cup of raw sugar. Handing Katie the spoon, Cheryl told her to keep stirring the concoction. At just the right moment, Cheryl pulled the saucepan from the heat before it boiled a second time.

Then she poured the steaming beverage through a large sieve that caught the spent tea leaves, and the faintly fragrant mixture was poured into mugs.

"Lots of people like Kenyan chai with cardamom and ginger mixed in," Cheryl said. "I like it plain, so that's usually how I fix it."

Katie took a sip and knew this was going to become her new go-to comfort beverage. It was thick and sweet and certainly helped the not-so-tasty ugali to go down.

Cheryl had explained that she only used a certain type of tea leaves when she made chai. She opened her tea canister again and showed the deep black contents to Katie. "See how finely they're chopped?"

"It almost looks like ground coffee," Katie said.

"Another tip is always to shake the canister first or stir the tea up with a dry spoon — just in case some bugs are burrowed in the chai. If the tea moves on its own before you put it in the boiling water, give it a good sift and remove the intruders before using."

"Got it." Katie considered adding that tip to her list of notes to self but had a pretty good feeling she wouldn't forget that one.

The same commonsense spirit of "adjust as you go, and make use of all your resources" was in effect the rest of the day, as Eli and his parents helped to settle Katie in her new digs. She was assigned Room #3 in Building A, located behind the main office. As a newer accommodation, the building was where the single, long-term visitors stayed at Brockhurst.

Her room was in the middle of a stretch of six individual rooms connected by common walls in a long building with a red tile roof. The rock composite construction made her room feel private, secure, and quite cool. She had no heater, but the bed came with two blankets. Under the single window by the front door was a narrow desk with a lamp. Beside her bed was an end table with another lamp, and across from the foot of her bed was a wardrobe-style dresser made of dark wood with engraving along the sides. Katie ran her fingers over the vine carving and admired the craftsmanship that had gone into it. She was impressed. This wasn't a precut piece of furniture like the bookshelf one of the girls in her dorm had tried to put together last year with a tiny screwdriver and glue.

The best part was that her room had an attached bathroom with a shower. She was used to living in a dorm where the toilets, sinks, and showers were down the hall. It seemed like a luxury to have her own bathroom only a few steps away from her bed.

"And here I thought I was going to be roughing it when I came to Africa," Katie said when Eli showed the room to her.

"It's still a jungle out there," Eli said. "You'll want to be sure to keep your bathroom window closed at night."

"Right. Your mom told me about the bugs and how to get them out of the tea."

"Bugs? I'm talking about keeping the monkeys out of your room."

Katie grinned. "Of course. The monkeys." She thought he was kidding about the monkeys but couldn't be sure since Building A backed up to some dense foliage as if the building were nestled on the edge of a forgotten jungle.

After leaving her luggage in her room, Katie and Eli went on a hand-holding, grand tour of the Brockhurst grounds. The conference center was beautifully landscaped and much more expansive than Katie had realized. The high altitude, rainy climate, green grass, and stone cottages spread across the vast conference center made her feel more like she was in an English village than an African locale. It seemed impossible that a monkey would ever find its way to such a place.

Eli stopped at a large, impressive, hand-carved bench that was strategically placed under a shady tree in the middle of a grassy area. "This is my favorite bench," Eli said.

Katie thought it was cute that he had a favorite bench.

"If you ever can't find me, try looking here." He stretched out to demonstrate how it was the perfect length for an afternoon nap and how the armrests had been built at just the right height if you were sitting at the end and holding a book. He smoothed his hand over the well-worn log that formed the perfectly curved backrest.

"A man named Martin made this bench. He was a big man from Belgium with huge hands and a deep love for this place. He taught me a lot about construction and woodwork. Whenever he would announce that he was going to start a new project somewhere on the grounds, I tried to get on the volunteer crew list."

"I'd like to meet him," Katie said.

"I'd like you to meet him too." Eli paused a moment and added, "It'll be in heaven, though. Not here. He left two years ago. He was eighty-eight and working on a wardrobe for Building A. It could have been the one in your room."

Katie remembered noticing the carved details running up the wardrobe's side. Even at a glance when she moved her things in, she knew it was a special piece of furniture.

Eli concluded his thoughts about Martin by saying, "One of the other guys working with him that day told me that one minute Martin was rubbing oil on the finished dresser, and the next minute his body was sort of crumpled on the floor. He said it was as if Martin's huge spirit rose and left his body in an instant, and all that was left was a pile of skin and bones. And those huge hands of his."

Katie had never heard anyone talk about a person's death like that. The raw, elemental atmosphere of this place seemed to evoke unfiltered discussions and responses.

Dinner that night confirmed her impression when they joined the rest of the staff and visitors for simple bowls of vegetable soup and soft dinner rolls in the main dining hall. Direct communication was best. Information wasn't couched in a way to make sure no one was offended. The spirit of the conversations was open, as if all of them were family and could speak freely, even if this was the first time they had met.

After dinner Eli led the way to his second favorite spot at Brockhurst, located above the dining hall. This well-designed lounge area was called the Lion's Den. At the far end was a private area with sofas in front of an impressive fireplace. At the other end was a nice little café called the Coffee Bar. Eli explained that this was one of the places where both of them would most likely end up helping out.

"Sounds good to me. When do we start?"

"Relax, Katie. Give yourself a chance to settle in."

"I feel ready to go. You can put me to work. Honest, I'm not tired at all."

Eli suppressed a grin. "Just wait."

Katie soon discovered what he meant. By seven o'clock that night she felt as if all her batteries had run out. Here she was in bed at the unheard-of Katie-bedtime-hour of seven thirty, thinking again about the monkeys. She still wasn't convinced when it came to Eli's warnings about the occasional brazen primate that found its way through the jungle growth and didn't hesitate to wedge itself through the bars that covered the bathroom window to ransack a room in search of snacks. Nevertheless, she made sure all her windows were closed before she slipped into bed that first night in her assigned room.

That may have deterred any marauding monkeys, but the closed windows didn't stop the distinctive, early morning birdcalls from finding their way to Katie's ears on her second morning in Kenya. They seemed determined to rouse her so that she would get up, pull back the curtains, and discover what the other sound was this morning. It was rain.

A sheet of silver rain splashed against the metal roof and ran in rivulets down the angled walkway. The morning light was dim. Katie's room was cold. She wished she could make a cup of her new favorite comfort drink. Especially on such a chilly morning.

Katie got up and dressed in several warm layers. She found a baseball cap she'd packed and was glad that at least her head would be covered since she didn't have an umbrella.

Charging her way uphill to the Lorenzos' cottage in the downpour, she knocked softly on the door. No one answered. She felt odd trying the doorknob and letting herself in. Cheryl had invited her to come to their cottage when she woke up, but she hadn't made it clear if they would leave the door unlocked. Katie didn't know the protocol when it came to letting herself in to use the kitchen.

Rather than knocking louder and risking the possibility of waking everyone, Katie dashed through the rain and climbed the steps to the Coffee Bar above the dining hall.

A wonderful sight greeted her. To the right of the entry, in a well-situated meeting area, a fire was lit in the large hearth. The slender red flames lapped at the stacked, dry logs, filling the area with warmth and a sense of comfort. Facing the stone hearth was a tattered sofa, and someone wearing a knit beanie cap was sitting on the sofa with his head bent.

Katie recognized the beanie and the free-for-all brown hair that tumbled out at the edges. Slipping out of her soaked jacket, Katie took off her baseball cap and shook her rain-kissed hair. The wood floor creaked as she made her way over to the sofa and said, "Hey, Tarzan."

Eli didn't turn to look at her.

Katie stepped around to the front of the couch and felt the delicious warmth of the fire. She smiled when she saw why Eli hadn't responded. His head was dipped because he had fallen asleep in front of the fire with his Bible open in his lap. In the same way he had slept so deeply on the bumpy van ride from the airport, he kept sleeping even after Katie sat beside him and put her legs up next to his on the hassock. She took off her shoes and wiggled her stockinged toes, relishing the warmth coming from the fire.

Katie leaned over to see where Eli had been reading in his Bible. It was open to the book of 1 Thessalonians. She looked closer and saw that he had underlined parts of chapter 3.

"May the Lord make your love increase and overflow for each other ... May he strengthen your hearts so that you will be blameless and holy in the presence of our God and Father."

Katie also noticed that Eli had written something in the margin that looked like it started with a *K*, but his arm was covering part of it so she couldn't see what it said. She considered tickling his nose so he would lift his hand to swat away the imagined bug while she caught a glimpse at what he had written.

Did he write my name in the margin beside those verses? Is he praying those verses for us?

Katie leaned back and smiled. It seemed like just about the most romantic thing a guy could ever do, to write her name in the margin of his Bible next to a passage about love increasing and overflowing and God strengthening their hearts.

Katie couldn't say she remembered ever reading all the way through either 1 or 2 Thessalonians, but she had a feeling they were going to become her new favorite books in the Bible.

Is this what you desire for us, Lord? Are you going to make our love increase and overflow for each other?

She read the underlined portion again. *Strengthen our hearts, Father. Make us blameless and holy before you.*

Katie drew in the soothing scent of the burning wood and felt as warm inside as she was feeling outside from the delicious fire that had turned her feet toasty. She looked at Eli, secretly wishing she could figure out how to cuddle up to him without being too invasive or interrupting his sleep.

Her snuggle plan was cut short when the door to the lodge opened. It sounded as if a stampede were going on, with everyone stomping feet and speaking in loud voices about this being the place to go for coffee.

Katie glanced at Eli. He had woken up and looked dazed, as if he didn't remember where he was or why Katie was there beside him.

"Hi," Katie greeted him.

"Hey." He looked at her more closely.

"Remember me?"

He grinned and rubbed his right eyelid. "So, what's going on?"

Katie chuckled softly.

"What?"

"Every time you wake up, you look like you have amnesia."

Eli kept a straight face. "What's amnesia? I used to know what it was, but I think I forgot."

"Oh, well then, let me help you with your memory. My name is Princess Hakuna Matata, and it just so happens I'm the most captivating woman you have ever met."

"I do remember that."

"Yes. But wait, there's more. You have vowed to come to my rescue if the jungle monkeys break into my cottage."

"Right. It's all coming back to me now. The monkeys." He squinted and tilted his head. "Princess Hakuna Matata, huh?"

"Yes. It's the only Swahili I could think of at the moment."

Eli pulled his beanie off his head and tried to smooth back his hair, which was pointless now that his hair had grown out and the natural wave pulled his locks every which way. "Your ol' personality seems to have finally caught up with you. I take it you're not feeling as skiddish as you were."

"Have I been skiddish?"

Note: Use of "skiddish" (+ variations) s/b "skittish"! GJ

Eli lowered his chin as if waiting for Katie to answer her own question.

"There's an explanation for my skiddishness. Over the past few days I have not been sufficiently caffeinated. You can change that all right now. You're buying, remember?"

"Yes, of course. I remember everything now. You followed me to Africa because of my wealth. All along I was hoping it was because of my charm, but I see how it is."

"Sorry you had to find out this way," Katie teased.

Eli closed his Bible and got up. "Come on, Princess Hakuna Matata. Let's go get caffeinated." He looked beyond Katie to see the group that had created the stampede. "Oh, good. They're here. Come on." He held out his hand, and Katie slipped her hand in his so he could help her to rise from the mushy sofa. She didn't know why he was so energized all of a sudden. "Did you talk to any of them yet?" he asked.

"Who? The herd that just entered?"

"Yeah, it's the group from Rancho Corona. They arrived a little after midnight. My dad and I helped to check them in. They had a great time in the village."

"This is the group from school that you helped to train? They're staying here?"

Eli looked at her. "Now who's the one with amnesia? I know I told you on the plane that they were coming."

She had forgotten about the group. Katie felt suddenly shy about holding Eli's hand. Her skiddishness returned and she didn't know why. They had held hands yesterday when they walked around the conference center, but no one knew her. She wasn't sure who was in the group from school and if they might know her or Eli. Clearly Eli didn't have any qualms about letting anyone and everyone know that they were together.

As she and Eli approached the group, Katie recognized three Rancho students, and all three of them happened to be people she liked and trusted. She had gone to part of the first meeting at school for this mission trip because she had hoped Rick would join her at the training so the two of them could go on the trip to Africa. But Rick said he had no interest in ever going to Africa, and that was the end of Katie's consideration of the trip.

She now realized that she could spend a lot of time comparing the differences between Rick and Eli, or she could let it go. Comparing them wouldn't accomplish anything. Rick was then; Eli was now. College was then; Africa was now. She was on a good path. There was no need to compare anything or to feel hesitant about being with Eli.

Yet she did feel hesitant. Just a little. The effect of seeing the group of the same students she had been around on campus such a short time ago made her realize how much had changed in less than a week.

"*Jambo,*" Eli greeted the group.

All eight people in the group turned and greeted Eli with enthusiasm.

"Hey, Katie!" One of the guys came over and gave her a side hug. "I didn't know you were going to be here."

"I didn't know either," she said blithely.

"What are you doing here?" he asked.

"I ... we ..." She looked at Eli. "We were just going to get some coffee."

"No, I mean, what are you doing here" — he spread out his arms — "in Kenya?"

"I'm going to be helping out. Here at Brockhurst."

"Really? For how long?"

The group all seemed to be staring at her, waiting for a reply. She could tell some of them were fixated on the sight of her and Eli holding hands. Katie tried to slowly pull her hand away, but Eli held on a little tighter.

"I'm staying indefinitely." Katie felt something inside her go wobbly when she said "indefinitely." It was a true answer from her heart, but it was so — indefinite.

"That's great, Katie!" One of the girls offered a supportive smile and nod. Katie remembered Kaycee Uy from the World History class they had together two years ago. Kaycee's straight, dark hair was longer now, but her warm brown eyes expressed the same kindness they had when Katie had last rattled off to her one of her rants about all the reading they had to do for their history class. Kaycee's encouraging expression meant a lot to Katie now.

"Do you know what time the Coffee Bar opens?" Justine, one of the other girls asked. Katie remembered her, because when Katie had to sign her in for an event, it took three tries before Katie had assembled the letters in Justine's last name in the right order: V-o-n-d-e-r-h-e-i-d-e. The last time Katie had talked to Justine, she was transferring to another college in Kentucky. This morning she looked like a country fresh girl, with her dark hair pulled back in a ponytail, her great smile showing off her straight teeth, and a happy gleam in her clear eyes. She looked way too awake to be in serious need of coffee the way Katie felt she was at the moment.

These were her fellow Rancho Corona friends. Katie didn't know why she still felt so reserved in front of them.

Eli lifted his arm to look at his watch while still holding Katie's hand. "I'd say the Coffee Bar should open in about a minute and a half."

Katie and the others looked at the closed sign and the unattended counter. Why did Eli think someone would come sliding in and be on duty in a minute and a half?

The answer became clear when Eli gave Katie's hand a tug and briskly led the way behind the counter. Apparently he was the volunteer employee with the morning shift at the Coffee Bar. Still holding on to Katie's hand, he led her farther behind the counter, where the others couldn't hear them, and asked, "Are you okay?"

"Of course."

He gave her a piercing look.

She lowered her voice and turned away from the group. "I felt a little embarrassed for some reason."

"Of me?"

"No, I'm not embarrassed of you. Not at all."

"Then what?"

"I don't know. I guess I'm embarrassed that this—you and me—is so soon. That we started 'going together' so quickly."

"According to your time frame, it may seem quick, but for me it's been a year."

Katie knew that Eli had set his affections on her when she was still dating Rick. Eli had hung in there, patiently waiting and praying.

She tried to explain what she had felt so that he wouldn't take her embarrassment personally. "I don't know what some of them might think about us being together."

Eli pulled back. "What does it matter what they think?"

Katie smoothed back her hair. "You're right. What does it matter? Why am I worried about that?"

"Exactly. If you're going to call yourself Princess Hakuna Matata, you need to remember what it means. 'No worries.'"

Katie smiled.

"If you're going to find pointless things to worry about, you're going to have to change your name."

"Not a chance, Lorenzo."

Eli gave her a grin. "Well, maybe we should leave the possibility of a name change open. Someday."

It took Katie a minute to put together the pieces and to realize that he was saying they should leave the possibility open that one day her last name might be changed to Lorenzo. She felt her face flush. Eli had gone to work grinding coffee beans, as if his last comment hadn't carried such weighty possibilities.

Katie didn't have time to process what he had just alluded to, because Eli had taken command of the Coffee Bar, and she was trying to keep up with him as he walked her through the steps to sign in, wash up, start the espresso machine, and serve the students who were placing their orders from the handwritten menu on the blackboard hanging over the counter.

Once again Katie felt her worlds collide. A year ago at this time she was learning the ropes at the café Rick managed. He was the one

showing her all about food service. What also felt strangely familiar
to Katie was that when Eli had come to a pizza night last fall, he had
ended up serving beverages to everyone and making himself right at
home as he looped Katie into serving alongside him. Here they were,
serving beverages again to probably at least one person who had been
at that pizza night.

As soon as everyone had been served, Eli said, "It's your turn.
What would you like? I'm buying, remember?"

"I didn't forget. I'd like one of those mochas like you made for
Justine."

"You got it." Eli first pulled some Kenyan shillings from his
pocket and followed the protocol on the way to take the money and
make change that he had explained to Katie earlier. She watched him
make her mocha and then asked what he was going to have so they
could go sit with the rest of the group.

In a lowered voice, Eli said, "That was all the money I had on
me; so how about if you drink as much as you want and save me a few
good swigs at the end?"

The first thing Katie thought was how impressed she was with
Eli's integrity. He could have made anything he wanted to drink, and
no one but Katie would have known that he hadn't paid for it. The
next thing she thought was how her favorite part of a mocha was the
last few sips.

"No way." She put on a stern expression. "You're not getting the
dregs of my mocha. You and I both know that those last few swigs are
the best. All the good stuff settles on the bottom."

"You are one determined woman, aren't you?" Eli returned the
teasing expression.

"Have you already forgotten how you tried to give me a parking
ticket at school last fall and how I fought to get out of it?"

"No, I haven't forgotten."

Reaching for her hair, Eli took a few strands and rubbed them
between his thumb and forefinger. The tender gesture matched the

tender expression on his face. "I haven't forgotten anything, Katie Girl. Not a single thing."

Katie pulled back, not sure what to do with his expression of affection. She gave him a playful, taunting look. "Nice try, Lorenzo. But you're still not getting my mocha dregs."

"I had a feeling you would say that." Eli leaned back, crossed his arms, and added, "And that's such a bummer, because it looks like you're going to have to find someone else to be your wild monkey patrol guy."

"What?" Katie put her hands on her hips. "You can't blackmail me like that."

"It's the way of the jungle, sweetheart. Share your mocha dregs or chase your own wild monkeys. It's up to you."

"Fine." Katie shot him a sideways look. He seemed to tower over her, grinning and looking like he was about to beat his chest and let out a crazy Tarzan holler.

Inside, Katie felt as if Eli had scooped up her heart in his brawny arms, and the two of them were swinging through the air on a jungle vine.

A nd you're sure you got a tetanus shot before coming here, right?"
The doctor looked at Katie over the rim of his glasses.

"Yes, I checked. It's listed on the papers I brought with me. They're in my shoulder bag over there."

Eli's mom lifted Katie's bag from where she had left it beside the desk in one of the guest rooms in Building C where Dr. Powell and his wife were staying. Cheryl brought the bag over to Katie so she could pull out the copies of her immunization forms.

It had been four days since she and Eli had arrived, and the odd little wound on her back was continuing to bother her. That morning she told Cheryl about how the injury had awakened her in the night because it felt hot and was throbbing. Cheryl took a look at it and said a doctor needed to take a look. Blessedly, Dr. Powell and his wife were staying at Brockhurst for two weeks before they returned to the village where they lived and worked in Sudan.

"Yes, this is all in order," Dr. Powell said. "You got all the right immunizations. That's the good news. But you definitely have an infection in the wound. I'm going to clean it out for you, and then we'll see if we can start you on an antibiotic. Do you have any allergies to any medication?"

"No, not that I know of."

"When was the last time you took an antibiotic?"

49

Katie couldn't remember. Aside from catching a cold or the flu every few years, she was a healthy person.

"Any other symptoms?"

"I'm really tired."

"Have you slept much since you arrived?"

"Not much. Only about four hours at a time before I wake up. It takes a while to fall back to sleep, and then I only manage to get in another couple of hours before I wake up again."

"That's not unusual. You'll adjust the longer you're here. The formula is that it normally takes one day for every hour of the time difference before your internal clock is set to the local time. What is the time difference from California? Isn't it eleven hours?"

"I thought it was ten," Cheryl said. "Or is that only with daylight savings?"

The doctor turned back to Katie and said, "Whatever the difference, the point is you've been here a few days already. Give yourself another week, and you'll be less fatigued. In the meantime, avoid caffeine and take short naps in the afternoon if you can. I'll see what I can do about some antibiotics for you. If I'm unsuccessful, you might have to take the prescription into Nairobi."

Katie noticed the expression on Cheryl's face that seemed to indicate she wasn't thrilled about having to go to Nairobi.

"Is that a problem?" Katie asked. She liked the idea of seeing the countryside in the daytime and going back to Nairobi.

"It can be," Cheryl responded. "We'll see. Last month we had a guest visiting us from Canada. She forgot to bring her blood pressure medication, and we had to take three trips into town and wait in long lines at several places before we finally located what she needed. The antibiotics shouldn't be as difficult." She turned to Dr. Powell. "Don't you think?"

"I'm afraid I never know. I'll look into it right away. Can you think of anything else you or Jim need while I'm hunting down the antibiotics?"

"No. We've both been managing to stay pretty healthy."

"That's always good to hear. I saw Eli working at the Lion's Den last night. He's looking the best I've seen him in years. His time away at college must have been good for him."

"It was very good." Cheryl offered Katie a small smile. "Katie went to school with him, and they both graduated a few weeks ago. She's planning to be here for, hopefully, quite some time."

Dr. Powell gave Katie's face a closer exam, as if checking for symptoms of a fatal crush. He must have found what he was looking for, because his diagnosis was, "Well, that's the best news of the day. For both you and Eli."

Katie nodded but didn't try to offer any sort of explanation. She thought of how the conversation had gone around the table yesterday morning when she and Eli "shared" her mocha and sat with the other Rancho students. Eli carefully had dodged every question that was an attempt to corner him into clarifying how serious he and Katie were about each other. The best line he used that morning was, "We're content to figure it out as we go."

Katie liked that, because she did feel content. Eli was finding all kinds of clever ways to make his feelings known to her, and her heart was responding to every small gesture and message he sent. But Eli was making it clear that the relationship was theirs to explore.

Dr. Powell patted Katie's wound with a cotton pad soaked in something that felt cold and smelled awful. She winced at the sting.

"My wife and I have a deep affection for Eli," Dr. Powell said. "Did he tell you we happened to be here six years ago when he went through his worst bout with malaria?"

"No. I didn't know Eli had malaria. Didn't he take his malaria pills?"

"You can get malaria even if you've taken all the precautions."

"I didn't realize that."

Dr. Powell finished cleaning and patching her wound and pulled down the back of Katie's shirt. He took another look at her immunization papers and glanced at his watch. "I need to meet some folks over at Building A. I'll let you know what I find out about the antibiotics.

Great meeting you, Katie. I'm sure we'll be seeing you a lot in the future."

"Not if I can help it," Katie said.

Dr. Powell and Cheryl both looked startled at her reply.

"I meant, you know, since you're a doctor, I want to stay healthy so that I don't have to see you often. As a patient."

"Oh, I see. Well, I meant that I would see you around here. It's a small community of people who come and go and use this place as a haven. I'm sure you'll get to know a lot of wonderful folks as they pass through."

"I look forward to that." This time Katie didn't try to be clever. She followed Cheryl out the door and into the rain.

It had been raining off and on for the last three days, and the walkways were slick. Cheryl held a wide umbrella over the two of them, and they walked close together back to the Lorenzos' cottage.

"I didn't know Eli had malaria," Katie said. "Dr. Powell made it sound as if it was pretty bad."

"It was. He pulled through, obviously, but it was a bad bout. Unfortunately, once you get malaria, you always have it in your system. The sweats and chills can show up years after you were first infected. The immunizations help tremendously, but they're not a guarantee you'll never get it."

Katie felt sobered by this bit of information. She felt as if she had done everything she needed to protect herself from any tropical diseases, and yet she already had managed to get an infection by not properly cleaning out her small puncture wound. She knew better than to leave it untouched all night as she had, with just a couple of tissues pressed up against it. If she had ignored the same injury back at school, she could have easily gotten an infection there as well. Malaria, though, was something she hoped never to have to deal with.

"I'm glad Eli was okay," Katie said. "I didn't know it was still so prevalent."

"Not everyone gets it." They walked a little farther before Cheryl added, "I've never contracted malaria. Jim has. And so did our son Andrew, of course."

Katie stopped walking. Cheryl came to a halt and turned to look at Katie. She stepped back to where Katie stood and held the umbrella over both of them.

"Eli has a brother?"

Cheryl looked surprised. "He didn't tell you?"

"No."

"That's understandable. Andrew passed away before Eli was born. He was only four months old when he died from malaria."

Katie felt a clench in her gut. She couldn't imagine what it would be like to lose an infant. "Cheryl, I didn't know. I'm so sorry to hear that."

Cheryl nodded and looked away. "I can see why Eli wouldn't have said anything to you about him, because Andrew was never really part of Eli's life."

Katie could see the pain on Cheryl's face even though she spoke with quieted emotion.

With equally quieted sympathy, Katie said, "But Andrew was part of your life."

Cheryl looked at Katie, and the two women exchanged gazes as the rain gently came down around them and made a soft pinging sound on the taut umbrella.

Katie wrapped both her arms around Cheryl and gave her a long hug. "I'm so sorry you lost your firstborn son. So sorry."

When Katie pulled back, she could see tears in Cheryl's eyes.

"Thank you for saying that, Katie. It was such a long time ago. Andrew was so small. He was a preemie, and he had respiratory problems from the beginning." Cheryl dabbed her tears. "We spent a lot of time at the hospital in Johannesburg during the brief four months of his life. There really was nothing that could be done."

Katie blinked away the tears that had rimmed her eyes and kept looking at Cheryl, not sure what else to say. She didn't want anything to pop out of her mouth that would sound dumb. Cautiously choosing her words, Katie said, "You guys have faced a lot of difficult situations living in Africa, haven't you?"

"Yes, we have." Cheryl drew in what appeared to be a deep breath of courage. "I'm not sure that what we've gone through is any more difficult than what everyone else experiences in a lifetime regardless of where that person lives."

Cheryl started to walk again, and Katie moved right along with her under the big umbrella. All Katie could think about was the terrible experience Eli had recounted to her that had happened to both him and his mom when he was eleven and they lived in Zambia.

Perhaps Eli's mom would feel comfortable talking about that another day. Not today. One sorrowful memory on a rainy day was enough.

"There are always obstacles in life," Cheryl said. "But we love it here. We wouldn't want to live anywhere else or do anything else. This is home to us."

"I can see that," Katie said. "For Eli this is home too. I saw it in his face the night we arrived."

"And is it starting to feel like home for you too, Katie?"

Katie didn't answer right away.

"Give it time," Cheryl said confidently.

The two women arrived at the cottage, and Cheryl shook out the wet umbrella. Katie opened the door. Eli looked up from where he was reading a book on the small sofa that was once again covered with papers and files. Katie had found Eli reading more than once over the past few days, and each time it surprised her. College was over. He didn't have to read books on theology or *Star Constellations of the Southern Hemisphere*. But he said he wanted to. Eli told her last night about how much he loved to read. Katie didn't know any guy who loved to read. This was one of the curious discoveries Katie was making about Eli. His personality was becoming more and more attractive to her.

Last night they had discussed how Eli probably learned to enjoy reading so much because the Lorenzos didn't have a television in their home. He hadn't grown up glued to it the way Katie had in her younger years.

"My parents called the TV the one-eyed babysitter. Whenever I acted up or got too energetic," Katie had told Eli, "they said I should visit the one-eyed babysitter."

They concluded that Eli and his parents were habitually reaching for a book the way Katie grew up reaching for the TV's remote control.

Eli closed his book as Katie and Cheryl entered the house. "What did the doctor have to say?"

"He's going to try to find an antibiotic for me."

"So it is infected?"

"Yes, unfortunately."

"Are you feeling okay?"

"Yes, pretty much. I'm still so tired, though. I was thinking I might sleep a little bit before lunch."

"Do you want me to bring you some lunch from the dining hall? That way you don't have to leave your room if you're getting good sleep."

"No, that's okay. I can set my alarm and make it to the dining hall for lunch." Katie turned to Cheryl. "You raised a really caring son. You know that, don't you?"

Cheryl smiled. "Is that right?"

"Yes, it is. As a matter of fact, last winter at school—it was February, actually. Valentine's Day." Katie grinned at Eli, feeling confident that he would remember the moment as clearly as she did. "I had a cold. A bad sore-throat kind of cold that you feel coming on, and then you just know it's going to take you down for several days, so all you can do is give in to it. Your son came to my dorm room and brought me a bunch of cold remedies from the drugstore."

Eli kept his gaze locked on Katie. He seemed pleased that she remembered but even more pleased that she was giving his mom a stellar report about his character.

"He brought me some stuff to spray in my throat that tasted like cherries and a box of something for my sinuses, and then he told me that the box said not to operate machinery." Katie laughed at the memory. "I mean, really, it wasn't as if I was in any condition at that moment to crank up a backhoe and plow a few furrows on upper campus."

Cheryl laughed.

"Hey, I was just making sure you knew all the warnings." Eli's grin was pretty irresistible.

Katie remembered something else about that Valentine's night. She remembered how Eli had prayed for her that she would get better quickly. He had taken her hand in his just moments before Rick burst into Katie's dorm room with a bouquet of flowers that were supposed to help make her feel better. Eli's expression of concern had helped her feel better and more cared for than Rick's grand arrival with the dozen roses.

The memory of Eli's steady, caring expression for her helped Katie to feel even more confident that she had done the right thing coming to Kenya and making herself so vulnerable.

"You can be assured that no one here will ask you to run a backhoe," Cheryl said. "Someone might put you to work in the tea fields picking tea buds or using a hand-operated hoe, but that's about it."

"Tea fields? You have tea fields?"

"Yes. Didn't you see them on the way in?"

"It was dark," Eli reminded his mom.

"That's right. It was late at night when you arrived. And with all the rain, it hasn't been very appealing to explore the area. Yes, we have the most beautiful tea field just over the hill. Acres and acres. I'll take you there once you're feeling up to a short hike. It's my favorite place to walk. So peaceful and beautiful. The light on the fields in the early morning is spectacular."

"I wish I felt better. I would love to go right now."

"It wouldn't be very enjoyable since the trails are muddy. But the rains are subsiding. We'll have plenty of good weather soon. You and I can go another day. Meanwhile, I need to pick up our clothes at the laundry. Eli, are you scheduled to work at the Coffee Bar today?"

"I'm there from one o'clock until nine. Dad said a group is arriving this afternoon from one of the well projects. I don't remember which one."

Katie headed for the door. "I'm going back to my room. I'll be at the dining room for lunch. And if I decide to sleep through lunch, don't worry. I'll be there for dinner."

"Wait." Eli reached for his jacket that was slung over the back of a kitchen chair. "I'll walk you down to your room."

Katie didn't protest. She let Eli hold the yellow umbrella as she linked her arm in his and leaned close while they walked together in the rain.

"I wish I didn't feel so tired and have this stupid infection going on. I'd like to start doing something useful, like help you again at the Coffee Bar."

"You probably should wait until you at least have some antibiotics in you to kick that infection."

"Infection-schmection. I'm here to serve. If it's not a good idea for me to be around food, I can at least carry boxes. When is your dad moving into the new office?"

"I'm not sure. A few days. Maybe a week."

"Whenever it is, I'm sure I'll be fine by then. Put me on the list for the moving team. I want to help."

"I know you do. But, Katie, here's the thing. It's not all about doing. It's about being. You need to just let yourself 'be' here first before you start doing stuff."

She didn't know if it was because she was tired or chilled from the rain, but Eli's words ricocheted around in her head without landing anywhere. What he said didn't make a lot of sense to her.

"What about you?" Katie asked. "How come you're not just 'being'? You're jetlagged too, but you're doing a lot. Your dad didn't hesitate to put you right to work."

Eli didn't respond.

"Is that not a fair question?" Katie asked.

"No. It's just something else."

"What?"

Eli stalled.

"What is it?"

He still hesitated.

Katie stopped walking and gave Eli's arm a tug. "Listen, you're the one who has been convincing me to be honest and open about what I've been feeling and thinking ever since we got on the airplane together. This is not a one-sided relationship, Eli. I'm being transparent with you. Now it's your turn. Tell me what's going on."

"It's my dad," Eli said.

He started down the pathway again and Katie fell into stride with him. "What about your dad?"

"He and I don't see eye to eye on some things."

"Is it me? Does your dad think I shouldn't have come?"

"No, it's not you. Not at all. It's me. About what my role is here. I want to get out to the villages, and I really wished I'd been able to go with the team from Rancho that went to a village last week. I like being with the teams."

Katie waited to hear why that was a problem.

"My dad assumed that when I came back I'd take over his role in the office so he could do more administrative work for the mission."

"Can't you do both?"

"Yes. And that's how things are here, as I know you've noticed. Everyone does several things. But I don't want to get stuck in the office. I don't want to be tied down to Brockhurst. I want to be on the move. I told him I wanted to write my own job description and see what he thought of it."

"And what are you going to put in your job description?"

"Team trainer, onsite team leader, facilitator in the villages, and scout to villages to determine best candidates for the next well project."

"Sounds like you've already written it."

"I have, in my head. But I didn't add anything about office work. My dad said the reason they're expanding the office was because he told them I was going to be onsite full-time." Eli let out a huff. "I just don't like him assuming things, you know? He never asked what I wanted to do."

Katie couldn't explain it but she felt closer to Eli after hearing he was having conflicts with his dad. At first his family had seemed so perfect. Ideal in every way. But now that she knew that Cheryl and Jim had lost a baby boy and that Eli was feeling pressured to live up to his father's expectations, she felt as if she fit in more, with all of her imperfections.

"It's good that you and your dad are at least able to talk things out." Katie had often wished she could experience that luxury with her parents.

"True. But here's the thing. It's been a long time since I've been under my parents' roof, and in our conversations so far my dad keeps talking to me like I'm a teenager. Before I was at Rancho, I taught at a mission school in southern Kenya. Before that I was in Spain. I haven't stayed with my parents for almost four years. I'm not sure it's going to work for me to stay in the room they have set up for me. I mean, I love them. Both of them. I love being with them. But I think if my dad is going to see me as a grown man, I have to be in my own space."

"Are you thinking of moving into the Monkey Motel with me?"

Eli pulled back and gave Katie a curious look.

"I don't mean with me. Stop looking at me like that. You know what I mean. You can move into one of the other rooms in that building."

"I'll probably go to the building at the top of the grounds near the laundry facilities. They call it Upper Nine, and they don't put guests there because the rooms are older. I wouldn't be taking a good room that might be needed for conferences and guests."

"That sounds reasonable."

"To us, yes. I didn't approach the topic with my dad yet. He was too adamant about the other thing with the office and my position here."

They were at the door of her room, standing under the overhang as the rain tap-danced on the red tile roof. Around them the elephant-ear-sized leaves of the thick foliage bowed from the weight of the rain and dripped with an uneven rhythm. She felt as if the cool air around them was pressing against her, taking her breath and causing her to shiver.

"Thanks for listening, Katie."

"Of course. Anytime. And thanks for the rile. I'll see you in a little wide."

"The rile? A little wide?" Eli questioned.

"A-little-while," Katie overcorrected herself. "You know what I meant. I must be more tired than I thought. I was going to say thanks for the ride, but it was a walk, not a ride. And then I said ... Oh, never mind. I just need to go to bed." She pulled the key to her door out of her shoulder bag and opened the door to her chilly room.

"You sure you're okay? Is there anything I can do for you?"

"No, I just need some sleep. That's all. I'm fine. Really."

"Okay." He gave her a warm hug. "Get some sleep, and I'll see you in a little wide. I'll even take you for another rile if you want."

Katie managed a half smile before she went inside and closed the door. The first thing she did was change into warmer clothes. She towel-dried her hair from the moisture that clung to her red, swishy mane and found a pair of socks, which she put on over the pair she already was wearing. Crawling under the covers, Katie pulled up both blankets and continued to shiver. She just couldn't get warm.

I should have asked Eli to bring me another blanket. Although I don't know if they have only a limited number, and I've already been allotted two blankets, while some people staying here might only have one.

As tired as she was, Katie wasn't able to get any sort of a nap going. Her thoughts kept bouncing all over the place. *Malaria, Andrew, anti-*

biotics, cherry-flavored throat spray, Rick, roses, New Zealand glacier water . . .

Katie remembered the bottle of New Zealand glacier water Eli had brought to her on Valentine's Day when she was sick. He said he remembered it was her favorite. She would love a sip of water right now. Her head felt hot. So hot. Katie kicked back the blankets and tried to cool off her poor, confused body.

This is awful. I feel like I have the flu. Please, Lord, no, not the flu. Don't let me get sick. Please let there be antibiotics for this infection. Please heal me.

Katie heard a knock on the door and was certain Eli had ignored her insistence an hour ago when she told him she didn't need anything. He must have come back to check in on her.

Katie called out, "It's open."

The door opened, but it wasn't Eli who entered. It was a woman Katie didn't know.

"Hi, Katie. Do you mind if I come in? I'm Dr. Powell's wife. He wanted me to bring you this." The short woman walked over to Katie's bedside and handed her a small, white envelope.

"Is it the antibiotics?"

"No, it's some amphetamine to help with the discomfort. He hasn't been able to locate any antibiotics yet."

Katie felt a sense of panic rise in her along with her fever. "Do I need to go to Nairobi to try to get some?" The thought of riding on that bumpy road the way she felt right now made her ache even more.

"I'm not sure. He'll let you know. Just rest. That's the best thing. Do you need anything else?"

"No. I mean, yes."

"What can I get for you?"

Katie paused. She wanted to say, "I need you to get Eli so he can take care of me the way he did last Valentine's Day." But instead she said, "Nothing. No. Never mind. Thanks for checking on me. I just need to sleep."

She left, and Katie rolled over on her side.

I feel like such a wimp. Dr. Powell and his wife must see an endless variety of terrible diseases. Here I am, acting delirious and fragile, as if I'm about to die.

She told herself all she had was a small, infected wound. And a fever. And a headache. Come to think of it, her throat was pretty sore too.

What's wrong with me? Am I getting seriously ill?

Katie pressed her hand to her forehead and tried to gauge her fever. She was perspiring but her feet were still cold.

This can't be good. What if . . . A paralyzing thought washed over her. *What if I have malaria?*

K atie checked her arms closely and tried to remember if any mosquitoes had bitten her over the last few days. She didn't recall any. But that didn't mean they hadn't found her and bit her when she wasn't looking. She could be infected with malaria, a very real, life-threatening disease at this moment and not know it.

This is ridiculous. I shouldn't be thinking these things. Just because Eli's infant brother died of malaria, that doesn't mean I'm going to die— if I do have it, which I probably don't. But what if I do?

Her heart pounded, and she wanted to cry, but even her tears seemed too afraid to make an appearance.

What's wrong with me? Why do I keep getting hit by these waves of panic? I feel as if I'm going to lose my mind. I am so afraid.

The moment Katie thought the word *afraid,* it was as if she'd named the culprit of her bouts of panic. It was fear. Intense, chaotic fear like she'd never known before.

For God has not given us a spirit of fear, but a spirit of power and love and a sound mind.

The verse that exploded in her thoughts at that moment was one Eli had quoted twice on their long flight, in the middle of their heart-to-heart conversations. The truth calmed her now as it had calmed her then. She reminded herself that the fear she was feeling wasn't from God. His Spirit gave her power, love, and a sound mind. No fear. She wanted those qualities to be present in her life right now. She needed them to overturn the doubt, fear, and instability.

Katie closed her eyes and prayed. As she did, she felt the sense of panic loosen completely and a longed-for sense of calm came over her. Her thoughts cleared. She stretched out her legs and breathed more steadily. A constant awareness of God's presence and his powerful protection over her filled her thoughts. He was here, with her, in this small room in Kenya. At this moment, he seemed even closer to her than he had when she was in California. Perhaps she felt that way because she realized how much she needed him.

Whatever the reason, her prayer that fear be abolished had an immediate and powerful effect: the panic was gone.

Another note to self: If you're going to spend most of your young adult years asking God to bring more adventure into your life, don't turn into a timid little coward when he answers your prayers in a big way. Trust him.

Reaching for the two pills in the envelope, she took them without water and told herself that all the unknowns could remain unknowns while she slept. She couldn't do anything at the moment to hunt down the antibiotics. She couldn't do anything if she had malaria. God knew. He cared. He could work out the details while she slept. Katie closed her eyes and felt as if she were being tucked in under an invisible blanket of peace.

When she woke, Katie noticed that the rain had stopped. She checked her watch and saw that it was 5:40 in the evening. A gleam of sunset light found its way through the open space between the two nearly closed edges of the window curtains and left an amber line across Katie's gray blanket.

The wound on her shoulder still hurt, but the rest of her confusing symptoms seemed to have calmed down. She felt hungry and considered it a good sign she was ready for dinner. Getting up and washing her face, Katie hoped she would feel like her old energetic self pretty soon.

She pulled her hair back into a ponytail, brushed her teeth, and changed into a less crumpled top. Pulling on her warmest jacket, she opened her door and took in the view of the verdant landscape drenched in melting, buttery light. It seemed like a different world from the one she had been sloshing through the past few days. The remaining raindrops on the deep green foliage gleamed like liquid emeralds.

Something small and fluttery flew around Katie in somnolent loops. At first she thought it was a moth. But it didn't behave like a moth. A twin to the languid creature joined it, and pretty soon Katie seemed to be caught up in the middle of a dance of these tiny insects with their thin, fairy wings.

She stood still and watched them flutter around her. Reaching out her hand, Katie nearly caught one. The twilight glow of the evening gave them a luminescence like she never had seen on any insect in the United States.

The door to the last room in Building A opened, and a short man exited wearing a business suit and carrying an umbrella. He was bald, had dark skin, and wore small, wire-rimmed glasses. He noticed Katie and said something in French as he walked toward her.

"Hello," Katie replied. "I'm sorry, I only speak English."

"Ah, yes," he said, switching to English. "American?"

"Yes."

"Are you on your way to dinner?"

"Yes. I had to stop and watch these moths or whatever they are. They're beautiful."

The man chuckled. "Those are not moths. They're termites. Flying termites."

"Termites? Are you sure?"

"Yes. *Absolument.* Where I live we call them flying peanuts."

"Why is that? Are they shaped like a peanut?"

"No. Because we eat them like a snack. Like a peanut."

If Eli were the one telling Katie this, she'd think it might be a big tease just to get a reaction out of her. But this man seemed serious.

"You eat these?" Katie watched as more of the "flying peanuts" fluttered around them with graceful ease. It seemed impossible that termites could be so elegant, let alone be the ideal African "to go" snack.

"Yes. Like this." The man waited until just the right moment, quickly snatched one of the termites, and held it in his fist.

Katie put her hand over her mouth. Her stomach did a flip-flop as she thought she was about to watch this man chomp into the termite.

"First, you pull off the wings."

"Pull off the wings?"

"Yes. You don't eat the wings."

"To be honest, I don't think I could eat the termite, actually. Wings or no wings. Sorry."

"Maybe you like them better roasted. We make them that way. They come out after the rains to mate, and they make these crowds like this."

Katie had a feeling he meant "swarms" instead of "crowds," but she knew what he was referring to. It surprised and humbled her that this man knew English so well. She would never be able to have a complex conversation with someone who spoke only French, German, or Swahili.

"After the rains, we dig a small hole and beat the ground with sticks. And they come." He opened his hand and let the tiny marvel go free.

Katie was fascinated. "You beat the ground, and they come?"

"Yes."

"Why do they do that?"

"I don't know." He grinned, revealing several gaps where teeth once had been. "So we can eat them, I suppose."

Katie smiled back at him.

"We get them together and ..." He made a pounding motion by cupping one hand and using his fist to demonstrate the sort of mashing and grinding one would do with a mortar and pestle.

"You grind them?" Katie asked.

"Yes, yes. We grind them into something ..." He rubbed his thumb and fingers together.

"Like a flour? Or a paste?"

"Yes, yes. Like that."

"And then what do you do with it?"

"You can cook it and eat it."

Katie wanted to flippantly say, "You might cook it and eat, but you'll never catch me doing that." She knew she couldn't say that. She needed to respect this man's culture.

"Shall we go to dinner?" he suggested.

Somehow Katie wasn't quite as hungry as she had felt a little while ago.

"I am Bin." The man took the first steps away from the flurry of termites and headed toward the dining hall.

"Bin?" *Like a trash bin? What an odd name.*

"Yes, Bin."

"Hi, Bin. I'm Katie. Where are you from?"

"The Democratic Republic of the Congo."

Katie planned to spend more time studying a map of Africa so she could mentally envision where each country was. She knew that French was the common language in many West African countries in the same way that English was the main communication form in many East African countries. She had picked up that detail the other night around the dinner table when Eli's dad explained which world power had the most influence on which parts of Africa during the colonization era.

Venturing a fairly educated guess based on his speaking French, she asked, "And that is located in West Africa, right?"

"Central Africa."

"What brings you here?" Katie asked.

"I am receiving training at the conference for pastors."

"Oh, you're a pastor. That's wonderful."

"Yes, it is wonderful. I have been in prison only two times for preaching the gospel. Now I am able to move about and come here to attend this training. God has been very good to me. Very good."

Katie tried to take in what he had just said—in prison *only* two times—and still he said God had been good to him.

They walked together silently for a bit. It was nice not to be walking in the rain. All around them the green grass and revived foliage seemed to show off how squeaky clean they were after the showers. Katie loved the fresh fragrance in the air. She felt honored to be with someone who took his role as a pastor so seriously that he would go to prison for his faith.

How different he was from any pastor she had ever met. And not just because of his gourmet taste for flying termites.

"What brings you here?" he asked.

"God, pretty much."

He gave her a sideways glance, as if he didn't understand her comment. Her wit didn't seem to translate well.

"What I mean is that I'm here because God opened up an opportunity for me to come and help out. I've only been here a few days. I came with a friend of mine, Eli Lorenzo. Do you know him? He grew up in Zambia."

"I don't know him."

"I will be sure to introduce you."

They entered the dining hall, and the first thing Katie noticed was the abundance of African men wearing suits. Others were dressed in their native garb with headdresses and colorful shirts or long robes that had designs running up and down both sides.

Her companion bid her farewell and headed across the room with his hand extended, ready to greet another man whose face lit up in an eager smile when he saw Bin.

The fellowship around the tables seemed more charged with energy than it had been any other night. Every man seemed to have lots to say and was eager to greet all the other conferees. Katie noticed Eli's parents seated across from one of the pastors. The three of them were engaged in such a deep conversation that none of them were eating.

Katie thought it best not to impose herself on their private circle, so she sat by a woman from Scotland who served in the laundry facilities. She was quite a bit older than Katie and had wide shoulders and a fair, smooth complexion. Her accent was fun to listen to. She told Katie she had been at Brockhurst for eighteen months and loved what she did, washing laundry.

Since the twenty-four cottages and the many motel-like rooms didn't come with individual washing facilities, all the laundry was done at a central location. Eli had familiarized Katie with how it worked and that she needed to pay various rates in Kenyan shillings for whatever she had washed. So far she had managed to rinse some of her things in the sink and hang them to dry over the bathtub.

"And what is it you love to do, Katie?" the woman from Scotland asked her.

Katie didn't have an answer. "Just about anything. I'm here to help."

"Yes, every young woman I have met from the West has come to help. They want to do something important and useful so they can go home knowing that they helped to change Africa." She picked up her teaspoon and wagged it at Katie. "The surprise you will discover is that you will not change Africa, my dear. No, Africa will change you."

The words stirred something deep in Katie's heart. She kept her unblinking gaze fixed on the woman.

With evenly paced words the woman said, "The key is for you to discover what you love to do, what you were created to do, and then do it for the people around you with love. That is the abundant life, dear girl, no matter where in the world you live."

Katie slowly swallowed her last taste of something that reminded her of rice pudding and thought about her dinner companion's statement. She wished Eli wasn't working at the Coffee Bar so he could have joined her for dinner. It would be interesting to hear his impression of what had just been said.

"Lovely sitting with you, Katie."

"Yes, lovely sitting with you." Katie wished she could remember the woman's name. She knew it would come to her later. She also knew it would be an important name to remember since she was one of the permanent residents.

Katie lingered a few minutes by herself, thinking and letting the wise counsel she'd just received sink into her soul. Lingering was a significant step for her. She was learning how to slow down a little and sit at the table after she had finished eating. She might have practiced that skill a bit longer, but she was eager to get over to the Coffee Bar to see Eli.

Rising from her seat, Katie carried her dinner dishes to an open window area where the uniformed kitchen staff received them, scraping and stacking them in what seemed like an orderly, British manner. Katie said hello to the young woman who reached for her plate and then thanked the woman for doing such a great job.

"You're welcome." The young woman sounded American. She had cinnamon-colored hair, fair skin, and lots of freckles.

"Where are you from?" Katie asked.

"Kansas."

"I guess you're not in Kansas anymore." Katie tried to make it sound like the reference to the *Wizard of Oz* was apparent.

The young woman smiled kindly, as if she had heard that joke one too many times. "What about you?" she asked.

"I'm from California," Katie said. "I went to Rancho Corona University."

"I've heard of that school. I have a friend who went there."

"Really? Who? I might know them."

"Sierra Jensen."

"Are you kidding me? I know Sierra. How do you know her?"

"I met her in Brazil a few years ago. I was on a short-term mission project, and she worked for the same mission organization. I knew she went to Rancho Corona because she was always wearing her university sweatshirt."

Katie nodded. "I've been wearing mine a lot since I got here. Have you kept up with Sierra? I haven't talked to her for a long time."

"No, I haven't."

"I need to check in on her. I'll tell her I met you." Katie paused. "Wait. What was your name again? I'm bad with remembering names lately."

"Kara Hawthorne."

"Kara from Kansas. Got it."

"Tell Sierra hi for me."

"I will. See you later."

Katie hoped Eli had his laptop with him at the Lion's Den. She could hang out at the Coffee Bar and email both Christy and Sierra. The three of them had met years ago when Katie and Christy had gone to England to serve on a short-term mission trip.

Katie's involvement at Brockhurst didn't feel like it was going to be a mission trip. This wasn't a "go play with the kids in a foreign country and tell them a Bible story" sort of one-week experience. This was the next season in her life. Not that she was exactly sure what that meant. But for now, this was it. This was her life. Now that the fear had lifted, she felt like she had more space to breathe and pay attention to what was going on around her. If only she felt better.

Katie sauntered upstairs to the Coffee Bar, and the first thing she heard was the rumble of deep male voices coming from the pastors gathered at nearly every table as they were caught up in important conversations. It sounded like she had indeed stepped into a lion's den, and, though these lions were quite tame, each had something to roar about.

Katie saw Eli before he saw her. He was in full swing as a barista boy. His hair was flipping every which way, and his white apron looked like a shield that had taken a few hits on the coffee grounds battlefield. But, as ever, he looked steady and content.

The customer he happened to be helping at the moment was the man from the Congo. Katie sidled up to the counter. "And add a side of flying peanuts to that, if you will."

Both Eli and the pastor looked at her in surprise. "You don't put them in coffee," the pastor said.

"I know. I was just making a joke. Never mind." Katie was becoming aware of how often her humor wasn't working here. Perhaps it was because the things that she thought were odd and worth poking fun at were commonplace for everyone else.

"Katie, this is Ben," Eli said. "We just met this evening."

"Ben!" *Oh, his name is Ben! Not Bin.* Katie kept the name mistake to herself and swallowed her smile. "Yes, we met earlier. Ben taught me about the flying peanuts."

"Did you try one?" Eli looked serious.

"No."

"They're a great source of protein."

"I'm sure they are."

"How are you feeling?" Eli called over his shoulder as he poured a cup of coffee for Ben.

"Better."

"Have you been ill?" the pastor asked.

"I have a small infection."

"May I pray for you?" Ben didn't wait for an answer. He bowed his head and asked God to put his great and powerful healing hand on Katie, to remove from her body the sickness and poison, and to deliver her from evil.

It was an unexpected prayer that felt natural in the roomful of pastors.

"Thank you," Katie said when he finished the prayer.

Pastor Ben looked at her. His eyes narrowed behind his wire-rimmed glasses, and he tilted his head slightly to the side. He looked as if he were listening for something. With a compassionate expression, he said her name in a rumbling sort of way. "Katie."

"Yes?"

"You have to remember the peace. The past will find you here, but it's for a different purpose than you think."

"Okay." His fragmented words seemed odd. She looked over at Eli. He wasn't paying attention to them at the moment because he was at the cash register making change for Ben. She had no idea if this was some sort of tribal blessing or what.

"Thank you." It was the only response she could think of.

Ben put his hand over his heart and held it there a moment as he bowed his head and then looked up at her again.

She didn't know if she should respond with the same gesture or just stand there. She opted for standing and trying to look respectful.

"Remember the peace," he repeated.

Katie nodded. "Okay." Again, she had no idea what he was talking about.

Ben picked up his change and the cup of coffee and walked away.

Katie looked over at Eli, who was now standing in front of her with a steady grin.

"I have something for you." He reached under the counter and pulled out a sealed white envelope that had some handwriting on the front and looked as if it had lumpy, small pebbles inside.

"Mail from home already?" Katie quipped.

"Better than that. Antibiotics from Dr. Harry at the Rift Valley Academy. Dr. Powell brought them to me about an hour ago."

Katie had never gotten teary-eyed over medicine before. She had never received mysterious, encrypted messages from short men who ate termites. She had never been told by broad-shouldered Scottish women to figure out what she was passionate about.

And she had never dreamed of Africa like this.

The third day after the rains subsided and after Katie had started on the antibiotics, she felt as if she finally had arrived all the way. Her body may have arrived when their plane landed in Nairobi, but her heart caught up with her a week later, very specifically at 6:45 on a Tuesday morning.

That was the moment Katie opened her door, and Eli stood there wearing one of his frayed beanies and with a daypack on his back.

"You ready?" he asked.

"Yes." In every way she believed she finally was ready.

The destination of their early morning trek was the tea fields. Cheryl had been promising to go with Katie, but Eli was the one who set the plan in motion and showed up right on time on her doorstep. Katie followed him, feeling cute and comfy in her favorite pair of jeans, a freshly laundered T-shirt, and a new-used pale green knit sweater she found in the Sharing Closet next to the laundry.

The Sharing Closet was a small room where left-behind clothing from conferees ended up, freshly washed and ready to give away. Brockhurst residents also donated clothes, which made it worthwhile, Katie discovered, to check in every so often to see if any new items had been added. The sweater she found there yesterday was a boon, and one she was sure would get a lot of use.

This morning was the green sweater's and Katie's maiden voyage to the tea fields. She had her cell phone camera ready and wore a pair of hiking boots she had bought at home at her favorite discount store, Bargain Barn. On Katie's first visit to the Sharing Closet, she realized it was a miniature Bargain Barn, and that made her happy in a way she was sure only her best friend, Christy, might understand.

"You look like you're feeling a lot better." Eli glanced at her and then reached for her hand.

Katie slipped her hand in his and gave it a squeeze. "I feel really good. How are you doing?"

"Great."

The two of them strolled hand in hand down the lower path that led to the entrance gate and the guardhouse. Eli greeted the uniformed guard in Swahili with a term that had become familiar to Katie. "Jambo."

The guard tipped his hat and replied the same. They turned down a dirt road and walked under a canopy of trees as a chorus of birds greeted the new day with gusto. A woman with a baby slung across her shoulders by a wide piece of colorful fabric came toward them, smiling and making eye contact with them.

"Jambo," Katie greeted her, feeling like a local.

As they continued to walk, more people from the nearby village appeared on the dirt road headed in both directions. Some of them were carrying bundles of something all wrapped up and balanced on their heads. Others had a child or two in tow and were nudging them forward the way any mother in any culture tries to keep her youngsters from stopping to examine every pebble and crawling bug along the way on a lovely, sunny morning.

Katie soon realized this was the morning commute. The people they passed were on their way to school and work, as most people around the world would be at seven in the morning. The notable difference was that no one was rushing—they all walked at a steady pace. No one was in athletic wear, jogging on the trail or riding an expensive bike to exercise before showering and jumping into an expensive car to dash to work. Here the commute was all the exercise anyone needed.

Katie could see over the side of the trail into a fertile valley where two dozen huts and an uneven assortment of metal-roofed shacks were flanked by even rows of carefully planted gardens. Smoke rose from an outdoor fire pit. A rooster crowed, and Katie noticed two skinny goats in the village that were tied to a post.

"This is so cool," she said in a low voice.

"You like this?"

"Yes. This is how I pictured Africa. Only hotter and drier with giraffes and zebras running around."

"I'm glad you said that; it reminded me I'm scheduled to take a group to the giraffe reserve in Nairobi on Friday. I signed you up. Do you want to go?"

"Absolutely."

"I thought you would. Also, it looks like the tour agency will vacate the new offices by this afternoon. Dad bought some paint, and I let him know we would help him paint tomorrow."

"Great."

"I told him we were experienced."

"Experienced?"

"Yes. Remember when we painted the apartment where Rick and I lived?"

"Oh, yes. How could I forget? Our big decorating debut. Or rather, Nicole's decorating debut. I wonder how she's doing with her big project of decorating Rick's new restaurant."

"Do you want to call her?" Eli asked.

"I don't have international service on my cell phone yet. Your dad told me how I can set it up, but I haven't done it."

"You can use my phone anytime you want. What's mine is yours."

They had let go of hands earlier down the trail. Katie wanted to reach over, take his hand again, and give it a squeeze to say thanks for his generosity. She held back, though, not sure if Eli had let go because it was improper culturally for them to hold hands in public or if it was just easier to walk on the uneven trail without holding hands.

She was fine with just walking side by side. "Have you talked to your dad about his expectations of what you'll be doing?"

"We talked briefly a few days ago, but my mom joined the conversation, and my dad said it sounded as if she was taking my side. She said she was only trying to help both of us to explore options."

"It doesn't seem like you got very far in the decision making."

"No, we didn't. I told my dad later that I thought he and I should talk it out, just the two of us."

"Did he agree to that?"

"Yes and no. He said he had thought about what my mom had brought up in the discussion earlier, and he wanted her to feel that she had a chance to give her input since I'm her son too."

"Eli, have your parents said anything about me?"

"Plenty."

Katie gave his arm a tug. "So what have they said?"

"They think you're wonderful, amazing, and adorable, and they hope you stay forever."

"Really, really? Is that what they said?"

"Oh, wait. That was what I told them about you. Let me see, what was it they said about you?"

Katie gave his arm a playful swat.

"I remember now. They did say something about you. They said they think you're wonderful, amazing, and adorable, and they hope you stay forever."

"Eli, I'm serious. Do they have any unexpressed expectation of what I should be doing?"

"No."

"Are you sure? Your mom is always so nice to me. I'd hate to think that I'm doing something wrong and she's too kind to tell me. Or that your dad is secretly wishing that I'd sign up to be a security guard or something but he's not saying so."

"A security guard?"

"They're the only ones around here who get to wear uniforms, and I think their uniforms are really nifty."

"Nifty?" Eli laughed. "Katie, no one wants you to be a security guard, all right?"

"Fine. But if any of those guys donates his uniform to the Sharing Closet, I'm snatching it."

"We don't dress up for Halloween here."

"Who said I was planning to save it for Halloween?"

"Katie?"

"Yes?"

She could feel Eli staring at her profile.

"Nothing." A hint of laughter was in his tone.

They walked a little farther down the red dirt trail, and Katie said, "Eli?"

"Yes?"

She waited a beat before responding. "Everything."

Eli laughed again, and Katie couldn't remember the last time she had felt this happy.

The trail curved upward and took them around a bend. When they made the turn, Katie stopped to draw in her breath. Spread out before them across the curved and rounded hills were acres and acres of tea plants.

"Wow," she murmured.

"Pretty amazing, isn't it?" Eli stood next to her, admiring the view.

"Amazing isn't the word. Magnificent is more like it. Eli, look at the light on the green leaves. I've seen pictures of tea fields but, wow! The photos never looked this amazing. Look at all those tea plants."

"I like the way the rows between the plants look like seams. If those narrow gaps weren't there in those long strips, it would just be a sea of green."

Katie noticed what Eli was talking about. The tea plants looked as if they were about three or four feet high and were situated close together so that they formed a hedge. But instead of looking like a single hedge that served as a wall, narrow rows had been cut in between the plants to allow harvesters enough space to walk up and down the hillsides and pick the small buds that grew on the top of the tea plants.

"Is it okay if we go down there and walk through the fields?" Katie asked.

"Sure, though one of the pickers might put us to work."

"Really?"

Eli laughed. "It's not as exciting as you might think. It's tedious work. They only pick the top inch or two of the buds and leaves."

"If I remember, those are called 'flushes,'" Katie said. "And the proper name for the plant is *Camellia sinensis*. I remember that."

"Impressive."

"So is this." Katie tried to take in the beauty of the fields before her and the way the sunlight was touching the *Camellia sinensis* leaves, gracing them with what looked like finely spun lace. She stared and stared but still felt she couldn't take it all in.

"Eli, I have to tell you something."

He put his arm around her, and she rested her head on his shoulder. "I didn't get this before."

"Get what?"

"You. This. I know I keep saying how different everything is here, but I'm beginning to understand why you were the one who seemed so different when I met you last year. You somehow managed to stay within this slower rhythm even in crazy California, and I thought you were ... I don't know ... different."

"Slow?"

"Yes. But not like mentally slow or emotionally challenged. You just lived at a different pace on the inside. I think I'm beginning to understand why it seemed to me that you were never in a hurry."

"That's a good observation. Does it seem to you that I'm not in a hurry about us, about our relationship?"

"Yes, I guess. But I'm not in a hurry either."

"Good. Because we have lots of time."

"Yes, we do," Katie agreed.

"Lots and lots of time," Eli repeated.

Katie's eyebrows furrowed. Cautiously, she lifted her head from his shoulder and looked at him. "Eli?"

"Yes?"

"What exactly is your idea of 'lots of time'?"

When Eli didn't respond right away, Katie asked again. "I mean, do you define lots of time as meaning a month? A year? A decade?"

"Until what? Until we get married?"

His abrupt conclusion caught her off guard. "Ah, don't you think we should, like, date first? You know, get to know each other, evaluate how we're doing, take the next step as it comes?"

"I don't really see us dating." Eli looked serious.

"You don't?"

"No. Dating is a California thing. How are you and I supposed to 'date' in Kenya?"

"Isn't that what we're doing right now? Isn't this a date?" Katie asked.

"No, not to my way of thinking."

"Then what is it?"

"It's us being us. You know how I told you before that in Kenya it's about being, not about doing? Well, this is us being us. Together."

"You're messin' with my worldview, Lorenzo."

"Good." He took her hand in his, and they walked farther into the fields.

They reached the entry trail to the first row of tea plants and then walked together down the waist-high row. Katie ran the flat palm of her hand over the top of the spring green leaves. The farther she walked, the more surrounded she was on every side with the gorgeous, vibrant green.

She was aware that their banter session had done nothing to clarify where they were in their relationship, and yet she felt settled, calm, and at peace. This wasn't California. This was Kenya. They weren't dating. They were going together. Okay, she could live with that.

Remember the peace.

The mysterious words from Pastor Ben came back to her. Was this what he meant? Was she supposed to pay attention to the times when she felt God's peace? Because she certainly was feeling it now.

"Stand right there." Eli pulled out his phone. "I'll take your picture."

Katie struck a pose, and Eli snapped a picture.

With a grin he said, "You are a woman who is outstanding in her field."

Katie didn't catch the joke at first, but when she did, she cracked up. "Nicely played!" She reached into her sweater's pocket for her phone. "Don't move. The sun is just right. Say, 'Camellia sinensis'!"

Eli busted up, and Katie caught an extremely cute shot of him surrounded by the tea plants and with the early morning sun giving him a freshly washed look. She checked the photo on her phone's screen. Eli had such a great manly look to him with his wayward hair and scruffy, unshaven face.

A slender man with a canvas sack strung diagonally over his shoulder came plodding up the road toward Eli and Katie. He apparently recognized Eli, because he called out a warm greeting that started with "Jambo" but included other words Katie didn't recognize.

The two men exchanged wide smiles. Eli introduced Katie to Itimu, and he cordially shook her hand. She was startled at how sinewy and rough his hands were.

"How is your mother?" Eli asked.

Itimu replied and asked the same of Eli. He asked about Eli's father, and Eli asked about his children. This went on for a few minutes as they both took the time to listen attentively to the other's responses.

Katie joined the conversation and had a lot of questions for Itimu. She wanted to know if the satchel he was wearing was for tea harvesting, and if so, could he show her how it was done?

He handed her the bag, she put it over her shoulder, and then he proceeded to demonstrate how to pick the small top bud and tuck it in the bag. As Katie moved down the row, picking tea, she kept up her flow of questions.

When she asked how long it took him to fill the bag, he replied that he wasn't sure. He worked until he was done, and then he went home.

Once the tea leaves were stretched out to wilt in the sun, Katie wanted to know how long it took before they were treated in their own particular way to determine if they were to be made into green tea, white tea, oolong, or black tea.

He didn't know how that part of the process worked.

She asked if the tea plantation raised and picked leaves that produced only one type of tea.

He couldn't say. He had never asked that question.

Finally, Katie asked, "How long have you been doing this?"

"Since I was eleven." With that, Itimu unfurled a fascinating description of the growth process of the tea plants. All the while he continued to pick the tea leaf buds and to place the small bits into the satchel. Eli took photos and joined them. For Katie, being in a real tea field picking tea leaves was a dream come true.

From Itimu she learned that the plants can grow into trees as tall as fifty feet high if they aren't trimmed and cultivated. The best teas grow at elevations of five thousand feet or higher, which is why this part of Kenya was well suited for the crop. He carefully explained how it takes anywhere from four to twelve years before a tea plant bears seed. After that seed takes hold, it can be another three years before the plant bears leaves that are ready for harvest. Itimu knew everything about the bugs, the rains, and the soil. He had a deep respect for the land and for what he did.

Several other workers lumbered toward them with their satchels in place. Itimu kindly requested his satchel from Katie, made his exit, and went to work with his companions.

Katie thought she and Eli were going to head back to Brockhurst, but Eli said, "I have a favorite lookout point. It's up this way."

"Of course you do. You have a favorite bench, a favorite spot in front of the fireplace, and now a favorite lookout point."

She followed as he trekked through a less-traveled section of the tea field where the cinnamon-colored earth was still damp. Their shoes left the first telltale marks that humans were taking this upper road since the last round of rains. The extra effort was worth it. They came onto a grassy knoll that overlooked the whole area. In front of them were the vast tea fields. Katie could see Itimu and his fellow workers in the lower right corner of the fields. In the central portion of the fields, at least two dozen people were at work. No workers occupied the immediate left side of the patch.

"Turn around," Eli said.

Behind them, through the trees and thick foliage, Katie could see a portion of one of the buildings at Brockhurst. "Wow! It's like being on top of the world."

"Wait until I take you to Mount Kenya. Or we could go to Kilimanjaro, if you like."

Katie remembered Eli saying months ago that he and his father had hiked partway up Kilimanjaro, one of the tallest mountains in the world.

"Will we see elephants, lions, or zebras?" Katie asked.

"I can pretty much guarantee you'll see some zebras as well as hippos if we go with one of the groups to Lake Naivasha for a day trip. As far as the elephants and lions, we might see some on Mount Kenya, but we're more likely to see those if we can swing a trip to the Masai Mara."

"And what is that?"

"It's a wildlife area to the south. We would have to sign up for a safari and stay overnight in tents. The tour guides would take us around in Jeeps that are specially designed to get into the right places to see the wildlife."

"I want to see it all," Katie said.

Eli smiled. "I thought you would. One wild animal at a time though. For now, how about if we have some ostrich meatballs for breakfast?"

"That's good, Lorenzo. Keep going with the clever punch lines. It's working for you this morning."

Eli took off his daypack, pulled out a thin blanket he had rolled up, and spread it out on the grass. Katie stood back with a questioning gaze, watching him unload his pack's contents. He pulled out a thermos and handed it to Katie. Next came two coffee mugs, which Katie held by their handles in her other hand. Eli withdrew a plastic container, something wrapped in waxed paper, and two bananas. He placed those items on the blanket, took the mugs and thermos from Katie, and motioned for her to sit.

"Eli, you made a picnic for us."

"Yes, I did."

"That's so sweet. Well, not sweet. I can't say I've ever thought of anything you've done as being sweet, per say. Clever, maybe. No, that's not the word. Oh, I know. Thoughtful. There, that's better. You made a picnic for us, and that was so thoughtful."

Eli reached over and pressed his forefinger to Katie's lips. "Hush," he said in a low voice.

A close-lipped smile inched up his mouth in an adorable curve. "Sit down and eat your breakfast, Princess Hakuna Matata."

Katie sat. She looked at the unopened containers then up at Eli. "Please tell me you were kidding about the ostrich."

"I don't kid about ostrich meatballs. One of the guys from the front office went down the hill to Nairobi last night. A restaurant there specializes in exotic game food. I'm sure we'll go there eventually. The guy knows that ostrich meatballs are my favorite, so he brought some back for me. Here we go."

Eli opened the plastic container, and Katie peered inside. The four meatballs looked like normal meatballs. She decided to remind herself of that as she took a bite. They were just meatballs. Normal, eat-'em-with-your-spaghetti meatballs.

Trying to keep her expression unchanged, Katie asked, "And what do you have in the other mystery wrapper?"

"Cheese."

Katie relaxed. Then she asked, "Do I want to know what sort of animal was milked to obtain the cheese in that wrapper? I mean, you wouldn't try to spring some sort of rhinoceros cheese on me, would you?"

Eli laughed.

"Wait. Are you laughing with me, or are you laughing at me? Because you know, there is a difference."

Eli laughed again.

"You're laughing at me. I know you are. Because look—I'm not laughing. Therefore, you can't be laughing with me."

Eli curbed his mirth and opened the thermos. He poured coffee into both of the mugs and then lifted one of the mugs as if to say, "Drink up." The fragrance of the steaming, dark brew was delicious and woke up Katie's taste buds. She wasn't a big coffee drinker, but the first sip made it clear that Eli had prepared some extra special sort of blend that morning.

Katie took another sip and looked at Eli. He was comfortably situated, with one knee up and the arm holding the coffee mug balanced on the top of his knee. His focus was on the fields below. His jawline gave away that he was holding back another bout of laughter.

"Eli?"

"Um-hum?"

"I have a feeling you're not going to let me leave here until I try one of these ostrich things."

"Yup."

"I also have a feeling you're not going to tell me what kind of cheese is in that wrapper."

"Nope."

"It's probably best that way."

"Yup." Eli's mouth curved up once again, but he kept looking straight ahead as he took another leisurely sip of coffee.

"Eli?"

"Uh-huh?"

"You know how you said you think I'm amazing and wonderful and that you hope I stay here forever?"

"Yes?"

"Well, I think you're pretty wonderful and amazing too, and I wouldn't mind staying here forever."

Eli turned his head to meet her gaze. His intense eyes studied her expression. "You're not making a joke, are you?"

"No, I'm not." Katie's expression was unflinching.

Eli put down his coffee mug, reached over, and smoothed back a few strands of her hair that had brushed across her cheek. If he was thinking of kissing her again, Katie knew this would be the perfect moment.

Eli leaned slightly closer and whispered, "Katie?"

"Yes?"

"You can say all the nice things about me that you want, but you know what?"

"What?"

"You still have to try the cheese and the ostrich."

W ell?" Eli watched as Katie swallowed her sufficient bite of ostrich meatball.

She cleared her throat and took a sip of coffee. "It's actually pretty good."

"Told ya."

"I'm sure it's not the ostrich that tastes good. It's the spices or the filler they use to hold it all together. I mean, it's not straight ostrich, off the bird."

"But you like it, don't you?"

"Yes, I do."

Eli looked pleased with himself. "Now try the cheese. Go ahead."

Katie looked at the thin slices of white cheese in the opened waxed-paper wrapper. It looked like Swiss cheese without the holes. "Just tell me if it comes from some African animal."

"It comes from an animal we have a lot of in Africa, okay?"

"Is it an animal that cheese would normally come from?"

"Katie, just try some. I'm not going to tell you anything else. Take a piece and put it in your mouth."

She complied. It tasted normal, like a mild Jack cheese. Kind of bland and boring, even. She swallowed. "Okay, I ate it. Now what animal did it come from?"

"A cow."

"Seriously?"

"Yes, seriously. I got it from Claudinei in the dining hall kitchen."

Katie picked a handful of grass and tossed it at him, spreading the green blades like chopped confetti all over their blanket, in the cheese, and on the ostrich meatballs. "Not fair," she protested. "You had me believing it was rhinoceros cheese or something."

"No, you're the one who let your imagination go on a safari." Eli tossed a few blades of grass back at Katie. "Rhinoceros cheese? Where do you come up with this stuff?"

"Where do I come up with this stuff? Hey, Ostrich Meatball Guy, it's not that big of a stretch from ostrich to rhinoceros. Especially after the lesson in flying peanuts last week."

"You really should have tried one when Ben offered." Eli reached for the other slice of cheese, rolled it up, and popped it in his mouth.

Katie shook her head at him and sipped her coffee. "Oh, Lorenzo," she murmured.

Her gaze was fixed on the heart-stirring green vista. The sunlight on the tea plants now painted the landscape with a spectrum of shades of green. Some areas of the rolling hillside were shadowed by puffy white clouds sailing overhead, making the green as deep and dense as an evergreen forest. In other areas, the direct sunshine seemed to hit the small leaves like a laser beam, igniting them so they burned with a silver intensity.

"It's so beautiful," Katie said. "So, so beautiful."

"You feel closest to God when you're out in nature, don't you?" Eli asked.

"Yes, definitely. You do too. I know because of the night last fall when we went with Joseph to watch the meteor shower in the desert."

"And the morning of graduation when we went to see the sunrise at Strawberry Lookout," Eli added. "That was a terrible morning."

"Why do you say that? I thought it was an amazing sunrise."

"The sunrise wasn't the problem. It was me. I was so mad at myself for the way I froze up."

Katie didn't remember Eli being less talkative than at other times during the school year. Although it was his idea to get up in the middle of the night and drive to the San Bernardino Mountains, just the two of them. Then Katie recalled how, as a matter of fact, the whole time they were at the lookout and for most of the ride back to school, he had hardly said anything.

"What was the deal? I thought you were deep in your own mysterious thoughts."

Eli leaned back and rested on his elbows. "No, I was punching myself around for not knowing how to talk to you. I froze once I had the chance."

"The chance for what?" Katie asked.

"I wanted to ask you to come to Kenya."

"You did?"

"Yes. Actually, more than that. I wanted to convince you that this was where you belonged. I could see you here, Katie. From the first time I saw you, I could picture you here, like this."

Katie drew in a deep breath. A sweet scent was in the air, and an even sweeter stirring was occurring inside her.

"Not everybody fits in Africa, you know? But you do. I knew that in my gut, but I couldn't find a way to tell you. So I spent all that time I was with you rehearsing hundreds of conversation starters and not finding a way to use any of them. By the time we were back at Rancho, I gave up. I knew I'd missed my chance to convince you to come to Brockhurst."

"And yet, look." Katie spread out her arms. "Here I am."

Eli looked over and gave her a long gaze. "Yes, here you are. Here we are. Together."

It felt to Katie as if they should plant a flag on this knoll and mark this as the moment their past caught the tail of their future. Their lives were overlapping in a way that was meshing their hearts together.

"It would have been too soon," Katie said. "If you had said anything about coming here that morning on the mountain, I wouldn't have been able to take it to heart. I wasn't ready to be open to this, to us. It had to work out the way it did for me to know God was leading me to come."

Eli nodded. "I know."

Katie reached over and rubbed the back of her knuckles across his scruffy jawline. She smiled at him, and he smiled back.

They took their time, telling each other more behind-the-scenes moments from their individual stories of the past year. Eli recounted times when he was around Katie and felt tongue-tied. She confided in him how she felt the night of the All Hall Event when she was in charge and was losing control of the crowd. Eli had saved the day when he took the microphone at Katie's request and connected the group to the game they were supposed to play.

"You're a natural leader," Katie said.

"So are you," Eli said.

"Yes, but you and I have different areas of leadership strength."

"Agreed." Eli sat up and finished off the last ostrich meatball. "Do you mind if we talk as we walk? I'm on grounds maintenance duty today, and I know George is going to be at the equipment shed waiting for me."

They packed up and hiked down the hill. Once they were on the dirt road, they held hands and playfully swung them back and forth as they talked, teased, and watched their friendship grow.

Katie found some time later that morning to place a call to Christy. It wasn't a long call, but Katie had enough time to give Christy a speedy update and to summarize how things were going.

"It all sounds amazing, Katie," Christy said. "Except for the infection. That was crazy. I hope you threw that bra away."

"I did. It was pretty bad."

"It sounds like things with Eli are dreamy."

"Everything is dreamy here." Katie was glad no one was around her in the far corner of the Lion's Den where she was using the internet phone service on Eli's laptop.

"Do you feel good about where things are headed with him?" Christy asked.

"Yes. I love being at Brockhurst. When we were at the tea fields this morning, it felt as if we had always been there or had already gone there a hundred times. It was like it was our place, even though it was my first time to see it. It's so beautiful, Christy. You can't even imagine how breathtaking this place is."

"You keep talking about all the things you love about Kenya. I want to know how you feel about Eli."

Katie was caught off guard. She thought she had been talking about her deep and growing affection for Eli. Maybe she had her love for Africa and for Eli a little mixed up at the moment.

"Eli is wonderful. I love being with him. I'm so glad I'm here. I love everything about this place. I really do. I honestly can see myself staying in Africa the rest of my life. Although, I admit, I'm in this lovely British bubble of a community where life is pretty easy."

"But you're going other places, aren't you? I thought you said you were going to see the giraffes."

"We are, the day after tomorrow. Tomorrow I'm helping to paint the new office for Eli's dad, and then the next day we're going to a giraffe reserve. I'm really looking forward to that."

"Be sure to take lots of pictures and send them right away."

"I will. I know you have to go. Say hi to Todd for me, okay?"

"I will. Miss you, Katie. So much."

"I miss you too. Love you guys."

"We love you too, Katie."

The next day when Katie and Eli were in the middle of painting the new office, Katie told Eli about Christy's request that they take lots of pictures of the giraffes.

"We can do that," Eli said. "I found out the group that's going is from Texas. Twenty-three people are in the group, and they're staying here for three nights starting tonight. If I remember correctly, their church has a sister church they planted a couple of hours' drive from here."

"And how did you end up being the unofficial tour guide for this group?"

"I volunteered. I always volunteer. I like having a chance to show other people around."

One of the head administrators came in through the office's open door and had a look at their progress. "It's looking good," he said.

"Thanks," Eli said. "We're going to have a lot of paint left over, so let me know if you want anything else done while we're at it."

"If that's the case, you can paint the lobby at the office. Mary has been asking for fresh paint in there for months. Years. You'll make her a very happy woman."

Eli nodded, and that was that. Katie knew their work as the official Brockhurst painters had only just begun. How could she complain about work like this? Working alongside Eli, enjoying the warmth of the breeze and sunshine now that the rains were gone ... Yes, this was a good way to spend a workday.

Eli started on the detail trim, painting along the floorboards on the final wall in the office as Katie finished rolling the wall by the door. A few minutes later, he stepped away from his wall and came over to stand beside Katie.

"I'm almost done," she said. "Are you ready for me to start rolling that wall?"

"If you think you have to cover it up, okay. I thought we could leave it as it is."

Katie turned around and saw Eli's handiwork. With a small trim brush, he had painted on the wall a big heart surrounding a second, smaller heart, a heart within a heart. In the inner heart were the letters "E + K." Inside the top of the larger heart were the letters "J.C." and a plus sign. Katie tilted her head, trying to decipher the code.

Eli must have read her confusion, because he stepped over to the wall and pointed out his equation with his paintbrush as if he were a teacher and the paintbrush were his ruler. "You will note that the E plus K equals Eli plus Katie."

Katie felt her face blushing. It was just so sweet. So unexpected. Eli had such an innocent approach to life and to their relationship.

"Now, you will observe," Eli continued, "that this larger heart encompasses Eli and Katie with an even bigger love. And of course the J is for Jesus and the C is for Christ. That's because the Lord loves

Eli and Katie, and he surrounds them with that love. Any questions, class?"

Katie felt a little misty-eyed. She stepped over to the wall and held out her hand for the brush. "May I?"

"Yes, you may." He handed her the brush.

Katie leaned down and dipped the end of the brush into the paint tray. To the side of the heart within a heart, she wrote "1 Thess. 3:12." The letters were wavy, and the numbers were uneven. Katie noticed Eli was the one trying to crack the code this time.

"I would have written Thessalonians, but I wasn't sure how to spell it."

His eyes lit up. "That's the verse!"

"I know. I saw it underlined in your Bible, and so I underlined it in mine." Katie swayed back and forth like a little girl who had just won an award for good citizenship.

Eli grinned. "Cool. We have a verse. Some people have a song; we have a verse. I like it."

"Do you have it memorized?" Katie still swayed like a proud schoolgirl. Before he could respond, Katie showed off her memorization skills. " 'May the Lord make your love increase and overflow for each other . . .' There's more, but I guess I need to study it some more."

Eli finished it for her. " '. . . and for everyone else, just as ours does for you.' " He held out his hand for the paintbrush. "May I?"

"Of course." Katie handed it over.

He added a "+13" after the number "12" and quoted, " 'May he strengthen your hearts so that you will be blameless and holy in the presence of our God and Father when our Lord Jesus comes with all his holy ones.' "

"Show off," Katie teased.

Eli knelt down and went back to painting along the baseboards. Without looking up at Katie, he said, "That's been our verse for a long time. You just didn't know it."

"What do you mean?"

"I've prayed those verses for you for a year now. I've prayed that your love for God and for others would increase and overflow, and I've prayed that God would strengthen your heart."

Katie knelt down beside Eli. "I saw that verse the morning you were sleeping by the fire. I saw you'd underlined it in your Bible."

"Did you see the date?"

"No. What did you write in the margin?"

"Your name and the day I first saw you at Todd and Christy's wedding."

Katie could hardly take in the sweetly eternal feeling that was connected to his words. "I was such a train wreck that day, running after their getaway limo ..."

"Your halo flying off ..."

Katie laughed. She almost had forgotten about the narrow wreath of flowers she had worn on her head as the maid of honor, and how it came off in her mad dash. Eli tried to give it back to her, and that was the first time they had spoken. She told him to throw it away. Instead, he saved it, and months later she saw it hanging from the rearview mirror in his car. When she asked him about it, Eli told her it reminded him to pray for her.

And now she knew what he had been praying.

"God answered your prayers," Katie said.

"I know." Eli grinned.

"Over the past year, God has definitely strengthened my heart. And my love has increased so much for people that were difficult for me to love, like my parents. Those are great verses, Eli. I'm going to keep praying them for us."

Their eyes met, and Katie felt as if both of them were looking deep into each other's hearts and finding open space, ready and waiting.

She spontaneously, naturally, leaned over and kissed him gently on his scruffy cheek.

Eli swiftly put down the paintbrush, took her face in his two hands, and kissed her like the world was coming to an end in the next three seconds.

They pulled apart, and Katie sprang to her feet as if an electrical current had shot through her. *Whoa.*

Eli looked at her, not blinking.

Neither of them noticed when Eli's dad had entered the office. Katie hadn't heard his footsteps, but she had been a little too preoccupied to pay attention to who might be passing by the open door.

She knew Eli hadn't noticed his dad either, because he jumped slightly when his dad spoke. "How's everything going here?" His words were slow and weighted, as if he was asking about a whole lot more than the painting project.

"Good." Eli stepped away from Katie and from the wall, as if that was going to somehow deter his dad from noticing the huge valentine that had dried nicely with their initials in the center.

Eli rubbed the back of his neck and didn't make eye contact with his father. Katie didn't feel they had anything to be ashamed of. She did think that maybe she and Eli should consider choosing a different verse rather than one about their love increasing and overflowing.

At least in some areas, that prayer appeared to be sufficiently answered.

Eli and Katie didn't have a chance to process their surprise kiss, because Jim asked Katie to help check in the just-arrived Texas group. Mary, who worked in the office, usually handled that job, but she had gotten sick, and Cheryl was trying to make sense of the room charts that had been left at the check-in desk.

Several hours later, everyone was in his or her assigned room with the correct luggage and a room key. Katie knew an easier way to handle check-in had to exist, because she and Cheryl had bumbled their way through the process.

Katie spent a lot of time dashing up and down the pathways with a ring of keys, trying to figure out how the numbering system had gotten so far off kilter. She eventually figured out that everyone had the key to the room next door, which meant neighbors needed to swap keys. Apparently Cheryl had read the charts incorrectly.

Once the group was settled, Katie returned to the office. It was locked up, but she peered through the window and saw that the walls were painted, with nothing remaining of the valentine. The memory of the moment and of the kiss would remain with Katie forever. She was certain of that.

Eli wasn't at dinner, and he wasn't working at the Coffee Bar. She knew she would see him the next morning when they boarded the tour bus with the group from Texas, but that wasn't exactly the best place for the two of them to debrief about what was happening between them.

She thought a lot about the momentum of their relationship as she was trying to fall asleep that night. What they had experienced was powerful and passionate. How could one kiss contain so much fire?

The next morning, weary but with a lot of enthusiasm, Katie stood beside the door of the chartered tour bus to welcome everyone onboard. Most of them remembered her from the check-in fiasco and had lots of comments about how that had gone.

"Is that not your usual job?" one of the older women asked with a look of contrived sympathy.

"Good guess," Katie said. "That was my first attempt, and I don't think they will put me on room check-in duty again."

"I should hope not," the woman said it in a cheery voice, but it still felt like sandpaper to Katie's heart.

Right before the woman boarded the bus, she asked, "And what is your position at Brockhurst?"

"I'm an extra." Katie hadn't premeditated her answer. It just tumbled out. "You know, like in a play when the extras have walk-on parts, such as the village carolers. Only I don't sing."

The woman looked even more confused. "You really should work within your passion and your skill set, young lady."

"I agree." To Katie's way of viewing the last twenty-four hours, passion wasn't exactly a problem for her. At least not around Eli.

The woman wasn't finished. "God made you for a purpose, you know. It doesn't bring him honor when you're wasting time doing things outside your gifting."

"Thank you for that insight." It was killing Katie to continue being gracious to this woman. Katie knew that she needed to find the best fit for herself at Brockhurst, but she also didn't respond well in her spirit to a stranger who seemed to think it was her duty to point out Katie's weaknesses and to give her advice.

Some people have no idea how much they hurt others.

Katie looked up and noticed Eli jogging across the gravel parking lot toward the bus. She put the woman's comments aside and felt a little embarrassed as she thought about their "whoa" moment yesterday. Her response reminded her of how she had been hesitant about holding Eli's hand when they were with the group from Rancho. She seemed to be not quite in sync with how Eli was viewing their relationship.

But then she noticed that Eli seemed off center as well. He looked at her and then looked away. "Thanks for covering for me. I got hung up at the office with the list. Mary's still sick."

Katie reached over and touched his arm. He met her gaze. "Are you okay?" she asked.

Eli lowered his voice and turned his face away from the people boarding the bus. "Yeah, I'm okay. We need to talk later." He leaned closer and gave her a tender little connecting touch by putting his forehead against the side of her head. It was awkward, but the message was received. It was still "E + K" inside his heart.

Once everyone was onboard, Katie climbed into the bus as well. It was much larger and more comfortable than the shuttle that had carted Katie and Eli to Brockhurst on their first night. Eli stood at the front behind the bus driver, used a microphone to welcome everyone, and gave some instructions.

Katie watched him from one row back where she had taken a seat next to a broad, older woman whom Katie knew from check-in was single and traveling with a group of mostly married couples. One of the feelings Katie was sure would be wired forever in her was knowing what it was like to be the leftover, odd-numbered person in a group of couples, since many of her best friends were married. She introduced herself, and the woman, warming right up to Katie, responded that her name was Susan.

As they listened to Eli, Katie recalled last semester when he had spoken at chapel about the mission his dad ran and how the organization was committed to digging wells in remote villages to provide for people who were dying from lack of clean water. His presentation had been so powerful and convincing that a mission team had formed spontaneously—the group Eli and Katie had seen the other night.

Concluding his welcome remarks to the group, Eli took his seat in the row in front of Katie. He turned, looked at her, and patted the empty seat next to him, as if indicating she could now move up and sit beside him.

Part of Katie wanted to do just that, but she didn't want to have her relationship discussion at the front of a bus where everyone could see them and some could easily hear them. Another part of her had a pretty good idea how Susan would feel if Katie moved to sit next to Eli.

"I think I'll stay here," Katie said. "You'll need to jump up and down the whole way, so you might as well take both seats. Besides, how can Susan and I heckle you in unison if I'm up there?"

"You came along to heckle me?" His words were teasing, but his eyes looked sad.

Katie bantered back in an attempt to ease the moment. "Yes, and to see the giraffes. My goals for the day are twofold. Heckle first, then hug a giraffe's neck. They're simple goals, really. Not ones I manage to accomplish every day, but today is looking like a good day to cross them off my bucket list."

Eli didn't counter with any equally witty quips. He turned around, pulled out some papers from his nicely organized folder containing the forms for the people on the bus, and started to read as if he were looking for something.

Susan had her eyes closed; so Katie let go of the idea that she needed to become Susan's bus buddy and tried to take down her exuberance a few notches. She pulled out her phone, which she had finally updated with an international service plan, and saw that a new email from Christy was waiting in her inbox.

Katie, it was so great talking with you! I've been thinking a lot about the way things are unfolding for you and Eli. It has to be pretty exciting to ponder all the what ifs and the what's nexts.

I really hope you enjoy the mystery of riding along inside the unknown. That mystery factor seems to be an important part of the journey on the way to falling in love. I don't know why, but it is. Let your relationship with Eli open slowly like a flower.

I'm looking forward to seeing those photos of the giraffes!

Love you, my forever friend,

Christy

Katie smiled as she closed the email. *Now, see, Christy can tell me whatever she wants, and I'll take it. She's earned the right to be in the inner circle of my life. But that lady who was boarding the bus, she's in the outer circle. She shouldn't think she has the right to scold me.*

Katie imagined a bull's eye and made a note to self: *Only listen to people who are in the center of your bull's eye.*

Those bull's-eye occupants were God, Christy, Todd, and Eli. In the next circle out, she could envision a bunch of other close friends, including Nicole, Julia, Doug, Tracy, and, yes, even Rick. While he no longer was in her inner circle, he was still her valued friend and brother in the Lord. Katie also put her parents in that circle. Even though she had a stilted and fairly uncommunicative relationship with them, they were her parents.

She thought of how surprisingly smooth her call with them had been during her first week at Brockhurst. It was short, informative, and for communication with her parents, pretty positive. Katie would almost say they were supportive of her decision. Her dad commented that he always thought she would end up in some "God-forsaken place" like Africa. Awkwardly expressed, but she would take it.

Katie leaned back, settling more comfortably into her bus seat. She liked this bull's-eye model that had formed in her thoughts, because it meant that women like the lecture-prone one who had boarded the bus earlier could try to project on Katie all the advice they wanted, but their opinions weren't weighted like those who were closer to the center. Those outer-circle people hadn't earned the right to tell her what to do. Not that God couldn't use their insights to direct or motivate Katie, but rather those people weren't empowered to boss her around or instill in her a sense of guilt or failure based on their opinions of who she was or what she should be doing.

Feeling pretty good about things at the moment, Katie looked over at her seatmate and made a comment to Susan about what a pretty day it was. Susan nodded without replying. She seemed to be very focused on the front of the bus.

"Do you get queasy on buses?" Katie asked.

Susan nodded again. The woman across from them heard Katie's comment and said, "Well, why didn't you say so, Susie? I have some motion sickness pills right here."

The woman opened up her large bag and pulled out what looked like a miniature pharmacy of wonder drugs. "Here you go. You need some water?"

Susan kept looking straight ahead and nodded. The woman across from them also had a mini bar of tiny water bottles and small cans of juice. "Water or apple juice?"

"Water."

Katie's phone bleeped, indicating she had an incoming message. Since Susan was in good hands, Katie pulled out her phone and saw that she had a text message. It was from Eli.

I MISS YOU.

Katie grinned and curved her shoulders inward, trying to keep her message back to Eli private.

MISS YOU TOO.

She waited for his reply, glancing up at his profile as his head was bent and he focused on his phone. DAD THINKS WE SHOULD SLOW THINGS DOWN.

Katie drew in a breath and unconsciously cleared her throat.

Eli glanced at her for a moment and then looked back at his phone.

Katie started a long question but then backspaced all of it and texted, HAKUNA MATATA. She wasn't sure she spelled it right, but she knew Eli would catch the message that they shouldn't worry about it. Then, on second thought, she quickly typed the same question Eli had asked her the morning they were with the group from Rancho. WHAT DOES IT MATTER WHAT OTHERS THINK?

IT MATTERS WHEN IT'S MY DAD.

Katie realized Eli had the privilege of welcoming his mom and his dad into the inner circle in the bull's eye of his life. Of course their opinions mattered. It mattered to Eli and to Katie very much.

SLOW IS GOOD. She sent the text and then quickly typed a follow-up. I THINK WE CAN STOP PRAYING ABOUT OUR LOVE INCREASING AND OVERFLOWING AND WORK ON THE HEART-STRENGTHENING PART OF OUR VERSE.

She watched as Eli read her message. He turned and gave her the best smile.

Katie smiled at him in return and felt peace coming back on ballerina slippers, doing a pirouette in her heart. Wasn't this what Christy had just talked about in her email, enjoying the mystery of riding along inside the unknown? Katie could slow down, wait, rest, and trust God for what was next. She knew that was the recipe for experiencing the deep sense of peace she had felt a number of times in her growing relationship with Eli.

What Katie also realized was that when she felt that powerful sense of peace, she wasn't afraid. The tormenting spirit of fear that had harassed her when she first arrived couldn't coincide with the spirit of peace God had given her.

As the bus rolled down the road on the way to Nairobi's outskirts, Katie looked out the window and watched the stunning views go by. A short time later, the bus stopped at a lookout spot, and Eli stood, grabbed the microphone, and explained that they were taking a fifteen-minute break to see the Rift Valley.

"Many consider this Africa's Grand Canyon," he said. "It's much more than that, though. The Great Rift Valley is a geological marvel. Right here, where we'll be disembarking in a few minutes, is where two tectonic plates are shifting. They're pulling apart from each other. Think of the immense force going on under the earth's surface. It always makes me think of God's power, as if he is taking a huge chunk of Africa in one hand and another chunk in the other, and he's stretching them in opposite directions."

As the driver maneuvered the bus into a narrow parking area, Eli went on about the way tectonic plates shift. The movement had created the second largest and deepest freshwater lake in the world, as well as the pressure that exalted Mount Kilimanjaro to rise to the height of over nineteen thousand feet, making it the fourth highest in the world.

"The Great Rift Valley covers six thousand kilometers. All of East Africa from north to south is affected by it."

It seemed he had a few more facts to share, but the bus driver had turned off the engine, and people were standing up, making their way to the front of the bus, eager to disembark.

"Fifteen minutes," Eli reminded them and put away the microphone.

As soon as Eli and Katie stepped off the bus, they were surrounded by locals who had set up a dozen souvenir shacks at this turnout where tour buses apparently stopped to give their passengers a look into the Great Rift Valley.

"Madam, will you look at this? Would you like to take home a blanket made of goat hair?"

"Sir, please, I ask you to look at this tribal mask and this spear that came from a Masai warrior. I will give you a very good price for both."

Eli said something in Swahili, and all the vendors who had gathered around Eli and Katie took off like mice.

"What did you say?"

"You'll see." Eli walked confidently into the middle of the area where the other tourists were caught up in looking at craft items and practicing their haggling skills with the local artisans.

"Be sure you take a look over the edge," Eli called out to the group.

No one seemed to heed his advice; they were busy shopping. Eli led Katie to the rickety-looking wood platform and stood right next to the splintered railing. Katie looked down, down to the deep valley below that ran as far as she could see.

"Wow. This is amazing. Absolutely amazing."

She looked over her shoulder and saw that only two people in their group had ventured closer to the edge, where they were taking photos. The rest of the crew was trying to convince the vendors to lower their prices on child-sized African drums and wood-carved elephants and giraffes.

For several long minutes, Eli and Katie stood next to each other, gazing at the miles and miles of wide open valley far below.

"Are you okay?" Eli asked, still looking forward.

"I'm good. You?"

"I'm good."

"You know," Katie said quietly, "it seems a little odd that your parents were so happy when we arrived, and they practically cheered when you told them that you kissed me at the airport."

"I know."

"And now your dad saw us kiss, and he's no longer a fan. Did you tell him it was only our second kiss?"

"It's not the quantity, Katie. I think it's the quality we're talking about."

She knew exactly what he meant. The passion infused in their second kiss made it quite different from the first one.

"My dad saw our verse on the wall, and he said we should keep going and add the next seven verses to our relationship."

"The next seven verses?"

"You'll understand what he meant when you read them."

Katie hated being kept in suspense. She also hated knowing tension had developed between Eli and his dad and that she was part of the unsettledness.

"I told my dad I wanted to move into Upper Nine, and he didn't think that was a good idea."

"Was it his way of saying he doesn't think he can trust you or something?"

"Maybe. I don't know."

Katie could tell this was dragging Eli down. "Are you sure you're okay?"

"It's just that my dad said something to me that I can't get past."

"What did he say? Can you tell me?"

"He said, 'You can make a baby with a kiss like that.'"

Katie was surprised, and tried to make a joke of it. "Last time I checked the science reports, I'm pretty sure it takes more than a kiss to initiate regeneration."

"You know what he was getting at. So do I. It was more than a kiss. It was ..."

"I know, Eli. I was there, remember?"

He finally turned and looked at her. "So the wise thing for us to do is to hold off on kissing. That's okay, right? We can abstain."

"Of course. Absolutely."

Eli looked relieved. He nudged her shoulder with his shoulder and said in a lowered voice, "It is kind of nice to know there's a fire inside both of us, though, don't you think?"

"Did you ever doubt it?" Katie asked.

"No, but it's still nice to know."

They stood together quietly for a few more minutes, not touching, but very much connected. Eli nudged Katie's shoulder with his shoulder once again, and she took the cue that it was time for them to head back. As soon as they turned around and walked toward the bus, all the vendors who had approached them earlier came out of their stalls like honey bees swarming around Eli and Katie.

"I forgot," Eli said. "This is what I asked them to do when we got off the bus. I asked them to bring me their best beaded necklaces for consideration after we had a reverent, uninterrupted view of the valley. I'd like to buy some necklaces for you, Katie. But I want you to pick them out."

Six vendors had circled them and were holding up an assortment of beaded necklaces. Some were made of tiny, colorful beads in patterns that seemed to have no specific order yet looked lovely and artistic. Other necklaces were made of big, chunky beads, while others were made of beads of various sizes and shapes. Katie was drawn to the necklace and reached out to touch it.

That vendor immediately lifted the necklace from the four draped across her hand and placed it over Katie's neck. "My sister made this one. It is very beautiful. I will give you a good price, madam."

"Do you like that one?" Eli asked.

Three other vendors held up similarly styled beaded necklaces and respectfully suggested that their price would be the best. They all spoke at once, and they all stood close, but surprisingly Katie didn't feel as if they were harassing her or being pushy. Each of them, in an in-your-face cultural way, was trying to assist her in making her selection.

She reached for a second necklace with black, yellow, red, and green beads that were in a distinctive pattern. Again, the chosen item was placed over her head, and the vendor said, "Only seven shillings."

"This is fine work," Eli said in English, picking up the end of the necklace and rubbing the beads between his thumb and forefinger. "But not for seven. I will give you four. And madam"—he turned to the woman who said her sister had made the necklace—"I will give you four. Eight shillings for both."

The two vendors shook their heads. "Six. Each. No less. The beads are painted by hand. You will not find better. Not in any of the marketplaces in Nairobi."

"I do not doubt what you say," Eli responded. "They are made with much care. The fine work is evident. But they are beads. Not precious stones. I will give each of you four, and not a shilling more."

Both vendors put up their hands as if in shock at his offer. "No, this is not a four-shilling necklace, as you can see. Note the details on the painted beads. Six. No less."

Katie was fascinated by the way Eli calmly negotiated the purchase. She had heard several people talking over meals about how haggling is expected and never to pay the asked-for price. Even so, looking at the condition of the vendors' overall health, their clothing, and their teeth, her heart went out to them. She wanted to give all six of them in the circle ten shillings each and walk away with nothing so they would have more inventory to display to the next tour bus that came through.

What Eli did next surprised her. He shook his head at the price of six shillings and lifted the necklaces off Katie's neck as if they were prepared to walk away.

An immediate protest arose. Eli held the necklaces suspended in the air over Katie's head. She stood motionless, feeling like a vintage clock in the shape of a cat whose eyes move from side to side with the tail while the rest remains still.

"Four," Eli said firmly, necklaces suspended over Katie.

"Five," both vendors said in unison.

"Done." Eli lowered them back over Katie's neck, gave a nod, and pulled the money from his jeans' front pocket.

Another vendor stepped up with a large, carved figure of an African woman with graphic details. It seemed that he assumed if Eli was doling out money for the woman beside him, then he would certainly want to take home such a statue. Eli put up his hand and didn't make eye contact. The vendor walked away.

Katie felt like she should say "Thank you" and "Have a nice day," or else her shopping experience wasn't concluded. However, the vendors with the beads were now working the crowd with some of the other women in their group and pointing to Katie so the Americans could see what all the rage was in African fashion.

"How much?" one of the women from Texas asked.

"Twelve shillings."

"That's not bad. I like this one. Here. Do you have change for a twenty?"

As Katie watched the exchange, she wanted to stop the woman and confide in her that Eli had bought two for ten shillings, not one for twelve. It all went so quickly and exchanged hands so effortlessly, she thought it was better just to leave things as they were. What an interesting variety of people these vendors must see each day.

Eli was at the center of the group now. Another tour bus was pulling up, and the busy, buzzing vendors dispersed from the Texas group and clustered around the not-yet-open door of the bus that had just arrived.

"If I can have your attention," Eli called out. It worked. The Texans looked to him as their leader. "We have only five more minutes before the bus leaves. I strongly encourage you to head over to the edge of the platform and have a look at what we stopped here to see: the Rift Valley. I don't want you to miss this marvel of God's creation."

Most of the group responded, and Katie could tell that brought Eli a lot of satisfaction.

"That was pretty impressive, Lorenzo." Katie looped the two long necklaces over her neck a second time, doubling them up and making the length feel more normal.

"You like your souvenir?"

"I meant the way you motivated the group was impressive. And I love the necklaces too. Thank you. Or, wait ... asante sana."

"You're welcome. Thanks for the encouragement."

"Anytime."

Eli reached over and ever so slightly brushed the back of his knuckles across her forearm. Then he took the lead and headed for the bus.

Katie looked up at the seamless blue sky and drew in a deep breath. The pure oxygen seemed only to fuel the fire that was burning inside her, the fire that burned for both Eli and for Africa. She was in love. She knew it. But for now, that was a truth that shouldn't be revealed to anyone. Not even Eli.

As if he didn't already know.

The bus ride into Nairobi provided Katie and the rest of the group with plenty to see. The city in daylight was a bustling place with people everywhere. Alongside every road they drove on, people walked with bags and bundles, and children in school uniforms strolled in groups. Men on bicycles held on to the back of trucks, catching a ride uphill. Bent old men slow-shuffled along on their way to somewhere. So many people were on the move that Katie found it hard to imagine where they were all going to or coming from. Little white shuttle vans were everywhere, picking up and dropping off passengers the way yellow taxis clogged New York's streets in every movie she had ever seen of the Big Apple.

The bus trundled past a large, open-air market in a field. The dry dirt seemed to rise in a constant cloud from the hundreds of people compacted into the confined space. Katie could see vegetable stands next to kitchen tables and chairs. She thought the market formed the African equivalent of one of the big-box stores in the States where everything was under one roof. Only here, there was no roof.

This bustling, humanity-filled part of town was the opposite of what their surroundings were like in the hills at Brockhurst. So much dust. So many people. So much traffic. She closed her eyes for a moment and tried to remember the image of the peaceful green tea fields at dawn. Opening her eyes, Katie saw the mix of cardboard lean-tos and current-year vehicles. Nairobi was a sprawling city of diversity.

One form of diversity that was missing was people with fair skin. Katie was keenly aware once again that she stuck out not only because she was a white woman but also because she had distinctive hair. She wondered if that was part of what made Eli stare at her when they first met. She would have to ask him sometime how much of an anomaly she was to him. Even though his skin was nearly as pale as hers, the red hair had to be an oddity. Katie realized that the more she got to know Eli in his familiar surroundings, the more she understood why he was the way he was.

The bus meandered through a shaded residential area, and Eli turned around and pointed for Katie to look out the window. She saw a large parking area and a glimpse of a single-story house with a porch, and then they were past it.

She looked at Eli with her eyebrows raised, as if to say, "Yes, so? It's a lovely old house in the African-colonial style."

"That's Karen," he said quietly.

Katie's eyes grew wide. She knew what he was talking about. Several days ago at lunch they had sat across from a Canadian couple who had visited "Karen." Katie realized what the house was: the home of Baroness Karen Blixen, the Danish author of *Out of Africa*, the woman who went by the pen name Isak Dinesen. The whole area was now developed into a suburb and had taken on the name Karen. The couple from Canada regaled Eli and Katie about what parts of the porch and house had been used for the film and how well preserved it was.

"We'll come back another time if you want to take a tour," Eli said, still keeping his voice low. "It's not on the schedule today, so I didn't announce it."

Katie let her thoughts wander to the future and the joy of knowing that she had many days to come in Kenya.

Before long the bus pulled into a parking area. "This is it," Eli said, standing up and taking the mic as the bus driver waited for another tour bus to inch its way out of the shady spot he wanted.

"All right, we're here. We're at the giraffe center, and we'll be here for a full hour. You'll find more information once you get inside, but to summarize, during the late 1970s, a number of areas in Kenya were being developed into subdivisions, and the wildlife in those areas was rapidly declining. The couple who started this center had learned that in western Kenya only a little more than one hundred Rothschild giraffes were left. They brought two of those giraffes here, to their home, and developed this area into a wildlife preserve for endangered giraffes. The park guide will have the current numbers, but I believe more than five hundred Rothschild giraffes are in Kenya as a result of the sanctuary created for them. So, go hug a giraffe's neck and be sure to head back here in an hour."

Katie gave Eli a smirk when he turned off the microphone and looked at her.

"What?"

"You got that line from me. That was my goal for the day, to hug a giraffe's neck."

"And heckle me. Did you forget that part?"

"I'm saving up all my heckles for the ride home."

Most of the group had hurried out of the bus, and Katie wanted to rush with them, eager to see the giraffes. But she waited for Eli, who was engaged in a conversation with the bus driver. Neither of them seemed to be in a hurry. Katie sat back down in the emptied bus and tried to see what she could out the window, but it wasn't much.

"Ready?" Eli finally asked.

"More than ready." Katie exited with him. He led them to the snack bar.

"Do you want something to drink?"

"What about the giraffes?" Katie squeaked.

"They have their own drinks."

Katie swatted at his arm. "Why are we here at the soda fountain, Fonzie? The giraffes are over there." She pointed to the elevated observation area across the grounds. She couldn't see any giraffes yet and guessed they had to climb up to the observation deck with everyone else.

"Trust me, it will be too crowded with the whole group going at the same time. We might as well kick back and wait till they're done. And what did you just call me?"

"Fonzie. Arthur Fonzarelli. You know, *Happy Days*? Soda fountain? Richie Cunningham?"

"Am I supposed to know who these people are?"

Katie forgot the home she had grown up in contained the one-eyed babysitter while Eli had spent his childhood reading about African wildlife preserves and retaining facts on Mount Kilamanjaro and the Rift Valley.

"Never mind. Listen, I want to go to the platform with the rest of the group. If you want, you could wait here for me."

"You really are excited about this, aren't you?"

"Yes!"

"It's just giraffes."

"Just giraffes! Eli!"

"Okay, okay. I get it. My everyday stuff is not your everyday stuff. Come on." He reached for Katie's hand. "Let's elbow our way in. I have to warn you, though. They're cute, but they drool."

Eli's term of "elbowing in" was a perfect description of what they had to do. The elevated observation area was designed to hold fewer people than were already gathered when Katie and Eli arrived. It wasn't just the Texas group. Another smaller gathering of visitors was lined up for a group photo.

All Katie and Eli could do was hang back and try to hear the uniformed park ranger as he answered questions and explained that, while they could see the giraffes in the open area in front of them, the giraffes wouldn't necessarily come over to the open-air observation tower. The tower was built at just the right height so that, if the giraffes did approach, they would be eye to eye with the visitors.

Katie stretched her neck, trying to see around the people in front of her. By the exclamations they were making, it seemed that the others could at least see some giraffes. But all Katie saw, in the distance beyond the open field with the acacia trees, were downtown Nairobi's tall buildings.

"There's another one!" one of the men from their group exclaimed.

Then Katie caught a glimpse of a tall giraffe stretching its long legs and bending its knobby knees. With graceful and rhythmic strides, the grand creature moved across the open area from the shade of one large tree to the shade of another. All cameras on deck went on a snapping frenzy.

The uniformed guide raised his voice so that everyone in the tight quarters could hear him. "Did you know that the giraffe is similar to the camel and the brown bear in the way it walks? They all lift both legs on the same side of their body at the same time. That gives them their distinctive gait."

He went on to talk about the different types of giraffes, which ones were endangered, and ways people could contribute to the African Fund for Endangered Wildlife.

While all of that was interesting to Katie, she was dying to get close enough to the railing to set her phone camera on zoom and take a picture of a giraffe, especially since she promised Christy she would.

One by one the tourists took their photos, asked their questions, and made their way down the stairs to the snack bar. Eli was right. They could have gotten something to drink, hung out for a bit, and then headed to the observation deck after the crowds subsided.

"Thanks for elbowing in here with me," Katie said to Eli.

"Did you take any pictures yet?"

"No. I'll slide up there now."

A group of a dozen people, who appeared to be traveling together and speaking what Katie thought was Dutch, left at the same time. Another half dozen people from the Texas group left, and just that fast the only people left on the observation platform were Katie, Eli, the park guide, and an older couple who were snapping a few photos.

"Would you like a picture of the two of you?" the park guide asked.

"Sure. Thanks. I mean, asante." Katie handed him the camera and stood next to Eli. He put his arm around her, and she felt her face flush. She was sure it was from the heat. Nairobi was quite a bit warmer than Brockhurst, and even though the area was open air, with so many people crammed together on the observation deck, it had become uncomfortable fast. The older couple left, and Eli and Katie remained with the park guide.

"Would you like to feed the giraffes?" the guide asked.

"Are you kidding?" Katie looked at Eli and back at the ranger. "Yes! Is that possible? Can you call them and get them over here?"

"I have a few tricks. These giraffes have been here a long time. They are used to people but can be shy with large crowds. I think they will come just for you." He reached his hand into a gunny sack filled with some sort of pellets and held his hand up in the air, shaking it back and forth.

One of the two giraffes by the large acacia tree turned its long neck in their direction and, leading with its neck extended, headed for them.

"He's coming this way!" Katie snapped pictures as fast as she could.

"She," the guide corrected her. "This is Daisy. She'll eat out of your hand. Here, keep your palm flat like this." He filled Katie's flattened palm with pellets, and she held it out to the approaching giraffe.

"She won't bite my fingers, will she?"

"No. Just keep your palm flat and open. Don't make a fist. She hates it when people do that. She'll use the side of her head to ram up against yours."

"Seriously?" Katie could feel her heart beat faster. Several of the pellets cascaded off the side of her excitedly trembling hand. In the dirt below, a snorting warthog came trotting out of the shade and bent its front two legs at the knee joint, as if it were bowing in prayer. The park guide pointed out the warthog's position and said it was the only way his snout could reach the ground to get the food.

"As interesting as a warthog can be, I'm sure," Katie said, "I'm keeping my eye on Daisy. Here she comes. Hello, girl. Aren't you beautiful? Whoa! That's a bit up close and personal, don't you think?"

Daisy didn't stand back and take the pellets from Katie's hand extended out into the sun. Instead, the giraffe stuck her head into the shady space of the observation area so that she was only inches away from Katie.

"What do I do?"

"Hug her neck," Eli said.

"Give her the food," the park ranger said.

Without realizing it, Katie had made a fist in an effort to keep the pellets from falling down to the eager warthogs that had gathered in a gang of five beastly looking thugs.

Eli scooped his hand into the gunny sack and presented Daisy with a full, flat-palmed snack before she realized that Katie was holding out on her. Eli stroked the side of her large head the way a prized horse would be lovingly groomed. "You are a beauty, just like Katie said. Do you want to have some of the pellets she has for you now?"

Katie opened her hand and felt a peculiar sensation as Daisy's extremely long and surprisingly dry tongue licked up the pellets in one grand swipe. All that was left was a string of saliva that was more than a foot long and connected Katie's hand to Daisy's mouth.

Even though her every instinct was to let out a great big "Eww," Katie was too awed by the elegant creature and her big brown eyes to make a fuss.

"Here, do you want some more?" Katie reached into the sack for more pellets and repeated the offering of snacks. "You do know, don't you, Daisy, that your tongue looks a little purple today."

"That's normal," the park guide said. "And I think she likes you."

"Well, I like her too. This is the coolest thing ever. Eli, could you take a picture of us? You don't mind, do you, Daisy?"

Eli reached for Katie's phone camera and kept snapping as the park guide replenished the candy tray of her flattened palm.

Several people from their group at the snack bar apparently had noticed that a giraffe had meandered over. So they returned to the observation booth and took photos of Katie, as if she were some sort of gifted "giraffe whisperer" who had convinced the spotted creature to come to her and eat out of her hand.

Katie noticed that the park guide didn't correct their murmured assumptions, but he did offer for them to hold out pellets to Daisy as well. For some reason, even though two men held pellets in their palms, Daisy paid attention only to Katie, as if this was their private tea party and no boys were allowed.

More people came to the small space, and all of them snapped shots of Katie, who now circled her arm around Daisy's neck as Daisy demonstrated how far her big tongue could extend.

"Eli, I'm feeding a giraffe out of the palm of my hand. Did you know that?"

"Yes, Katie, you are. And for the record, I am standing right here."

"I know, but seriously, how cool is this? I am feeding a giraffe out of the palm of my hand."

"So you said."

"It's not a dream. This is so, so cool. Or as my friend Doug would say, this is awesome!"

Just then, Daisy turned her head away from Katie and the crowd.

"No! Don't leave. Was it something I said?"

With her long neck leading the way, Daisy lopped through the cluster of snorting warthogs and headed back to her companion under the acacia tree. Apparently too many people were on the deck, because it once again was filled with visitors standing shoulder to shoulder.

With a sigh, Katie blew a kiss to Daisy and thanked the park ranger.

"Come back anytime," he said.

As soon as she was back on the bus, she took out her phone to look at the photos Eli had taken. He had caught some great shots, including one that showed a long, swinging string of giraffe saliva that hung from Daisy's mouth to Katie's hand.

"This is the one I'm going to send Christy first." She held up her phone so Eli could see the shot.

"I told you they drool."

"But she was so cute."

"I told you they were cute too." Eli was flipping through the photos. He stopped and studied one of the shots with a big smile glowing on his face like a sunrise.

"What? Did you find another good one?"

He turned the phone's screen toward her. It was a shot of her feeding Daisy with all her attention focused on the gentle beast and a look of wide-eyed wonder on her face. Eli was on the other side of Daisy, stroking her long neck and peering around her great head to get a full view of Katie. The look on Eli's face was great. He looked so happy. So content. He was sharing his world with someone who was in awe. It almost looked as if Eli were as starstruck with Katie as she was with Daisy.

"You didn't know I had the ranger take some pictures of us, did you?" Eli asked. "Send that one to me, will you? And send it to Todd and Christy too."

Katie tapped out an email to Christy that read:

I will never forget this moment for the rest of my life.

Then she attached the two photos and sent the email off to the other side of the world.

Before the bus arrived back at Brockhurst, Christy had replied with an email that had the word "Smitten" in the subject line. Her email read:

Katie, this is amazing! Wow, look at that expression on Eli's face. He is captivated by you. Mesmerized. I love this photo of you two. As for the saliva one — eww!

Katie thought about Christy's comment over the next few days while she worked with Eli in the Coffee Bar, joined his parents for morning devotions, and helped to paint Mary's office in the administration building. Every day was great. Eli wasn't hiding that he was smitten with her, and she had no reason to pretend her feelings were anything other than mutual.

Having put their kissing-compatibility factor on the back burner, they turned their focus to further chances to get to know each other, discuss a variety of topics, and enjoy the beauty all around them as the days warmed up.

What they didn't do was discuss "them" or what was next. They simply did what was next as the projects kept coming their way and enjoyed being together. Katie didn't ask about how things were going between Eli and his dad. She knew he would talk about it when he wanted to. She also knew he still wanted to relocate to Upper Nine, because she heard him talking about possibly using the rest of the paint to redo his new room if none of the other offices needed a fresh coat. Katie took the talk about Upper Nine as an indication that Eli's dad was at least trusting him more and hopefully seeing him as an adult who was ready to make his own decisions.

But Katie was especially appreciative when Jim came to her and invited her to join him, Cheryl, and Eli on an overnight trip to one of the villages where a newly dug well was scheduled for completion in a week. To her, it meant that Jim saw her as being trustworthy, useful, and part of the team. That was important to her.

Cheryl asked Katie to help her start the immense project of organizing the new office space now that the paint had dried and the boxes and equipment finally had been moved in.

"Well, I've made one significant discovery," Katie told Cheryl when they were about four hours into the project.

"What's that, Katie?"

"I've discovered that this sort of work isn't my specialty."

"Really?" Cheryl stopped breaking down the empty cardboard boxes. "I'm surprised you would say that. You've gotten so much done. We've never had those supporter files organized the way you have them all together now."

"I'm not saying I won't help out with stuff like that. It just doesn't energize me. I wish I knew what my gifts and calling were. Maybe it's in the village, and I'll see it when we go tomorrow."

Cheryl pulled out the second office chair from the desk that faced where Katie was sitting and said, "What does energize you?" She grinned. "Besides Daisy the giraffe."

Katie had been teased by Eli and his parents over the past few days for the number of times she talked about feeding Daisy out of the palm of her hand.

"I don't want to be a zookeeper when I grow up, if that's what you're asking."

"No, I'm asking what really gets you going. What projects have you done in the past six months that you felt God's hand was on? I can think of one."

"You can?" Katie thought about the stories she had told Cheryl regarding her position as an RA and how she had organized an All Hall Event and the Spring Fling. Neither of those was on her list of things she would love to do again. She had told Cheryl that if it weren't for Eli's resourcefulness, both of those events could have crashed and burned.

But when she mentioned those tasks, Cheryl responded, "I wasn't thinking of either of those."

Katie couldn't remember organizing any other projects.

Cheryl raised an eyebrow. "Well, that's even more of an indication that you were using your gifts and working inside your calling. What about the fund-raiser you did at Rancho Corona for East African wells?"

"That didn't feel like work. I mean, it was a tremendous amount of work," Katie quickly added. "Especially that last semester with classes and RA duties. But it didn't drain me."

"Exactly. That's how it is when you're inside your gifting."

Katie let that thought sink in. "I think I see what you mean. Sort of. I was really passionate about telling people what you guys do here, and it was easy to get people to make donations. I mean, even this guy who was a vice president or something at the bank made a contribution when he saw what I was giving from my ..." Katie stopped herself. Very few people knew about the huge inheritance she had received from a great-aunt she had never met and how Katie had designated a number of generous contributions from those funds.

Cheryl stood and closed the window and the door to the office. In a low voice she said, "Katie, I have to tell you something."

Katie wondered if this was going to be the uncomfortable conversation she had anticipated when Eli's mom would ask about her "intentions" toward their son. Or at least try to find out Katie's point of view on their relationship. Obviously, Cheryl didn't want anyone to overhear them.

What Cheryl said next caught Katie off guard. "I know about the money you gave to pay off Eli's tuition."

Katie was stunned. "How did you know?"

"Eli told us that my brother paid off his tuition, but I knew Jonathan didn't have resources like that. Especially since he's a college professor, and it was right before he was getting married. I asked Jonathan about it, and he said he didn't pay for Eli's tuition, but he knew about it because Julia was somehow involved."

Katie leaned back and wondered what Julia, her former resident director from Rancho Corona, had said to Cheryl.

"I'm afraid I was unrelenting with Julia. I wouldn't let it go after Jonathan said that Julia knew the donor. It was such a large amount, I felt as if we needed to find a way to thank whoever it was or somehow pay them back."

Katie felt as if she had been punched in the stomach. How could Julia betray her trust like that? Katie had asked her to keep everything she knew about the inheritance confidential.

Cheryl continued, "Poor Julia had never met me, and there she was, newly married to my brother, and I kept hounding her. She finally told me the payment came from a young woman, a student from her dorm, who had inherited some money. She explained how she had helped this young woman make several contributions. I didn't know it was you, Katie."

"So Julia didn't tell you it was me? She didn't say my name?"

"No."

"Then how did you know it was me?"

"Your name was listed on a report of donors who had made sizable contributions through the fund-raiser you organized."

"Didn't the bank just transfer one final amount of money to the bank here?"

"Yes, but they also sent a breakdown report for the large amounts. I was the only one who saw it. Your name was on the report with the amount you gave. I put two and two together, and ... Katie ... I hardly know what to say. Thank you, and I'm sorry to put you in a place where you must feel vulnerable and exposed. Please know that Julia didn't betray your confidence."

"Does Eli know?"

"No. Neither does Jim. I thought about telling Jim recently, but it's your information and up to you to do with it what you want. I do apologize, Katie. Sincerely."

"You don't need to apologize. I'm glad you told me, and I'm especially glad you explained it all to me. It's an odd thing to have money in the bank, you know?"

"No, actually, I don't know." Cheryl offered Katie a tender smile.

"It's kind of a burden in some ways. I mean, I don't think about it a lot. It's just money. It's a resource. I want to be wise with how it's dispersed, so that's why I had Julia walk through the process with me with the lawyers and everything. It was my inheritance, in case you wondered where it came from."

"I'm glad you don't feel as if your trust was betrayed, Katie. I've wanted to tell you that I knew just so it was out in the open between us."

"I appreciate that," Katie said. "And I've wanted to say something to you for the past few weeks."

Cheryl's expression made it clear that she was open and receptive. That helped Katie to feel as if she could confide in her.

"I've wanted to say thank you for taking me in and making me feel welcomed. I know that I pretty much invited myself, and you've been very gracious. So thank you."

"Your arrival wasn't a complete surprise." Cheryl smiled. "I had a feeling you'd be coming. We're glad you're here, Katie."

"I'm really glad I'm here. And that brings me to the other thing I wanted to say."

"If the reason no one is giving me anything permanent to do around here is because you're expecting me to go back to California, then I think you should know that I don't see that happening. And that's not just because of Eli. I mean, of course he's a huge part of the reason why I came, and things are great between us from my point of view, but he's not the only reason I'm here. This is where I am supposed to be right now. I know that."

"It's good to hear you say this, Katie."

"Well, there's more I should say, and you probably already know this, but Eli and I are fine with taking our time figuring out what's next for us. I mean, us as a couple. He needs to decide what he's going to do here and so do I. We're not pushing our relationship ahead too fast, in case you were worried about that. We really are taking it slow."

Cheryl gave an affirming nod as if she'd already heard the same sort of report from her son.

Katie was glad to see that what she was saying seemed to be resonating well with Cheryl. Since she was on a roll, she kept going and leaked some more blunt truth. "I know that things are tense between Eli and your husband right now. I'm hoping the two of them will be able to work through their disagreement quickly. The thing is, I don't picture Eli as someone who could sit at a desk in this office and spend his days calling drilling companies or writing letters to donors. I see him being happier doing all the jobs he put down on his own list."

"He has a list?"

From the look on Cheryl's face, Katie could tell she'd said too much.

"He was going to talk to you guys about it."

"I see," Cheryl pulled back.

The office suddenly seemed to be getting smaller and smaller. Katie bit her lower lip and tried to think of what to say next.

Cheryl took the lead and said, "Why don't we put this topic aside for the moment. We can talk about it later."

"Good idea." Katie excused herself, saying she needed to go check on something. It was a lame excuse, but it got her out the door and into the fresh air. What she needed to check on was her emotional balance.

Trucking her way up the path to Eli's favorite bench, she kept scolding herself for not keeping her mouth closed. Things had been going so well. She'd felt a level of confidence opening up when Cheryl revealed she knew about Katie's inheritance. That openness obviously did not carry over to Katie being involved in Eli's conflict with his parents regarding his future position with the ministry. That was something Eli needed to settle with them without her involvement.

Katie remembered a line she'd overheard Claudinei say in the kitchen a few nights ago. "Throw it into the river. Let the crocodiles chew on it instead of you."

At first she thought Claudinei was talking about some food that had gone bad, assuming he was telling one of the guys on the kitchen staff how to dispose of it. As she handed over her dinner tray she discovered that the topic was problems, not food. The young man had apparently been telling Claudinei about his worries, and the chef was telling him to go toss them into the river for the crocodiles.

Katie wished she could gather up what she'd just said to Cheryl and go throw her over-zealous statements into the river. She would much rather see the crocodiles devour her words than have them gnawing away at her.

For a moment Katie considered turning toward the Lion's Den. She was pretty sure Eli was still working at the Coffee Bar that afternoon. If she could kidnap him and take him to the bench with her, she'd tell him about her financial situation and apologize for interjecting too much information into her heart-to-heart conversation with his mom.

At the fork in the path, something inside Katie convinced her that this wasn't the right time to pounce on Eli with all this information. She took the trail to the right and headed for the bench in order to have a chance to think and pray alone. Katie knew she could apologize at dinner for saying too much to Eli's mom. She was good at apologizing for such things.

Until then she had only one strategic thought.

Note to self: Zip your lips. Or else someone here might want to throw you to the crocodiles.

Katie had discovered early on that Brockhurst was a haven for many tattered souls. She had come to believe that in a way, she was one of them. Others found their way to the conference center after serving in long and difficult circumstances. The cool air, green lawns, comfortable beds, and extended hospitality of the permanent circle of residents at Brockhurst made this a place of restoration and peace. Katie felt it. Everyone who came on the grounds felt it. She was convinced that God had kissed this patch of Kenyan earth.

The night before the Lorenzos and Katie left for the village to celebrate the completion of the new well, Katie saw firsthand once again what a blessed place Brockhurst was. A hollow-eyed woman with four children stepped into the dining hall and tried to navigate her little flock through the buffet line. Several permanent residents from Brockhurst assisted her, carrying the trays for the young children and directing them to an open table. Katie watched as the children nibbled a little bit of this and that as their mother stared at her untouched meal.

Cheryl entered the dining room and made a straight path to the table with the newcomers. She sat beside the young mother, hugged her, kissed her on the temple, and then sat with her, saying nothing. Every time one of the children would look up at Cheryl, she had a calming smile for him or her and a few gentle words. The woman accepted the steaming cup of comforting chai someone brought to the table and offered to her. Katie watched as the woman sipped slowly, her eyes fixed and unblinking.

Eli joined Katie at the table where she had been sitting with a couple who had just arrived from Indiana and were waiting for their medical supplies shipment to arrive at Brockhurst before they went to their assigned village in Sudan. For the past few days both Eli and Katie had been unusually busy around the conference center with a variety of tasks assigned to them. They hadn't had a chance to speak privately for almost a week.

When Eli sat down next to Katie he started chatting with the couple from Indiana about the weather, the banana pudding, and other trivial topics before the visitors decided they would go for a walk before sunset. Since they had their backs to the mother and her children, they hadn't been watching what Katie was seeing.

As soon as they left the table, Katie asked Eli, "What happened to the woman your mom is with? Are she and her kids okay?"

"It's not good," Eli said in a low voice. "They were in Somalia and had to evacuate the medical compound. Callie and the kids got out, but they don't know where Evan is."

"Evan is her husband?"

Eli nodded. "Callie used to live here. As a matter of fact, she came here right after she graduated from Rancho Corona. She was my dad's office assistant for a couple of years and met Evan when he came to Brockhurst on his way to a medical mission trip to Somalia. They got married here and have been in Somalia for almost nine years. We have to pray, Katie. No one knows where Evan is, or if he's still alive."

Eli's words pierced Katie. Being at Brockhurst, she heard a lot every day about what was happening all around East Africa. Some of the reports of drought and disease were terrible and gut-wrenching. But this was the first time Katie had seen the look of true horror and terror.

"Let's pray for Evan now," Eli said.

They bowed their heads close, and Eli prayed. Katie silently agreed with him as he prayed aloud. When he finished, she found she couldn't add anything else, so she murmured "Amen" and reached for her glass of water. All she could think was, *Africa is not a safe place. I am not safe. I shouldn't be going to the village tomorrow.*

As soon as that arrow of fear punctured her thoughts, others followed. Katie felt her faith bleeding out all over the conversation she started with Eli. "Do you ever feel afraid that something like that could happen here?"

"Sometimes. Not often."

"What's to keep the Kenyan government from having a change of power and ousting all the Christian ministries?"

"God."

"I know God protects us, but not all the time, right? I mean, isn't this the country where the US embassy was bombed? How long ago was that?"

"It was August, 1998. We had a lot of people who came up here from Nairobi for refuge that month."

"Weren't you afraid then?"

"We were prepared to evacuate."

"Evacuate to where? Where would you go?"

"The airport was open."

"What if the airport closed? What if ..."

Eli reached over and covered Katie's hand with his. She felt her spirit calm slightly.

"Do you remember the night we went out to the desert with Joseph?" Eli asked.

"Yes."

"Do you remember seeing all those meteors and how they were set on a course, headed straight for the earth?"

"Yes."

Eli's handsome face had the look of a wise old man, as if he personally held one of the secrets of the ages and he was going to impart that wisdom to Katie. She had never seen that look on him before. It reminded her of his mother's expression the night they arrived and again that afternoon while they were moving into the new office and she hugged Katie after their heart-to-heart conversation. It was the look of serenity.

"Katie, any one of those meteors could have come through the earth's atmosphere and crashed into our planet. But they didn't. God held them back." He leaned in closer. "No matter where we live, immense forces are coming at us all the time. The only ones that get through are the ones God allows."

Katie gave Eli a stern look. It wasn't that she didn't agree with him. She did. She'd had those same sorts of thoughts after the night they watched the meteor shower. What she didn't like was that it was such a hard truth to accept at a moment like this. Her eye was on Callie and her little children as God was allowing a meteor to crash through their lives.

"Katie, look at me."

She turned her focus back onto Eli. "Don't be afraid."

As soon as he said the word *afraid*, she recognized the familiar weapon that had brought on such anxiety before.

"I am afraid."

"I know. You don't have to be. Whatever happens in your life goes through God's hand first before he allows it to come to you. Todd taught me that when we were together in Spain, and it changed my perspective on so many things. I know I've told you this before, but, Katie, we have to remember that we're not victims of all the horrible things that happen on this fallen planet. We're victims of grace. God's expansive grace. It all comes from him and is allowed by him. Even the terrible and destructive things in life."

Katie glanced again at Callie. Cheryl had draped her slender arm across Callie's shoulder like a comforting shawl and was speaking soft words as she made eye contact with each of the four children. Katie thought about how Cheryl had been attacked when the Lorenzos had lived on a medical compound in Zaire. Eli had told Katie about how he had come home from school, found a man attacking his mother, intending to rape her, and how his knife had found its way across her throat.

Eli had arrived at just the right moment, and the attacker lashed out, wounding Eli before the man fled. Both Eli and his mom were fortunate to receive the medical attention they needed to stitch up the cuts.

If anyone knew what terror felt like, it was Cheryl. If anyone here knew what it felt like to be a victim of grace and had earned the right to speak comfort and hope to this young mother, it was Cheryl.

"Are you all right?" Eli asked Katie.

She turned to face him and nodded. "Thanks for what you just said. I needed to hear that. Life seems more intense here sometimes." She let out a deep breath.

"Speaking of intense, I heard that you had an intense conversation with my mom a few days ago."

"Yeah, I was going to tell you about that. I'm sorry."

"Sorry for what?"

"I said too much. I told her about the list you were making for your job description."

"You did? You talked to her about that?"

"Yes. Didn't she tell you?"

"No. She told me the two of you talked about you and your role here."

"We did. I wouldn't say that part of our conversation was intense, though."

Eli's eyes had narrowed. He lowered his voice and asked, "Why were you talking about my position? That's something I need to work through with my dad. We haven't had a chance to sit down and talk about it."

"That's why I'm trying to apologize. I realized immediately I shouldn't have said anything. I'm sorry I did."

Their eyes were locked in a searching gaze. It seemed to take Eli a few moments to let go of his frustration. He drew in a breath and said, "It's okay. Don't worry about it. I need to get things settled with my dad. You didn't know that we haven't talked yet."

"Thanks for the grace, Eli."

He gave her a half a grin and seemed to pick up on the fact that she chose to use the word *grace* after the points he had just made on how God is ultimately in control. "It's probably a good thing that you brought it up with my mom. I need to talk with both of them. Hopefully I'll have time to do that tonight."

"So, does this mean I didn't completely ruin your life?" Katie asked with a hopeful expression.

"Not yet," he answered with a straight face.

Eli nudged her with his shoulder and she nudged him back.

"I feel like I haven't seen you in weeks," Katie said.

"I know. It's been wild around here."

They were both quiet for a moment. "Are you ready for our long drive to the village tomorrow?" Eli asked.

"No, but I will be by the time we leave in the morning."

"I can't wait. It's been a long time since I've been to a village. I'm eager for you to get a feel for what it's like. I think it's going to become clear to my dad once we're there that that's where I belong."

Katie paused. "Wait. Are you saying you see yourself living in a village? Full-time?"

"I wouldn't mind that. Would you?"

"Me? I don't know." It hadn't occurred to Katie that Eli's ultimate aspiration might be to live permanently in a village. When she allowed herself a few fanciful peeks into their possible future, she pictured them in their own cottage at Brockhurst. Visits to the village would be side trips every few months. How did she miss this significant piece of Eli's dream for the future? His future and possibly their future.

"Are you saying you haven't considered living in a village? Seriously?"

She wasn't sure what to say. She countered with a question of her own.

"How about if you ask me again after I've actually been to a village? I'd like to go have a look around and check out a few mud huts before I give my final answer."

Eli still looked surprised at her response but he nodded slowly and said, "Do you think this is fear stuff again that's making you feel uncertain?"

"No," she said decisively. "It's big-picture stuff, Eli. I mean, this is all new to me. I've never been to an African village before."

"Okay." He held up his hand before she got ramped up. "I understand."

"Good." Katie leaned back and folded her arms. "I'm glad you understand, because maybe I'm the one who needs to understand better. What exactly do you see yourself doing? In the villages, I mean. Would you be on a permanent team that goes around and digs the wells?"

"No. There's a lot more to the projects than the digging crew. The mission receives tons of requests for wells. Someone needs to go to each village, assess the need, and outline the steps required, because it's different for each location. Then someone needs to do extensive hygiene training so the original problems that polluted the water source don't reoccur."

Eli pushed his plate aside. "The other thing I'd like to do is work with the teams that come to Kenya to help. In some of the locations, it takes weeks to carry in the rocks, sand, and other components before the well can be built. It does no good to bring people over here unless they have an idea of what's going to be required of them. And they need someone to keep them on task once they arrive in the village. It's a lot more complicated than just digging a hole in the ground and installing a two-ton pumping system."

Katie knew that. She just didn't understand until now that Eli saw his position requiring extended stays and going from village to village.

"What about you?" Eli asked. "Can you see yourself being involved in that sort of work? Helping in the villages?"

"I don't know. I mean ..."

She didn't want to say anything like, "Where you go I will follow," because obviously she demonstrated that by following him to

Africa. But was she ready and willing to follow him to the villages for extended stays so she could haul cement up dirt trails?

Katie also knew she didn't want to sound like his dad, pressing Eli to set up a desk in the new office and stay in the Brockhurst bubble. If Eli was created to live in the villages, then that's what he needed to pursue.

"I don't know what to say. I'm trying to figure out where I fit and understand what it is that you want me to do. It's not all clear to me yet."

Eli leaned back. "Then you and I need to talk about this."

"Yes, we do. Actually, there are several things we need to talk about." She glanced over her shoulder to make sure none of the other people in the dining hall were listening to them. "When can we do that?"

Eli glanced at his watch. "Maybe tomorrow. On the way to the village."

"But your parents will be in the car. We need to talk privately."

"Then let's try to talk once we get to the village." He got up and reached for his plate. "Do you want anything else to eat?"

"No." Katie couldn't believe he was walking away from her. She knew he had a habit of taking small portions to begin his meal, as if making sure there was enough for everyone, which there always was. Then he went back and took more if he was still hungry. He usually only took more of one thing, which was whatever he liked the most at that meal. Katie watched the back of his head as he went back toward the buffet. She tried to wrap her mind around the thought of living in an African village. What if there was unrest? Would Katie end up like Callie one day? Huddled at a Brockhurst dining room table, her children looking like waifs as they waited for news of Eli's well-being in a wild, remote village somewhere?

A little rhyme danced in Katie's thoughts. *First comes love, then comes marriage, then comes a mud hut in an African village.*

No, definitely not feelin' it. She and Eli had some serious discussing to do. Somehow he seemed to think the conversation was going to happen either on the way or after they arrived in the village.

The next morning, Katie was ready for the road trip and stood waiting by the administration office with her duffel bag packed with layers for hot and cold weather as well as her hiking boots and her pillow. She had a collection of pillow cases that she had purchased at Bargain Barn while she was in college, and she had brought the assortment with her. Each pillowcase had a different animated character that conjured up fond memories of her youth. Today the Little Mermaid was about to accompany Katie on this adventure.

Eli's dad pulled up in one of the small, well-used, and thoroughly bruised cars that were shared by the residents at Brockhurst. As he got out and took a look at Katie's huge duffel bag, Eli and Cheryl arrived down the path with little more than knapsacks.

"Let me guess," Katie said. "I overpacked."

"It's fine," Cheryl said. "It'll all fit."

Katie noticed that the three of them were wearing several layers of clothes and had sweatshirts tied around their waists. She knew then that she should have at least left her pillow behind if she wanted to appear suited for village life.

Taking the backseat behind the driver, Katie turned so that her legs were at an angle. There wasn't enough space to put them straight. Cheryl settled into the backseat beside her, and Katie tried to hide her surprise and disappointment that Eli wasn't sitting with her. She had come to the conclusion last night after their talk in the dining room that if she was going to be telling Cheryl and Christy and anyone else who asked if she and Eli were taking things nice and slow, she needed to allow their important conversations to come at their own pace as well.

After all, how could she be a true "Princess Hakuna Matata" if she kept worrying about everything?

The first hour and a half of the journey, it didn't matter who Katie was sitting beside. All her interaction was with the beautiful scenery in the Kenyan highlands. She had her window open and kept the camera on her phone busy.

The town they drove through was packed with people on foot. The car was slowed down on the narrow road when they got stuck behind a local man on his way to market. He and his harvest of what looked like sweet potatoes were on a cart made of flat wood planks that was hitched to a skinny donkey. The man stood on the cart with his legs apart and his hands gripping a length of frayed rope. It seemed to Katie as if they were watching an extra in a movie about the Middle Ages. Nothing here had changed in hundreds of years.

Nevertheless, the shops that lined the main street of town showed evidence of the influence of Christianity on Africa over the past half century as well as the technology of the twenty-first century. Most of the shops had their names painted somewhere out front, and most of the names hinted at some sort of biblical reference. Katie saw the Guardian Angel Beauty Shop, the Alleluia Grocers, the Holy Ghost Laundry, and the Shekinah Glory Mobile Phone Store.

The Shekinah Glory Mobile Phone Store had a bright logo for the cell phone service provider painted across the entire side of the building, and they had a line of people waiting to get in.

"Are they having a sale?" Katie asked.

"Probably not." Eli's dad glanced to the side of the road and kept driving.

"Then why are so many people at the cell phone store?"

"Nearly everyone in Africa has a cell phone," Cheryl said.

That surprised Katie.

Jim added, "The number of people here who have computers or even laptops is very low. More Africans use mobile phones per unit than any country in the world."

"What does that mean, exactly?"

"In other words," Cheryl explained, "an East African village might have one hundred twenty people living in huts and have a generator to produce limited electricity. They have no televisions or computers. But they have a mobile phone."

Katie wondered if things were more advanced in the villages than she had assumed. She never pictured cell phones in any of her mental images of life in Kenya's remote regions.

"It doesn't mean the cell phone service is always reliable," Eli added.

"A lot more things here make sense than you think at first glance," Jim said. "People are quick to adapt. Kenya has moved ahead of most African countries with their school program, for instance. The government pays for eight years of school for children and includes lunch. In many rural areas the parents send their children to school so they will be fed that day. In the past they kept them home from school so they could work in the fields. This started in 2003 and has been quite successful."

"I have noticed lots of children walking along the road. I thought it was unusual that they were all in school uniforms," Katie said.

"The parents pay for the uniforms. It's worked out well."

As they motored through a more rural area with hills and fields, the road became bumpy. Katie braced herself, but Cheryl didn't. She bobbed and swayed along with the bumps as the scenery continued to spread out before them with fantastic vistas. Cheryl pointed out groves of papaya trees and banana trees. Katie noticed that the small herd of cows they passed looked pretty skinny. What surprised her most was that the entire time they had been driving, she saw people walking along the side of the road. So many people. All of them coming and going on their own two legs. She saw some people on bikes but not many. A young Kenyan man passed them on a motorcycle.

They came to an immediate halt when a young goat strayed from the pack of five that an older man was herding along with a stick. The wayward goat stopped in the middle of the road, and Jim nearly hit it.

"That was close," Cheryl said, as soon as all was clear, and he drove on. She said it with the same tone that someone would use to tell the time.

Calm and unrattled, Cheryl reached into a woven basket next to her feet and pulled out a book to read. Eli settled into one of his sleep-anywhere positions with his head against the side of the door. No surprise there.

Katie knew there would be no space for personal conversations for any of them on this long drive. She didn't like the unsettledness that came from not knowing who had said what to whom about which topics. Katie realized that every family has their own communication dynamics. If it were up to her, she would bust open all the hot topics and get them out there for all four of them to discuss.

She had a feeling, though, that it would go better all the way around if she used this as an opportunity to learn some patience and let Eli take the lead on when he wanted to talk and how he wanted to approach the unsolved topics.

As the car sped down the road, Katie congratulated herself for improving in the area of being a "big blurt."

The silence was soothing after the excessively busy week. Katie found herself dozing off for short stretches of time. Each time she awoke, the magnificent landscape soothed her senses all over again.

When the sun was high above them Jim turned into the small, dilapidated gas station in a clearly British-influenced town called Nyeri. After filling the tank, they drove about a half a mile and parked near a large hotel that had a restaurant Cheryl said was one of her favorites.

Katie soon discovered why it was a favorite place to stop. The restaurant was outside on a terrace under umbrella-covered tables. Katie would have thought they were eating at a California restaurant except for the peacocks walking around on the large grassy area that stretched out past the terrace. The view beyond the grass was of rolling hills and jagged rock formations. In some ways it reminded her of the sort of background seen in an Italian painting from the Renaissance.

They ate fish, potatoes, and a green vegetable that looked like zucchini but tasted different. It could have been the spices used in the preparation. Or it could have been some other vegetable and not zucchini at all. She had learned it was best to gratefully eat what was offered to her, and say an extra little prayer that even if she didn't like it that her stomach would. Fortunately this mystery vegetable made her stomach quite happy.

After they ate, the four of them strolled the grounds, talking about Kenya and how gorgeous it was and how surprising and exciting.

"I've never grown tired of the beauty here," Cheryl said as she pointed out the red ginger plants.

"There's a Swahili saying for all of this," Jim said. "It's *Uzuri wa Afrika*, which literally means 'the beauty of Africa.' When you can't find a way to describe what you're seeing, you just chalk it up to the beauty of Africa."

They walked a little farther, and Katie quietly asked Eli, "How do you say, 'I'm smitten' in Swahili?"

He gave her a funny look and didn't attempt a translation.

Leaning closer to him, Katie playfully said, "You see, you thought I was chasing you when I got on the plane, but now the truth is out. My big crush is really on Africa. I'm smitten. Sorry to break it to you this way, Lorenzo."

With a straight face Eli said, "I should have seen this coming. How can I compete with an entire continent?"

Katie grinned. "You don't have to compete. I think you know that."

He smiled back and took her hand. "I'm glad you love it here, Katie. Really glad." The path they were walking on had brought them back to the lobby entrance to the Aberdare Country Club.

Katie was reluctant to leave. Everything was so civilized and proper.

When they returned to the car, Eli was selected to drive. Katie ended up in the backseat with Jim. As he put on his seat belt, he said, "Cheryl, you should tell Katie the Treetops and Queen Elizabeth story."

Eli started the car and slowly backed out of the parking spot. Katie thought about the way he had driven around campus last year in a golf cart that Katie referred to as a "clown mobile." That was a different sort of vehicle than this one, and it was a different sort of terrain. She certainly wouldn't want to be handed the keys and invited to drive the rest of the way to the village.

Eli did great, though, and within a few minutes, Jim was asleep in the backseat, demonstrating where Eli's genetic disposition to sleep on the road came from.

"Mom, what about the story you were going to tell Katie?"

"Oh, yes. Queen Elizabeth. When she came to Kenya for a visit in 1952, she and Prince Philip stayed at Treetops. It's a hotel not far from here. The rooms are at treetop height. She sipped tea on the open veranda while the elephants and other wild animals came to the watering hole below. Her father, King George IV, had been ill but seemed to have recovered, so the trip to Africa didn't pose a conflict."

"Was he the one who stuttered? I remember seeing a movie about him," Katie said.

"Yes, that was the same king," Eli answered for his mom.

"What happened is that he took a turn for the worse and passed away while Princess Elizabeth was at Treetops. Since communication between England and Africa was so slow, she didn't know her father had died until after they had left Treetops, and they stopped for lunch at the Aberdare Country Club, where we just ate."

"Really? The queen of England ate at that same restaurant?"

"Yes. Only she didn't yet know she was the queen of England. Word hadn't reached her. The great statement about Treetops is that Elizabeth went up the stairs to her room that night as a princess, and when she descended those same stairs the next morning, she was the queen of England."

"I love stories like that," Katie said. "I mean, it's sad that her father died while she was in Africa, but what a rite of passage that moment was. She was doing what was on the schedule for that day, and by the time she put her head on her pillow that night, everything had changed."

As Eli drove, Katie thought about the story of Isaac and Rebekah in Genesis. One of her Bible professors had taught on that particular story with a lot of added details. Katie remembered how Rebekah had gone to the well one morning as always, and by the end of the day, everything had changed.

Rebekah offered to draw water from the well for the camels of Abraham's servant, who had been sent on a mission to find a wife for Isaac. She was singled out at the community well and returned with the servant knowing she would become Isaac's wife.

Katie remembered how her Old Testament professor had paraphrased Rebekah's comment on first setting eyes on Isaac and the two of them met halfway in the field. The Bible records that Rebekah said, "Who is that man?" Katie's professor jokingly said, "And Rebekah exclaimed, 'Hubba-hubba, who is the hunk with the Weedwacker?'"

Aside from that bit of professorial humor, the part Katie remembered most and had underlined in her Bible was the passage that said Rebekah became Isaac's wife and he "loved her." Her professor at Rancho had pointed out that while the Bible tells a lot of stories about how couples met and married, the word *love* rarely is mentioned.

That's what Katie wanted. She wanted to be loved. Was Eli a man who would love her for the rest of his life? Or would his work come first? It was an important question for Katie to consider.

Katie was grateful when they stopped again for gas at a petrol station in a remote area. They climbed out of the car and stretched their legs while Jim filled the gas tank and Eli filled a large, red gasoline container.

"How much farther, do you think?" Katie asked.

"A couple of hours. Are you road weary?" Eli asked.

"I'm doing okay. How about you? Is all the driving getting to you?"

"Not yet. I don't mind driving. I like it more than my dad does. What about you? Do you want to drive for a while?"

"Ah, that would be a resounding no. Thanks for your generous offer, but I'll pass. You're doing just fine." She patted him on the back.

Eli turned his back to her. "Scratch right there."

She scratched his upper shoulder, and he continued to curve his back, rounding his shoulders forward and making happy sounds as if Katie's fingernails were ministering angels.

"A little closer to the middle. There. Now down."

Katie got going with both hands and gave Eli's warm back a good scratch. She laughed at how he seemed to crumple at her touch.

"I didn't know my sawed-off fingernails could have such a soothing effect on you."

"You have the golden touch, Katie. This feels great."

She scratched some more and realized the local people as well as Cheryl and Jim were watching them. Katie patted Eli on the shoulder and said in a low voice, "I think we have an audience. We probably look like a couple of monkeys."

Eli made monkey sounds and scratched his armpits.

Katie cracked up. Eli never stopped surprising her.

"Katie, why don't you take the passenger's seat this next stretch?" Cheryl suggested, herding them back into the car.

Katie got in gladly and pulled the seat up as far as it would go so Jim had lots of leg room. He had bought some bottles of water at the filling station, and as they took off, they had music, bottles of clean water, and a wide view out the front windshield that was spotted with dirt and dead bugs.

"Katie," Cheryl said gingerly, "how do you feel about being in a village for an extended period of time?"

"I don't know. I'll tell you tomorrow after I've been in a village for an extended period of time."

"What about living in a village? For weeks at a time or longer?"

Katie could see where this was going, and her guard went up. Had Eli talked to his parents last night about their conversation in the dining hall? More importantly, had he talked to them about his father's expectations of his role within the ministry? Was Eli set on living in a village?

"I don't know," Katie said, trying to sound as lighthearted and breezy about the topic as possible. She really wanted to have this discussion with Eli before chatting about it with his mom. "I have to be honest; I do like having my own bathroom."

Eli darted a look at her and then returned his focus to the road. She knew she could be reading too much into his look, but it did seem that he was hoping she would withdraw her comment and cast her vote for village campfires instead of a sink and toilet.

The topics that had been hinted at but not fully opened on this journey were beginning to weigh on Katie. She liked things uncomplicated and out in the open. The best way for that to happen was for Eli and her to discuss these things privately, not with his parents. That meant she had to wait. And waiting was never a comfortable exercise.

She was glad when Eli's dad changed the topic a little while later. "Katie, is your mobile phone picking up a signal here?" Jim asked. "Mine isn't. I'm trying to check on the weather to make sure we're not heading into rain with those dark clouds ahead."

She pulled out her phone and turned it back on, since she had turned it off to save the battery. "It looks like it's working." She handed it to him so he could do a weather search.

As Jim was looking up the weather report, Katie's phone sounded a distinct buzzer. A few seconds later it sounded again.

"Do you have a call coming in?" Jim asked.

"No, that's an old alarm. I set it last year for anytime I received a text from my fellow RA, Nicole. When we were on duty this past year, lots of times we had to get ahold of each other right away."

"This alarm sounds only when that particular person is trying to contact you?" he asked.

"Yes."

"That would be handy. What's the app for that?"

Eli glanced at Katie as she was directing his dad to what he wanted to find on her phone. "That's what you need, Dad. Another phone app."

"We all have our hobbies, son."

Katie smiled as she took back her phone and turned off the buzzing from Nicole's message. It had been a long time since that alarm had sounded, and Katie felt melancholy hearing it. She missed Nicole and the time they had spent together in the dorm for their senior year of college. More than once Katie had wondered how Nicole and Rick were getting along in their newly sprouted dating and working relationship. Rick was opening a new café, and Nicole had been working with him on the huge project for quite a few months. Having worked with Rick when he managed the Dove's Nest Café, Katie knew that the close, daily interaction could either make or break their attraction to each other.

Opening her text message file, Katie read Nicole's note. ANY CHANCE YOU CAN CALL ME? ASAP? CALL ME BEFORE YOU CHECK YOUR EMAIL.

Katie didn't think this was a good time or place to call Nicole. Aside from the high service fees she would have to pay for the international call, it wouldn't be private in the car. Katie knew it would be better to wait until they were back at Brockhurst, and she could use the internet phone service she had set up on her laptop so they could have a nice, long conversation.

She was about to put her phone back in her bag, but her curiosity was too strong. What email had Nicole sent that she didn't want Katie to open yet?

Knowing Nicole, it was probably an email with an attached photo of the way her decorating scheme had turned out for Rick's café. Katie wasn't especially wowed by vinyl-covered booths or paint colors on walls the way Nicole was. Katie thought the email could wait.

She put away her phone, and they drove into the dusk as the scenery turned dusty brown and took on the golden haze of the sunset.

"Did you see if rain is predicted in the village?" Katie asked.

"No. The clouds seem to be just passing through," Jim said.

"How's Nicole doing?" Eli asked.

"I don't know. Her text said to call her, but I'll do that when we get back to Brockhurst."

"Do you think she's okay?"

Katie hadn't considered the possibility that something was wrong. Nicole's email might have bad news that she wanted to tell Katie first. Reaching for her cell phone again, Katie let her imagination sprint down a dismal trail. Tapping her foot as she waited for her dozen or more emails to load, Katie saw the subject line come up on Nicole's email: *Save the date.*

She relaxed her shoulders. "It looks like an invitation for a birthday party or probably for the grand opening of one of the restaurants Rick and his brother are opening."

Katie couldn't remember off the top of her head when Nicole's birthday was or when Rick's café was supposed to open.

Clicking on Nicole's email, she wanted to see what upcoming event she would have been saving the date for if she were still back in California.

Katie read the message and didn't blink. She barely breathed.

Save the date:

October 3

Rick and Nicole are getting married!

E li." Katie stared at her phone. No other words formed on her lips. "Yes?"

Katie was aware that he was glancing at her and then looking back at the road.

"Is something wrong?" he asked.

Katie still didn't know what to say.

"Is Nicole all right? What did she say?"

Without looking at Eli, Katie said, "She's getting married."

"She is? To Rick?"

"Yes, of course. To Rick. Rick and Nicole are engaged. I'm in shock. The wedding is in October." Katie's stunned thoughts turned to her default mode of sarcasm. "We're supposed to save the date."

"Did you know they were that serious about each other?"

Katie turned off her phone to save the battery. Or maybe she just needed to feel she had the power to hit some sort of "Make it stop" button. She knew that Eli's parents could hear everything she and Eli were saying from their position in the small car's backseat. Katie didn't care. They all had talked openly about Rick before and how Katie had gone out with him for more than a year. Eli always had nice things to say about Rick as a former roommate. Katie always had nice things to say about Nicole, her former fellow RA.

She didn't know what to say now.

"Nicole is a sincere person. Rick has a lot of vision." Eli kept his eyes on the bumpy road. "They'll make a good team. A good couple."

If she weren't so stunned at the moment, Katie probably would agree. What Eli said was true. Rick and Nicole would make a good team. As a matter of fact, when she found out a few months ago that Nicole had it bad for Rick, she helped to match them up. She knew then that in a lot of ways they would be better together than she and Rick had been. And Nicole and Rick managed to develop a really strong relationship and had been very good for each other in a lot of ways.

What hit Katie so hard was that Rick had managed to get in touch with his true feelings and take the lead in acting on them. He had decided after only a few months of dating Nicole that he was ready to commit himself to one woman, and Nicole was that woman. Katie was astounded. She didn't know where to put that thought. For so many months she had worked out scenarios in which she was that woman. Rick's one woman. But, no. It was her friend.

"I'm happy for them," she said, sounding emotionally flat even to herself.

"Are you really?"

Katie looked at Eli. He glanced over at her, and she nodded. "Yes. I'm shocked, but I'm happy for them."

Eli gave her another glance, this time with an encouraging grin attached to it. He reached over and gave her hand a squeeze. "I guess when you know it's the right person for you, you just know."

She felt her heart stir. He had just made that declaration in front of his parents.

"Do you think that's true, Eli? Really?"

"Yes. Really. I do. Don't you?"

Katie wanted to believe it. She wanted to agree. But at this moment, she couldn't find a way to add her own affirming comment. What was it Christy had said about riding along inside the mystery of growing a relationship? That's how she felt right now.

Eli let go of her hand and put both hands on the steering wheel to navigate the bumpy stretch ahead. Katie noticed that he turned on the headlights because the daylight had faded quickly, and the dark African night was rolling in, covering them with an inky blanket of darkness. The only lights were the car's headlights and the stars that Katie could see out the windshield. The moon wasn't in front of them, nor did it seem to be providing any light. It was the darkest night Katie had ever seen.

Eli hit a bump and slowed down. A minute later he hit another big bump, and when he did, the engine made a strange clunking noise.

"That didn't sound good," his dad said.

The car coasted; the engine had shut itself off.

"Hold on," Eli called out. "The steering wheel is locked."

"Put it in neutral," his dad said.

"I already did."

"Try the brakes."

"Got my foot on them."

Katie braced herself. She could see nothing but rutted road ahead of them. No cliffs or drop-offs.

"There's a level, open spot up there," she said, straining her eyes. "It looks like a turnout."

Eli coasted into the area, working hard to force the steering wheel to turn the tires to the right. He pressed on the brakes, and the car stopped with the left side of the car still on the road and the right side on the turnout.

"Let's see what we have going on under the hood," Jim said. He was out the back door before Eli even had his seat belt off.

Katie noticed that none of the Lorenzos seemed overly concerned at this turn of events. All three of them were acting as if this happened all the time, and once again they seemed content to go with the flow. Katie could hear Jim directing Eli where to shine his flashlight. The two of them remained hidden behind the car's raised hood. Then it sounded as if one of them was underneath the engine, tapping on something.

"Nothing obvious under here," Eli said.

Katie and Cheryl got out and peered at the engine with the guys. Not that either of them could say what they were looking for.

"I guess we pray for a mechanic and see what God brings us," Cheryl said.

As had been the custom often at Brockhurst, they stopped right there, joined hands, and prayed. Then they put together a plan for taking turns with the flashlight to "pay a visit to the cheetahs," which was code for going off to find a private spot to go to the bathroom. The guys went first, leaving Katie and Cheryl standing in the light of the car's headlights.

It was so dark that Katie kept looking up into the vast night sky. The stars, like pinholes in the velvet carpet of heaven, permitted the tiny points of glory to slip through. She thought of Queen Elizabeth coming down the stairs at Treetops and Rebekah going to Isaac in the field. Two very different women who had life-changing moments on ordinary days. From that one event on, they knew what their lives were about. They entered what was next and lived it out. Katie wanted that. With or without Eli or any other guy in her life, she wanted to know what God had created her to do. But she had to admit, she would rather go the distance with Eli than without him.

The guys returned and handed over the flashlights. Katie headed off into the brush with Cheryl following close behind.

"Clap your hands, Katie."

She obliged and made critter-shooing noises while Cheryl swished the flashlight. The next five minutes weren't as bad as Katie thought they might be. Cheryl came prepared with what they needed and made the experience seem natural. They returned to find Eli and Jim stretched out on the car's closed hood, gazing at the stars. Katie smiled.

Eli held out his hand, inviting her to clamor up and stretch out beside him. She didn't care how dirty the car's hood was or how many squished bugs on the windshield were going to now attach themselves to her shirt. She was in Africa, watching the night sky and stretched out next to Eli. This was a memory moment that overlapped the meteor-gazing night in the California desert and yet had a pristine beauty all its own. This was a different continent. These were different stars, and in many ways she was a different person than she had been last fall.

Eli, however, was his same, steady self.

Jim spoke softly, pointing out the constellations. Cheryl pulled a bag of her own version of trail mix from the backseat and passed it down the line while she stood next to Katie on the passenger side of the car. The four of them munched their evening meal of peanuts, pumpkin seeds, and dried pieces of papaya and banana while passing a bottle of water around.

In the distance, they heard a chilling sound of some sort of animal. The call was faint but distinctly a wild creature.

"What was that?" Katie asked.

"I'm not sure," Jim said. "But I'll tell you one thing. We'll be sleeping in the car tonight."

"I'll take the driver's seat," Eli said.

None of them protested, because they all knew that Eli could sleep anywhere. Jim took the passenger's seat, and Katie and Cheryl shared the backseat. Katie put on her faithful Rancho Corona sweatshirt and was grateful for the silly luxury of having brought her pillow. She put it between her and Cheryl, and the two women fell asleep sharing her pillow with the Little Mermaid pillowcase.

Through the night they slept in snatches. They would doze off, and then someone would hear a sound outside and rustle enough to wake everyone else. The night sounds increased. At one point, they were certain they heard a car approaching. Eli got out with his flashlight, prepared to wave them down. But no car lights ever appeared on the road.

By first light they were up and out of the car, eager to stretch. The world around them seemed much friendlier, even though it was just as void of human activity as it had been last night when they were rolling along on this road.

Katie was slowly chewing her handful of trail mix from the morning ration when she thought she saw someone walking down the road toward them. "Is that a person, or am I seeing things?"

Eli shielded his eyes from the sun that had just risen in the east.
The light shone behind the man as he walked and cast a glow on him
so that at first it seemed he was there, but then the light swallowed
him, and he seemed to be a mirage.

"Dad, I think someone is coming this way."

Jim and Cheryl joined Katie and Eli at the front of the car.

"Do you have yours?" Jim asked Eli in a low voice.

"Yes."

Katie didn't know what they were talking about, but she could
guess that in the same way both of them had flashlights connected
to their key rings, they also had some sort of weapon they would be
willing to use if necessary.

The dark-skinned man coming toward them at an even pace was
wearing a white shirt and had something under his arm. It didn't seem
to be a weapon. When he was within fifty feet of them, Katie saw that
he was holding a chicken under his arm. The perplexing part was trying to figure out where he had come from and where he was going.

"Jambo," Jim called out.

"Jambo." The man grew closer. "You have some car troubles?"

"Yes. We're not sure what's wrong. Can you tell me where you've
come from? Is there a place up the road that might have a mechanic?"

"Let me have a look." He handed the chicken over to Jim as Eli
popped open the car's hood. The man leaned over and put his long
fingers into the engine like a pianist would place both hands on the
keys of a baby grand. He seemed to pull something here and attach
something there.

"Try it now." He stood up straight and waited.

Eli slipped inside the car, turned the key, and the engine started.
Katie let out a cheer.

"Did one of the wires or tubes shake loose?" Cheryl asked.

"Yes."

"Asante sana." Jim held the chicken back to him. "We're so grateful."

The man held up his hand, calmly refusing to take back the
chicken.

"It's your chicken. Here. We can't accept this."

The man put up both hands. *"Mpaji ni Mungu."*

"Mpaji ni Mungu," Eli and his parents responded in unison.

The chicken fluffed up as if trying to get out of Jim's grasp. "Here, Cheryl, you were always better with these things than I was." Jim handed Cheryl the chicken, and with ease she tucked it under her arm as if it was a puffy, feathered handbag.

Eli settled back into the driver's seat and peered at the engine as it rumbled. "Dad, did you see what it was that needed to be reconnected?"

"No, I was holding the hen."

The men looked at each other, and then Jim asked their timely visitor, "What was it that came loose?"

All four of them looked up and looked around. Their morning mechanic was gone.

"Where did he go?" Katie peered down the long, straight rural road in both directions.

The four of them exchanged glances, their faces expressing the same look of amazement.

In a matter-of-fact way, Jim said, "We shouldn't keep the engine running. We can't afford to waste the petrol. Let's get going."

They took the same spots where they had slept last night. Eli drove.

"What was that he said to you and that you guys repeated?" Katie asked.

"It's sort of a blessing," Eli said. "Like the way people in the US say, 'God bless.' Here they say, 'Mpaji ni Mungu.' God is the sustainer."

The chicken remained under Cheryl's arm in the backseat between her and Katie. Twice Katie turned around and looked behind them, expecting to see the man stepping out of the shrubbery that was scattered at intervals along the road and continuing his trek with his back to them. But he was nowhere to be seen.

Now that they were back in closer quarters again and had the foul fowl to add to the fragrances, Katie remembered noticing something else about their unexpected roadside assistant. He smelled nice. That was unusual for someone who was in a remote area and had been walking some distance carrying the stinky chicken. He should have smelled more like the rest of them did. Instead, he smelled like fresh air.

"I just have to say something," Katie said after they were ten minutes down the road. "Does anyone else think that guy was an angel?"

"Yup."

"Yes."

"I think so."

"Okay, just checking." Katie looked out the window and let the profoundness of what had just happened sink in.

14

One of Kenya's distinctives that Katie had come to adore was the light. As they journeyed the final two hours to the village, the morning light awakened the day with long shadowed contours that seemed like gentle fingers rousing the earth from its night's sleep.

Katie felt the warm light settling on her shoulders as the golden fingers stretched through the car's back window. In front of them lay miles of dry red dirt, pale blue skies, and an occasional baobab tree posing like a great ancestor standing patiently under a wide, leafless umbrella. The familiar greens of the hill country were gone. No tea fields would thrive in this arid space.

She reached for her water bottle and downed the last few sips. They had only one or two more bottles of water with them in the trunk, and she didn't want to ask for any of that supply even though she was still thirsty. It made her realize how valuable clean water is in a remote place like this.

Gazing out the window, Katie watched Africa go by. Everything in her wanted to ask, "How much farther?" but she resisted.

She didn't have to wait much longer. About two hours after their car was mysteriously and miraculously repaired, Eli turned down a side road and kicked up a cloud of dust behind them. Katie could see several huts just past the line of shrubs. Three barefoot boys came running toward the car, smiling, waving, and calling out to them. As soon as Eli turned off the engine and the dust settled, at least two dozen children had gathered around the car and were all talking at once, peering into the side windows.

"Have you got the chicken?" Jim asked.

"Yes. I'll hand it over to you when we get outside." Cheryl tucked the clucking hen under her arm and opened her door. The chatter of the welcoming committee rose, and it seemed as if a hundred arms with open hands were reaching for Cheryl at the same time.

Eli turned around and looked at Katie. "Are you okay?"

"Yeah, I'm good. I'm not sure how to open my door, though, without hitting one of these kids."

"Slowly. Like this." Eli experienced the same greeting his mom had. Dozens of hands touched him, and a stream of rising chatter surrounded him. Jim was already out of the car while Katie hesitated.

As she cautiously opened the door, the cluster of children drew back just enough to make room for her. The moment she stepped out, the children around her seemed to take another step back as their eyes widened. They stared at Katie in silence for a moment.

Then, as one, they rushed toward her, reaching out to touch her red hair. They called to the other children, and suddenly all the children in the welcoming committee were circling Katie, staring at her, and reaching out to touch her hair.

"I forgot to warn you this might happen," Eli said. "I doubt any of them have ever seen a redhead before. Are you doing okay?"

Katie felt herself sliding into the moment with her whole heart. She leaned down so they could touch her hair and look into her green eyes and point at her, chattering like a bunch of chipmunks. Eli came up beside her and spoke to the children in Swahili. They responded eagerly, and he translated for Katie.

"They want to know how you got all the spots on your skin."

"Do they mean my freckles?"

Eli said something to the kids and pointed to the freckles on Katie's bare arm. Some of them gave him doubtful looks. Others took on somber expressions of awe, while a few of them covered their mouths and giggled.

"What did you tell them?"

"I told them that when you were born, God was so delighted that he sent a hundred angels to kiss you while you were in your mother's arms. Every place where the angels kissed you, they left a tiny dot. That way, if you ever forget how greatly you are loved by God, all you have to do is look at your skin, and you will remember."

Katie was so touched by Eli's fable, she felt her throat tighten. Several of the little girls in front of her were looking at their arms and legs and pointing out to each other where they thought they found an angel kiss on their skin.

"We need to take our greetings to the chief," Eli said. "You ready?"

"Sure." As soon as Katie started to walk with Eli and his parents toward the center of the village, a bunch of little girls reached for her hands as if they were self-appointed special escorts. Other children circled her and Eli, and one little girl stretched her hand around Katie's right wrist and held on tight.

They entered the center of the village and were greeted by lots of adults who were sitting in the shade or coming out of their mud huts that were covered with roofs made of dry twigs and grass. From one of the larger huts, an elderly man emerged wearing a button-down shirt made from bright yellow and black printed fabric. He wore glasses and a pair of khaki shorts, but on his head was an intricate headdress made of feathers and beads.

Jim greeted him in Swahili and gave a respectful nod of his head as they shook hands. Cheryl lowered her head as well and held out the chicken as a present, which the chief took with quiet words exchanged between the three of them. It seemed the chicken was the perfect gift to bring and was greatly appreciated.

Jim introduced their son. Eli spoke in Swahili and dipped his chin to honor the chief. The two of them shook hands warmly. Then it was Katie's turn. All the children let go and stepped back as Katie became the focus of the chief's attention. He seemed to study her face and hair with fascination.

"Jambo." It was the only Swahili Katie knew. She hoped it was the right thing to say in a moment like this. When no one moved or said anything, she added, "Hakuna matata?"

Eli gave her a signal that she should back away quickly and not try any more clever phrases.

The chief moved his attention back to Jim and handed off the chicken to one of several women who were standing nearby. The two men walked away from the others as they talked together and headed for the shade of a large tree behind the chief's hut.

"What do we do now?" Katie asked.

"Hang out for a while. After my dad gets the update, we'll probably go to where the workers are finishing up the well, and if it's done, we'll have a short dedication ceremony."

"And then what?"

"We'll take it as it comes, Katie. Don't worry. Hakuna matata."

Katie thought it was a lot cleverer when she had said it to the chief. When Eli said it, she felt as if he were scolding her. All this was new for her. He should realize that and try to be a little more patient and understanding.

Eli was listening to the discussion between the chief and his dad. He turned to Katie and in a lowered voice gave her the update. "It looks as if we came at just the right time. He's saying that the guys working on the well had some problems two days ago, so they're just finishing this morning. Dad thought the project was already completed. This is ideal. We'll be able to see the first trial run in about an hour."

"Perfect!" Katie said.

Eli's expression lit up. "The other good news is that a small film crew is here from the BBC. The team that dug the well is from the UK. This is going to be great promotion for what we're doing here."

"Wow, that couldn't be better," Katie agreed. Several of the children were tugging on her arms and trying to tell her something.

"They're inviting you to play a game with them," Eli said.

"Is it all right if I go with them?"

"Of course."

"Are you coming along to help translate?"

"You won't need me. You'll figure it out."

For a moment, Katie read extra meaning into his statement, as if Eli were saying she could carry on her life from here on without him and she would be just fine. She didn't know why she complicated things by giving herself crazy little relationship nuances to fret over. But there it was, sitting in the pit of her empty stomach. *You don't need me.*

The girls pulled Katie to the side of one of the huts where they had arranged a line of sticks and pebbles. They played something that resembled hopscotch, and Katie did her best to join in. The girls would all chatter at once when she did something wrong. They smiled approvingly when she got it right. For twenty minutes, she jumped, turned, stood on one foot, and felt her stomach grumbling. More than she wanted something to eat, Katie really wanted something to drink. She couldn't remember ever being this thirsty. The sun was rising in the sky, warming the earth and making Katie even thirstier. How did these people live in this remote village for all these years and not have access to clean water?

Katie knew from the presentation Eli had done in chapel and the fund-raiser she had organized that the lack of clean water was a solvable problem. In places like this village where the nearby streams had become polluted or dried up, a well could be dug, and from deep in the earth, clean water would come up. The ongoing need was for equipment funding and teams that drilled for water in these remote locations.

Katie looked at one of the small girls who stood across from her waiting her turn for the game. She was thin and was dressed in a large T-shirt that advertised a character from an American TV show. How that soiled T-shirt found its way to this village would be an interesting bit of information. Her hair was cut very short, and her lower lip was cracked. Aside from the few obvious differences that came from the rural living conditions, Katie thought of how, in many ways, the little girl looked like any little girl in the States. One major difference was that when she was thirsty, she couldn't drink some water and then return to her play. When she was thirsty, she remained thirsty.

Someone who worked for the mission needed to do a better job of communicating Africa's need for clean water by getting people to imagine what it would be like to be thirsty, really desperately thirsty, and to have no clean water available to drink. Katie wondered if the film crew from the BBC would let them use their documentary footage to put together a presentation for the US.

Eli came looking for her and appeared just as excited as he had been earlier. "How's it going here?"

"Good. You look happy."

"I am. I'm so amazed at what they've accomplished here. It's going to transform this village. Makes me wish we had ten million dollars so we could do this for every village on the list."

One of the girls tugged on Katie's and Eli's arms and kept saying something in Swahili.

"What did she say?" Katie asked.

"She said, '*Mimi na wewe pete na kidole.*'"

"Very funny. What does that mean?"

"It's sweet. It means, 'I and you are like a ring and a finger.'"

Katie wasn't sure she understood. "Is she saying that you and I seem like we're engaged?"

"No."

"Married?"

"No, Katie, it's like the two of you are so close that you are like a ring and a finger. She's saying she likes you. She wants to be with you."

"Oh, that's sweet." Katie gave the girl a hug, and she hugged back even harder. The other girls were sitting in the hut's shade, their energy spent.

"Eli," Katie said, her little ring girl still at her side. "You know how you said you wished you had ten million dollars to use for all the villages on the list?"

"Yes."

"Well, there's something I've been meaning to tell you. I'm not sure this is the best time, but I want you to know that I don't have ten million dollars, but I do have a lot of money. I mean, a lot."

Eli laughed.

She kept a straight face. "It's the truth, Eli. I had a great-aunt who passed away last year, and she left her estate to all the relatives who went to college, but it turned out I was the only one who did. So I inherited all the money."

He tilted his head and gave her an incredulous look.

"I ended up with a big inheritance, and I was thinking it would be great to do more to make the need for clean water known to people. Maybe you and I could talk to your dad about a marketing fund or something to get the word out."

"Katie . . ." He gave her a look of pity, as if the sun had fried her brain.

"Don't look at me like that. I'm telling you the truth. This is one of those things I was referring to the other night in the dining hall when we had some serious topics we needed to discuss. This is one of those topics. I probably should have waited, but there it is. I have a lot of money."

He still had no response.

"I don't think about it very much, but . . ."

"I don't believe you." Eli pulled back.

Katie was surprised. "It's true. I don't think about it."

"No, I mean I don't believe you have a stash of money in the bank. I've watched how you've lived for a year, Katie. I know you. I would have known about this."

She wished with all her heart that she had done this differently. Drawing in a deep breath and blowing the air out through her dry lips, Katie said, "Okay, I didn't want to ever tell you this, but your school bill was paid off in full, right?"

"Yes, I told you that. My uncle Jonathan paid it."

She asked Eli where his uncle would come up with that kind of money, and then she quoted him the exact amount.

Eli's jaw went slack. "That was from you? You paid it?"

Katie rubbed her forehead and looked down. "I shouldn't have blurted that out."

Cheryl came from around the corner of one of the huts and called out to them, waving for them to come to the well. Eli walked robotically, and Katie and her gathering of little girls followed him.

"I'm sorry, Eli. It is shocking. I forget that. I never wanted anyone to know. Except Julia. She helped me with the lawyers, the bank, and everything. But hardly anyone else knows. Except your mom. Your mom knows."

Eli stopped walking and turned to give Katie a wounded look. "You told my mom?"

"No, I didn't tell her. She figured it out from the bank statements for the fund-raiser." Katie pursed her lips together and wished again that she hadn't leaked more information.

"Is that why we did so well with the fund-raiser? You spiked the donations?"

"I didn't spike them. I just gave. A lot. Cheerfully. Eli, you're acting like I've done something wrong."

"I can't believe my mom knew but I didn't. Does my dad know?"

"No, I don't think he does. Your mom said she wasn't going to tell him or tell you since it was my place to tell people. I thought that was really sensitive of her, to hold a confidence for me like that."

Eli turned to Katie. "Is there anything else I should know?"

"No." She tried to lighten the mood. "That's the only surprise I have for you today. Check in again tomorrow."

Eli's expression made it clear he wasn't joking about this disorienting piece of information. They met up with his mom, and he kept his eyes ahead, walking faster than the two of them toward the area where the crowd had gathered.

"Eli," Katie called out.

He kept walking and didn't turn back.

"Is everything okay?" Cheryl asked.

Cheryl gave Katie a comforting pat on the shoulder as they joined the crowd of villagers. "Give him some time. It takes a while to sink in." Katie knew that once again she would have to wait for the right time to have a larger discussion with Eli that would clear the air and settle the tension that was building between them. She really hated waiting.

Everyone was gathered around a cement platform that had a raised rim circling the outside. In the center was a tall, sturdy pump. Katie had seen a number of pictures of wells like this one that had been put into use in other parts of Africa. But this was the first one she had seen in person.

The villagers drew in closer, waiting, talking in quieted tones, eager for the something special that was about to happen. She noticed that the two-man BBC film crew standing across from them didn't have their camera in place yet, so she guessed it was going to be a little while before the ceremony began.

One of the guys from the film crew came striding over to the side where Cheryl and Jim stood about ten feet from Katie and Eli. He shook hands with Jim and Cheryl, and then Jim pointed at Eli, who raised his hand in a casual wave.

The impromptu ceremony began with a declaration in English from the head of the well diggers that the project was completed and they were ready for a trial run. Katie pulled out her phone camera as the chief stepped forward and pronounced a blessing on the well. Many of the women of the village stood by with buckets in their hands, waiting with wide-eyed expectation as the chief selected one of the children to come and stand with him. Together the elderly chief and the young boy put their hands on the pump handle and lifted it up and then pressed it down.

Another little boy stepped forward and held a small aluminum cup under the opening. With a quick zoom, Katie's camera captured the look on his face, showing the intensity of his deep thirst and his eager anticipation. A cup of cold water in Jesus' name. Hope that the promised end to their thirst would soon be fulfilled.

The villagers began to chant, *"Maji, maji,"* which Katie quickly learned meant "water."

The answer came in a sputter that sent the boy with the cup closer to the spout. He lifted up the vessel to catch the first few drops that came out like a sneeze. Then suddenly a fountain of life-giving water gushed from the spout and doused the boy, filling his cup to overflowing.

He laughed and lifted his hands as he opened his mouth. The water poured over his head and face and soaked his body. The cup was tossed aside as all the other children rushed forward and danced in the glorious abundance of clean water.

Some of the women raised their faces and their voices toward the heavens. Others inserted their buckets, taking their fill. The water continued to flow. Cheers, laughter, and sounds of amazement echoed around the circle of joyful spectators.

Katie held up her phone, trying to capture the moment. She could hardly see because of the tears that flowed from her eyes. Dozens of hands were reaching out to touch the miracle. She could hear Eli laughing his best, soul-deep laugh.

One by one the ecstatic villagers filled their buckets and their cups and drank their fill. The thin little girl who had coaxed Katie into playing with them earlier came up to Katie holding the aluminum drinking cup that brimmed with water. She smiled broadly and waited for Katie to take the cup and drink from it. Katie sipped the cool, clean water and handed the cup to Eli. He downed all that remained and handed the cup back to the little girl, who happily returned to fill it again.

Katie smiled at Eli. He didn't smile back.

Coming closer, Eli's expression reamined serious. "You and I have a lot of things we need to talk about."

"I know."

"This sudden news about your inheritance is disturbing."

"Disturbing?"

"Yes, disturbing."

Katie didn't know what to do with that. Eli looked genuinely ticked off. She wasn't sure she'd ever seen him this upset. It was a crazy contrast to the exuberance of everyone around them at that moment.

"I guess it's almost as disturbing as my finding out that you plan on spending the rest of your life in a mud hut," she responded.

"I never said that."

"Oh, really?"

"No. Where did you come up with that?"

"I came up with that conclusion from reading between the lines of all your comments and your parents' comments."

"Well, you're not accurate in what you're saying, Katie."

"Oh, I'm not? Well, what a surprise. All I can go on is what I'm hearing here and there, because you haven't told me what you're really thinking."

"We need to talk about all that."

"When?" Katie lifted her chin defiantly. "When are we going to talk about it?"

"Now," he said firmly.

"Fine. Start talking."

Katie hated the feeling that she and Eli were about to have their first all-out fight, and she hated that it was in the wake of such a great celebration.

They stood two feet away from each other, Katie with her hands on her hips, and Eli with his arms folded across his chest.

Just then the guy from the film crew stepped up behind Eli. Katie glared at him, hoping he would take the hint and leave.

Instead of leaving, his eyes grew wide. With a gasp, he spoke her name.

"Katie?"

Her arms went limp at their sides.

The world around her seemed to turn into watercolors and dissolve. "Michael?"

In one grand sweep, Katie's old high school boyfriend pushed past Eli, pulled Katie close, and fervently kissed her on the lips.

Katie couldn't move. She couldn't speak or even blink. Michael's hair was shaved so that he was nearly bald. His skin was tanned, and his shoulders were broader than they had been in high school. But that narrow nose, those thick eyebrows, and those dark, brooding eyes couldn't be duplicated. Neither could that kiss. It was Michael, all right.

And he was going to mess things up for her something awful. She just knew it.

"Katie, darlin', what are you doin' here on the other side of the world?"

Before Katie could form an answer, Eli stepped in, wedging his shoulder between Michael and Katie. He turned and gave Katie a look she had never seen on his scruffy face. Fury burned in his eyes.

"Eli, this is Michael," she said quickly. "Michael, do you know Eli? His dad is Jim Lorenzo."

Neither of them spoke. They both stood with their shoulders back, sizing each other up.

Michael's expression suddenly changed, and a contrite look came over him. "Are the two of you married? Is that it?"

"No." Eli and Katie responded in unison.

Michael's eyebrows went up. "Engaged?"

Again the mutual "No" was given in perfect harmony.

"Ah, good. I thought for a moment there I'd be needin' to offer an apology."

"You do need to apologize, Michael," Katie said firmly.

"Do I now? The way I see it, I'm still waiting on an apology from you for the way you broke up with me."

"I … I …"

"See?" He pointed at Katie with a twinkle in his eye that was so familiar. It was his charm that caused her to fall for him in high school. He seemed to have perfected his skills in the half decade since she last saw him.

"You know you owe me an apology. Katie, go ahead. Ladies first," he said brazenly.

Without looking at Eli, Katie said, "You're right, Michael. I didn't handle things well back in high school. I'm sorry for the way I broke up with you. I really am. I apologize."

"Apology accepted."

It was silent for a moment.

"Your turn." Katie narrowed her eyes and studied Michael's smug expression. "Go ahead, say it. Say that you know you shouldn't have kissed me like that."

"You're right." Michael's grin expanded. "What I should have done was kiss you like this." With that, he tried to reach for Katie again.

Before she could pull back, Eli blocked Michael's path. The two men scuffled for a few seconds like a couple of impalas locking horns.

"Unbelievable!" Katie threw up her hands in frustration and walked away, letting out a furious huff. Her little maids in waiting skittered to her side, wet and grinning and eager to be the ones to hold her hands and lead her off to play another game with them.

Jim, along with the other videographer, had made their way over to Eli and Michael to see what the fracas was about. Katie glanced at them over her shoulder and then kept on going, feeling as if the fire in her belly was about to ignite and she would self-combust.

"Katie." Cheryl trotted up. "Is everything okay?"

"No, everything is not okay. Nothing is okay. I can't believe what's happening. This is over the top. Why is he here? I can hardly breathe."

"Come on." Cheryl took Katie by the hand and led her and her little followers to one of the mud huts. Cheryl called out something, and a reply came from inside. "We can go in here," she said.

Katie ducked and entered a cool, dark space where a grass mat covered part of the dirt floor. An elderly woman sat at the corner of the mat, holding a cup of water. Her nearly toothless smile was the first thing Katie focused on as her eyes adjusted to the shadows. The woman motioned for them to come in, to sit, to rest.

In a rounded corner of the hut, Katie noticed a modern saucepan balanced on a propane camping stove and a ceramic bowl with two bananas.

Cheryl and the woman spoke as Katie adjusted herself cross-legged on the mat. Only two of the young girls had followed Katie into the hut. Clearly the indicators of a woman in angst looked the same in every culture. Empathetically, the little girls stayed close to Katie as she took deep breaths and tried to calm down.

"You are welcome here," Cheryl translated. "You may speak, rest, or eat—whatever you like."

"Thank you." Katie turned to the woman. "Asante sana."

"Is there anything I can do for you, Katie?" Cheryl asked.

"No. It's not as if there's anything that can be done. It's crazy that he's here, though. I mean, what are the odds of Michael being here now?"

"How do you know Michael?"

"He was my boyfriend from high school. He's brash and arrogant. I broke up with him because he wasn't a Christian, and he was pulling me away from my close friends and the Lord. It wasn't a good relationship."

"You dated him even though he wasn't a Christian?"

Katie gritted her teeth. She wished she hadn't revealed that detail to Cheryl. It had taken her long enough to convince Eli's parents that she was in Kenya to serve and that she was a fine and upright choice

172 Robin Jones Gunn

of a girlfriend and even a possible future wife for their son. Giving Cheryl another reason to doubt Katie's stability or maturity as a Christian wasn't what she wanted to do.

Although, at this moment, Katie didn't know what she wanted.

Cheryl's calm voice washed over the moment. "It's okay, Katie. My first boyfriend wasn't a Christian either. If I hadn't met Jim when I did, I don't know what sort of life I would have ended up with. God knows what he's doing. He is the sustainer."

Cheryl repeated her last line in Swahili, and the older woman, along with Katie's two little attendants, echoed the blessing. "Mpaji ni Mungu."

"Mpaji ni Mungu," Katie replied under her breath.

"Are you okay staying here?"

"Yes. Thank you."

Cheryl gave her arm a squeeze. "It's all for a reason. You know that."

"What possible reason?"

"I have no idea."

Cheryl left with a smile, and Katie felt her shoulders relax. Part of her wanted to shake off the little girls the way she would shake off ants that had decided to use her arm as a bridge. But these girls couldn't be shooed away. They didn't know what catastrophic things were happening inside her at the moment. Or maybe instinctively they did. Maybe they knew something emotional and intense was happening with Katie, and they were doing what women of all ages and all cultures do in such a time—they were offering their support and comfort.

Her hostess motioned for Katie to lie down on the mat and rest. The woman had no trouble shooing the little girls away. Trying her best to get comfortable, Katie curled up on the mat and used the open palm of her hand as a makeshift pillow. She fell asleep almost immediately and woke to the sound of hushed giggling.

It took her eyes a moment to adjust to the hut's dim light and to remember where she was. Two new little girls were sitting cross-legged, with their hands over their mouths, watching Katie from only a foot away. The older woman was gone.

"Was I snoring?" Katie asked.

The girls giggled again and reached over to touch her hair. Katie pulled herself into an upright position and smiled at the girls. She reached over and touched their hair. They giggled again and talked to her, pointing at her head.

"Yes, I know. It looks like my head is on fire, doesn't it?"

The girls didn't indicate that they understood anything she said. They playfully reached over and touched her hair and then pulled back their fingers just in case they were going to get in trouble for their boldness. One of the girls left, and the other clambered onto Katie's lap. She touched Katie's face with her finger and then touched her bare arm. She touched it again and again.

"Are you counting my freckles? Let me know your final count. I've always wondered how many there are."

The little girl, Katie realized, was the same, thin child who had attached herself to Katie when they had arrived. She looked fresher now, undoubtedly having had a prance under the water spigot and partaking of all she could drink. Just that fast, her general appearance seemed enlivened. Clean water was going to transform this village.

"Let's go outside," Katie suggested. "I want to take a picture of you."

The girl followed Katie's lead. They stepped into the afternoon brightness, and Katie spotted Eli sitting in the shade of one of the huts, listening to two elderly men. His face was positioned toward the hut where Katie had been napping, and as she emerged, he seemed to watch her every move. She felt that he was watching out for her. Checking in on her. Making sure she was all right.

Four more little girls pranced over to Katie and staked their territory up and down her arms. They led her over to a shady spot away from where Eli was and persuaded her to sit down. She obliged and crossed her legs, making herself comfortable, expecting that they would show her how to play some sort of game.

Instead, several of the girls went to work, chattering away and meshing their narrow fingers into her hair, pulling it straight up.

"Wait, what are you guys doing? You're not checking for lice, are you? There wasn't an infestation of fleas in the hut where I just took a nap, was there? Why am I asking you? You can't understand a word I'm saying."

Then she realized they were braiding her hair. All of them, at once, as if busily readying her for the big party that night. Katie sat back and let them try their best to get her straight, silky hair to cooperate. She felt like a culturally adjusted Cinderella, surrounded by eager little chattering mice that were going to help their "Cinderelly."

One of the girls ran off and came back with some sort of thin, grassy-like twine. Apparently they discovered that Katie's hair was so sleek it unbraided itself as soon as they let go of it. Katie could only guess how ridiculous she was going to look with four hundred tiny braids all over her head, and each braid fastened with a bit of shrubbery.

"You girls are doing me a favor, you know," Katie said, cracking herself up since none of them understood her. "Instead of having two guys fighting for my attention tonight, I'm pretty sure your beautifying efforts will send both of them running as far away from me as they can get. And you know what? At this point, I think that might be a good thing."

One of the girls patted Katie's cheek as if to indicate that Katie was supposed to hush and not move around so much or she would mess up their safari-salon techniques.

Katie sat patiently as the girls attended to their task. It was relaxing in an unexpected way. She had never done much with her hair, and she definitely hadn't had anything done by her mother with her hair when she was a child. It struck her that ever since she had arrived in Kenya, a variety of nurturing expressions had been made to her by several women. She wondered if the experience of having that kind of love shown to her in tangible, physical ways had contributed to the way her spirit had settled itself, and she felt more quieted and calmer than she ever had.

Katie realized it wasn't just Africa and Kenya's beauty that had settled her spirit in such tender ways. It was the women. She had always wanted more caring, older women in her life. She wanted an attentive mother and a doting aunt like the one Christy had. She wished she had women to mentor her like Julia had done last year as the resident director. Having Cheryl in Katie's life as a steady rock of a woman was a beautiful thing. Katie felt blessed.

That was until she looked up and saw Michael coming toward her.

"Now that's a different look on you altogether," he said, checking out her many braids.

"Keep moving, mister. Nothing to see here. These are not the droids you're looking for."

Michael laughed. "Oh, Katie Girl, you've still got it, haven't ya? I have never met a woman before or since with the same wit." He bent down to be in her line of sight. "Are ya doin' better? I heard you weren't feeling well."

"I'm fine."

"In that case, you look like a cartoon character."

"Thank you."

"Just keepin' it real. Isn't that what you used to tell me?"

"Well, then I must say that you look like someone who is about to walk away and leave my peeps and me to our special girl time."

"Okay, I get it. I can take a hint."

"Really? Sure fooled me."

"Listen, Katie, you don't have to be so rough on me. I got the update. You're with the missionary kid. I get it. I was too expressive with my greeting, and I apologize. Where I come from that was a perfectly acceptable greeting between two old friends such as you and me. I thought you'd be onto that. My mistake."

Katie wanted to say something pithy, but obviously Michael was trying to offer his version of an apology. She backed down and didn't reply.

He took her silence as an invitation to sit across from her. "I'm not surprised that you're here."

"You're not?"

"No. You talked about coming to Africa when you were in high school."

"I did?" Katie didn't remember that. She did remember what Michael talked about in high school. "You used to talk about becoming a film director."

"That I did. You remembered."

Katie thought he looked a little too pleased that she recalled that detail. "So it looks like we both got our wish."

"I'm working my way to where I really want to be. Doing a documentary in Africa isn't my idea of being a film director, but it's work, and it's a start."

"And it's with the BBC. That's impressive."

"Actually, it's not. I'm here with the BDC, the British Documentary Company. It's a nonprofit. My cousin had a connection and got me in. Like I said, it's a start. What about for you? What are you doin' here, really?"

"I told you, I'm with the Lorenzos. I'm helping out."

"Helping out with what?"

"Whatever needs to be done at the conference center where we live."

Michael looked surprised. "That's not you, Katie. You're not an assistant to anyone. You're a leader. Why aren't you doing something for the mission that uses your great skills?"

Katie let out an awkward sounding snort of disagreement. One of Katie's hairstylists checked her face to make sure Katie wasn't reacting to her hair being tugged in all different directions. When it appeared that Katie was okay, the stylist went back to work.

"What was that all about? Are you mocking my comment about your skills?"

"I haven't found my place yet, okay? It's probably here in the village. That's what I'm trying to find out."

Michael shook his head.

"What? You don't think I could handle living in a village?"

"I don't doubt for a moment that you could handle living in a village. You can handle anything life throws at you. But I heard about the fund-raiser you did at your college, how it pulled in a tidy sum. Good on ya."

Katie wasn't able to take his praise, so she discounted the compliment by saying, "Yeah, well, I heard that someone spiked the donations, so it wasn't that big of a success."

"Not from what I just heard in the interviews. Didn't the fund-raiser motivate a group of college students to come over here? We went to the village where they worked, just two days ago, as a matter of fact. From everything we heard and saw, the college work team was a great success. Why won't you take a little credit for being their source of motivation?"

Katie shrugged and looked down.

"I know it's not my place to be makin' suggestions about how you should live your life, Katie. But it seems obvious to me that you were made for that."

"Made for what?"

"For motivatin' people and gettin' them to do things they wouldn't normally do. If you want to do some good for this organization, why don't you appoint yourself the official marketing specialist or whatever title you want? You can duplicate what you did at your school at other universities around the world. I have a contact at Queens University in Belfast. I could connect you with him, and he would be all over this sort of thing. Once they see the documentary, they're going to be linin' up to come here as teams. Who's going be the one to organize all that and get the fund-raisers goin'?"

Katie felt as if a thousand fireflies had lit up at the same moment inside her imagination. The ideas were fluttering around like the flying termites, just a quick snatch away from being easily caught. She felt enlivened as she listened to Michael's suggestions. Yes, this was it. This was what she wanted to do.

"You like that idea, do ya? Your face never lied to me, Katie. I see it in your eyes. This is what you were meant to do. It's obvious. How did you miss it?"

"I don't know."

Michael laughed. "I never thought I would hear those words from your lovely lips."

Katie bit the inside of her lower lip, thinking of all the great ways she could work on this by connecting with not only universities but also church groups. She had the template of how she and Eli had worked together to put on the fund-raiser as well as the training at Rancho. They could work together to do the same sort of program many times over. This was it! This was what she could do.

"It's brilliant, Michael."

He laughed again. "I'm the one who says 'brilliant,' remember? You're the one who calls something like this a 'God-thing.'"

Katie grinned at Michael for the first time that day.

"Ah, there it is. I knew you still had a smile in there for me somewhere. See, I didn't forget everything you taught me. I remember all the God-things, Katie. I really do."

Katie's thoughts had run ahead to what she needed for this project. "So, we can have a copy of the documentary you're filming, right?"

"Sure, not a problem."

"Would it be okay if we put an excerpt on the website?"

"Yes, we can help you with that."

"And you'll get me the name of your contact at Queens University in Belfast."

"Again, not a problem. He's my father-in-law."

"We'll also need ..." Katie stopped. "Wait. Did you say he's your father-in-law?"

"Yes."

Katie raised her eyebrows and stared at him.

Michael tilted his head and gave Katie a mischievous grin. "Did I not mention that I'm married?"

"No. You didn't happen to mention that."

"Ahh, well I am. Happily, as a matter of fact. You would like her. She's a good one. She got me to church. I knew you would be in her corner on that."

Katie still couldn't believe it. "And how would your wife feel if she knew you were running around Africa kissing other women?"

"I only kiss the ones I seriously dated. Shall I add that list up for you? Three. And you're the only one of the three I've seen so far on this trip, so my reputation isn't as spotted as you seem to think."

"It's still not normal to greet someone with a kiss like that."

"And I say, for me, it is."

They glared at each other, as if they had come to a standoff. At that moment, Eli made an appearance, striding toward them with his focus set.

Katie looked up at Eli and smiled. She couldn't wait to tell him about her breakthrough in knowing what it was that she could do for the organization.

"Everyone is gathering." Eli's eyes were set on Katie and her crazy hair. The girls had finished their creation, and all but one had gone across to the shade of another hut where they were busying themselves with another willing patron who had much shorter and coarser hair.

"I told her she looks like a cartoon character," Michael said. "And then I asked her to marry me, and she said yes. Too bad. You missed your chance."

"Michael, don't say stuff like that. And, Eli, don't listen to him. He has a warped sense of humor. But here's an interesting news flash. He's married."

Eli looked like he was trying very hard to swallow the words he wanted to say. The response that popped out of his mouth was, "Congratulations."

"For what?" Michael asked. "Having a warped sense of humor?"

"Congratulations on your marriage."

"Thanks. And for the record, Katie and I have made our amends. So in case you're thinking you've come over to defend her honor, we're squared."

Katie remembered how Michael had a way of slipping out of his sarcastic tone and turning serious. This was definitely that sort of transition. She hoped Eli picked up on the adjustment. Katie felt more comfortable around Michael now that she realized his status, and she hoped Eli did as well.

Michael said, "You know how they say that when you know, you know? Well, it's true. I knew. She knew. Right away. Within the first month after we met. It was all over but the negotiating. That took a year and a half."

Michael paused, and Katie watched Eli's expression. Eli seemed to be trying to discern if he could trust Michael or if he was being sarcastic again.

Rising to his feet, Michael turned to go. "I hope the negotiating doesn't take that long for you two. Life's too short."

Katie met Eli's gaze and held it for a moment. She wondered if all the relational bumps they had experienced the last few days were about to be smoothed out. Was this the turning point? Were they ready to acknowledge that they were a great pair? All they had to do was figure out who got to pursue his or her ideal vocation and who was going to make the sacrifice to support the other one's vision.

If that was true, she was ready to start the negotiations with her fresh insight into how she and Eli could work together and set up a desk in the office. She already knew where they would put it — up against the wall that held their hidden valentine heart. They could get to work right away on fund-raising. This possibility hadn't been on Eli's radar when he made his declarations about wanting to be involved in the villages for extended periods of time. Surely he would change his mind about that now.

"I don't agree with him," Eli said after Michael was out of earshot.

"About what?" Katie wondered if Michael's insinuations that Eli and Katie were headed for marriage were too much for Eli to grapple with at the moment.

"I don't think you look like a cartoon character."

"Thanks."

Eli held out his hand to help Katie stand up. "Did the two of you really settle things? Did he apologize?"

"Yes and yes." She rose and brushed off her backside, but she knew it was pointless. The dust from the dry earth had managed to cling to every inch of her. Even that didn't bother her the way she thought it might. It's different being dusty and dirty when everyone else around you is. A shower would be nice, but she didn't crave the luxury and decided she made a pretty good outdoorsy woman.

"Actually, we had a really good talk. And Eli, I need to apologize to you. I shouldn't have gotten so aggravated and upset with you earlier. I know you and I have a lot to talk through, and I also know that we'll be able to have that talk eventually."

"Yes, we will. I'm sorry I took my anger out on you too."

Eli pulled her close and whispered in her ear, "Mimi na wewe pete na kidole."

"No fair using Swahili. Say it in English."

"No." He started walking to the tribal gathering area, and Katie had to scurry to keep up with him.

"No? What do you mean, no?"

"You already know what it means."

She knew it wasn't the "God is the sustainer" blessing, nor did it contain the word for "water." Then she remembered. The little girl who had clung to her all morning had said that phrase to her. Katie repeated the meaning in English. "I and you are like a ring and a finger."

Eli grinned at her and, as they walked, bumped his shoulder up against hers in his chummy way.

Katie bumped his shoulder back. "We still have a bunch of stuff to talk about."

"Yes, I know. We'll talk after this evening's gathering."

As they walked toward the center of the village, a cluster of Katie's little tribal fairies gathered around her and scrambled to be the one to hold her hand. For the first time since Katie had arrived in Kenya, she felt as if she had clarity and direction about what she was supposed to do. It was such a liberating feeling. She couldn't wait to get started.

Earlier, in the hut, Cheryl had told her that everything had a purpose. Katie no longer felt the need to contest that comment. Everything was falling into place. Even the crazy pieces were starting to make sense.

Nothing but good times ahead.

The good times started as soon as they entered the center of the village where everyone had gathered. Even though Katie knew she must look ridiculous with her head full of itty-bitty braids laced with foliage, and even though she must smell pretty gamey after being in the same clothes now for two days, she waltzed her way to the evening meal a step behind Eli, with her entourage close behind as if she were the queen of Sheba.

She had no way of knowing what she looked like—aside from Michael's comment about the cartoon character resemblance—since no mirrors were anywhere around. Katie knew she wouldn't find any clear pools of water either, where she could catch a glimpse of her reflection. The only way she could gauge her appearance was in the expressions of those who looked at her. What an interesting and different way that would be for a young woman to grow up.

Katie wondered for a moment if part of the reason so many of the young women she knew who had poor self-esteem ended up that way because they had spent their lives gazing at themselves in a mirror instead of being the mirror others gazed into.

Cheryl came up to her and smiled. "Look at you! The girls did a great job on your hair." She repeated something in Swahili, looking the girls in the eye and clearly praising them for their efforts.

Cheryl's short white hair was matted down in front with perspiration from her efforts with the village women in preparing food. Her shirt was untucked and stained in several places. She looked happy though.

Katie fixed her expression so that it would mirror back to Cheryl that she was beautiful inside and out and looked perfect just the way she was.

"I'm so glad you're able to be here with us and experience all this, Katie."

"I am too." Katie wasn't sure what she expected of this great celebration. It seemed as if the number of villagers had doubled since earlier in the day. Either many of them were off elsewhere during the well's dedication or the area where they gathered was a smaller space and that made the group seem larger.

One of the women in a colorful caftan stood in the center of the gathering and sang. Her song was composed of rich, low notes that repeated themselves and kept to an elemental, repetitive rhythm. The song was more of a lyrical chant than a melody, and it acted as a call to cluster, as everyone formed a large circle and bent their knees slightly so they could bob along with the song.

Some people clapped in beat with the meter, forming the percussion section. Half a dozen women stepped into the circle and danced a bobbing sort of dance with their elbows bent and their forearms extended to the sides. Their hands were open, and their smiles were wide, as if they were about to greet one another warmly. Clearly this was a song of celebration and a dance of praise.

A few small children joined in, imitating the movements as if they couldn't keep their feet from dancing. Two young women entered the circle and danced beside the older women, emulating their moves. Then two teenage boys stepped in and added high-kicking moves with their legs.

Katie pulled out her cell phone to capture the festivities. More villagers had entered into the chanting-style song, and the ones who weren't dancing remained in the circle formation and clapped in rhythm with the beat. The song kept repeating the same lines, and Katie wished she knew what the words meant.

One of the women reached out her hand to Cheryl, inviting her into the dance. Cheryl stepped forward, and with surprisingly similar motions, she danced along with the women. Katie never would have guessed Cheryl had it in her to move so effortlessly and in perfect rhythm. Jim was invited next, and then all of the men from the well-digging team.

Katie watched as Michael joined in while the other videographer chronicled the event. Michael clapped and moved with an odd, locked-knee sort of sway. She hadn't gone to any dances with him in high school and had no idea he was so rigid. Katie felt embarrassed for him in a way, but she knew if she had been summoned to join in, her movements would have been laughable. She looked around for Eli, who had woven his way through the crowd. He was standing near one of the young men, saying something to him.

A few moments later, the sounds of a drum began, and the singer was joined by two other song chanters who changed the tune. The little girls still clustered around Katie took the change as their invitation to join in. All six of them pulled on Katie's arms and drew her out on the dirt dance floor. They circled her, all clapping and swaying, bobbing and grinning. With the little girls it seemed there was no wrong way to do this, so Katie let go and got in touch with her inner African boogie princess.

She was certain she looked hilarious with her braided hair flapping every which way and her white-girl moves that probably imitated a trained cockatiel pacing about on its perch, performing for a few pellets. *Who cares! I'm going for it.*

The little girls giggled, and Katie laughed with them, her chin up, her heart tossed to the heavens. Then, to add a bit of California culture, Katie tried a dance move she remembered practicing in high school when she and her girlfriends would dance at their sleepover parties. It didn't seem to impress the girls here any more than it had impressed the girls from Kelley High. Katie laughed it off and kept going with the African beat, wondering if somewhere in the crowd

Eli and Michael were watching her and feeling a little sorry and even embarrassed for her.

The drums changed the tempo one more time, and the chanting fell off so that it was only the drums, two of them now, that were dictating the next dance. Some of the dancers slipped into the livelier pace with more staccato movements. But Katie, along with Jim and Cheryl, stepped out of the limelight. Soon all the women stepped back, and only the village men continued to dance. With their shoulders back and arms to their sides, their sinewy legs did all the rhythmic movements.

Eli stepped forward and joined the dozen men who were dancing. Katie smiled. *This ought to be good.*

She remembered several times at school over the past year when Eli had come across as awkward when trying to imitate common greetings and clever joke movements that were familiar to those in the Southern California culture. He didn't really get the high five or knuckle bumps and had been slow to pick up the moves.

Here, in front of Katie's eyes, his coordination skills sprang into action. Katie's jaw dropped as she saw him slide into the lineup of dancers and follow their moves as if he had done this his whole life. He was good. Very good. His movements were natural and heartfelt. It was as if Eli heard the song, felt the beat, and was able to interpret the motions with easy duplication of the men around him.

Katie wasn't the only one who was surprised. One of the men from the well-digging team stood close to Katie and said, "It's like one of those dance competition shows, isn't it? Where did he learn to do that?"

"He grew up in Africa. It's in his heart." She couldn't take her eyes off him. This was a side of Eli she had never seen, never imagined. Once again she felt twinges of regret that she had judged him so hastily when she first met him.

The drums came to an abrupt halt, and so did the dancers. Food was brought out in baskets and bowls. Clean water was poured out of gallon-sized plastic containers. Eli sauntered over and stood next to Katie, his face beaming.

"Whoa, Lorenzo! You've got the moves, boy."

He grinned at her, looking happy, content. "You weren't too bad yourself, for a California girl."

"You're just saying that to make me feel better. I was a total goofball out there."

"Yes, but you were a very cute goofball."

Katie looked at the half grin Eli seemed to be hiding, and she pointed a finger at him. "Okay, Lorenzo, I see it right there. You can't hide it. The truth is about to come out. You do think I look like a cartoon character, don't you?"

He gave her an exaggerated look of innocence and then, with a grin, he said, "Well, okay. Maybe a little. But a very cute cartoon character."

Katie smirked at him then reached over and touched his arm. "Eli, I need to apologize to you again."

"Apologize? For what?" His expression turned serious.

"Yes. I need to apologize for a couple of things, actually. First, I apologize for the way I treated you when we first met. I looked down on you, ignored you, and gave you a hard time every chance I got."

"You don't need to apologize for that, Katie."

"I think I do. I didn't give you a chance to be yourself and to be accepted for your cultural differences and your oddities."

"My oddities, huh?"

"You know what I mean. I didn't honor the diversity. There, how's that for a politically correct way of saying it?"

"It's all right, Katie. It's understandable. I didn't fit well in California. That's in the past. You accept me for my oddities now, don't you?"

"Yes. I'm just so much more aware of my little oddities. I feel like you're giving me more grace than I gave you. So, thank you for that. And I know we said we were going to talk about this later, but the other thing I want to apologize for is waiting so long to tell you about

188 Robin Jones Gunn

the money. I can see how that would make you feel as if I didn't trust you or something."

Eli gave a slight shrug, as if he already had tossed that tense encounter in the river and it was floating away, headed for the hungry crocodiles.

"It would have been nice to know so I wouldn't have been caught off guard. But it's okay. Don't worry about it, Katie. You don't ever have to apologize for being yourself around me. There's no hope for the rest of the world if you stop being you. I'm depending on you to stay true to yourself in every situation."

"I can do that, but you need to know I can't guarantee your safety when my truest self is loose. I mean, talk about chasing wild monkeys."

Eli grinned. "I'll take my chances." He reached for her hand and gave it a squeeze. "We're going to go far, Princess Hakuna Matata. You'll see."

Katie felt as if the ever-glowing embers of the Eli-fire that had been carefully guarded in the corner of her heart were fanned into flames. Sparks rose, dancing like fireflies to an exotic beat. This moment with Eli, both of them covered with dust and perspiration and surrounded by little girls trying to hold hands with both of them, was a million times better than her prom night had been or any expensive dinner date with Rick or any birthday she had ever celebrated. This was the most golden evening of her life, and Katie didn't want it to end. Ever.

But by the time all the stars had come out of hiding and showed their shining faces to the assembly below, the moment had waned. Young children curled up in their mothers' arms and fell asleep. The old men leaned back contentedly, emptied of all the stories they had given as their verbal dessert to any who drew close enough to hear.

Eli walked Katie back to the car to retrieve her duffel bag. The digging crew had offered their tent to Katie and Cheryl and had volunteered to camp with Eli and the other guys on a big, blue tarp they had stretched out under the stars.

They stopped at an area that was lit by a Coleman lantern where the additional drilling supplies were stacked up. Eli seemed to have something to say before escorting Katie to the tent where the rest of the English speakers in the area could hear their conversation.

"We still have a couple of things to talk about," he said.

To Katie it seemed that what needed to be said for the moment had been covered in their earlier, golden conversation. They didn't need to talk at length now. In the morning they could go for a long walk and discuss all the things that had been left unexplored for the past few weeks, including Eli's interest in doing fieldwork for extended periods of time. Katie was pretty confident that once he heard her inspired idea of how they could work together on fund-raisers, he would change his focus. She knew his parents would like that idea. To Katie's way of thinking, they could talk about that openly in the car on the way home tomorrow.

"You like it here, don't you?" Eli asked.

"I love it. This was an amazing day."

"It was."

"I can see all kinds of possibilities for the future."

"Good. I feel the same way, Katie. You will have to learn some more Swahili, though."

"I was thinking the same thing. You can start to teach me anytime."

"Okay, I can do that. Gladly."

"I have some great ideas for how we can raise awareness and prepare more teams to come into the villages," Katie said enthusiastically.

Eli looked pleased. "You know, I've been praying that everything would be clear to you after you spent some time in the village."

"Well, then God really answered your prayer, because of all people, it was Michael who helped me to see that it's the ideal position for me. And it's so obvious. I don't know how we missed it."

"Michael helped you to figure out?"

"Yes. Crazy, I know. Your mom said earlier today that everything has a purpose, and I saw what she meant when I talked with Michael. He helped me to see that I'm suited to start more fund-raisers at colleges and churches. I can use what you and I put together for the fund-raiser at Rancho as the template and then adjust for each group we work with. The documentary will help people to see what's going on here, and you and I can organize the work teams that will want to come and help. It's absolutely perfect. It's like you said: you and I are going to go far, Eli."

"Wait. Katie, what are you saying?"

"I'm saying that you and I can work together in the office and expand the work in the villages but, more importantly, multiply the fund-raising efforts."

"Were we having the same conversation here? Where did that come from?"

"From the conversation I had with Michael."

"I thought you were saying that you like being here, that you feel comfortable in the village."

"I do."

"Then I'm confused. I thought you had come to the conclusion today that you wanted to work with me."

"I do."

Neither spoke for a moment. Then Katie clarified her answer. "I want to work with you in the office at Brockhurst and do all the things I just listed: expand the fund-raising, bring in more teams. It's the perfect position for both of us."

She watched the expression on Eli's face take on a shadow, and when it did, she realized they were not thinking the same thing.

"You thought I was saying that I want to travel with you to the villages, didn't you?" Katie surmised.

"Yes. And you thought I would jump at a position in the office if it was something interesting like what you and I did together at Rancho."

"Yes, I did. I got ahead of myself." Katie could see how, in her exuberant imagination, she had sailed right past Eli and his vision for the work in the villages and projected onto him what she wanted to do.

Neither of them spoke for another painfully still moment.

"We both need to think about this before we talk it through any further."

"I feel ready to talk about it now," Katie said.

"I don't."

"Okay." Katie realized she'd had a nap that afternoon in the hut. She might be a little more rested and thinking more clearly than Eli was. Waiting until the morning was probably a good idea.

He rubbed the back of his neck. "I thought you and I were on the same page, but now I'm not sure we're even in the same chapter."

Katie's heart took a dive. Why had she felt so certain that this was the answer? She still hoped that Eli would realize how right her plan was for them. Surely he would when he saw the whole picture in the same way she had seen it so clearly when she was talking to Michael.

"Come on. We should get to the tent." He picked up her duffel bag and walked like a man with a heavy burden.

The tent was near the truck and the drilling equipment, which was located not far from the well, and at the moment, the area was well lit.

Katie thought of Rebecca and how her ordinary day at the village well in the book of Genesis had a very different result than Katie's day at the village well. Rebecca left the village the next morning knowing she was going to marry Isaac. Katie would leave here in the morning knowing even less about her future with Eli than when they arrived.

Cheryl was already inside the tent when Katie said good-night to Eli with a hug and crawled into her corner.

As grateful as she was for the tent, Katie wished they were all sleeping outside under the stars. Dark nights in remote places while gazing up at a canopy of stars was something Katie loved sharing with Eli. She wanted to be close to him, to see his profile as he studied the heavens. She hoped he would be able to sleep tonight and not be exasperated about their off-track conversation. Katie decided she wasn't going to worry. She wasn't going to be afraid. God would work it out. He would make everything clear for both of them.

Katie tussled around at first trying to find the most comfortable way to turn her head with all the outcroppings. It was a bumpy experience.

"Cheryl," she whispered, "are you still awake?"

"Yes."

"Can you help me take out these braids? I can't sleep with them in my hair. It's like lying on a pillow of snakes."

"Here, sit up. You take your right side, and I'll take your left."

The unbraiding of Katie's coiffure took less time than the braiding. She unzipped the screen of the tent and tossed all the bits of vine outside. For a moment she lingered, gazing up at the sky filled with stars. She whispered a prayer for Eli and then zipped up the door and returned to her side of the tent where her Little Mermaid pillowcase welcomed her untangled head of hair.

The light of the new day streaming through the partially opened door of the tent was what woke Katie. Cheryl was up and out of the tent, and when Katie peered outside, she saw that the men were gone and the tarp and sleeping bags were rolled up and ready to be packed. Peeling out of her warm sweatshirt, Katie quickly changed into a clean T-shirt. She stayed with the same skirt she had worn for the last few days, because it seemed pointless to put on a fairly clean pair of jeans when her legs were so dirty.

Slipping into her shoes, Katie crawled out of the tent and wished she had a mirror. With both hands, she could feel the way her hair had crinkled and fluffed up after the billion-braid experience.

I bet I look like a Chia Pet.

Going straight to the well, Katie saw a dozen villagers gathered around, filling buckets of the precious gift. Katie greeted them and waited her turn. She was pretty sure she was getting more of a stare-down than usual because of her morning hairdo, but until she stuck her head under that spigot, she couldn't do much about it.

As one of the little boys primed the pump for her, Katie cupped both her hands and caught the refreshing burst of water, which she quickly splashed on her face and neck, dripping water all over her shirt. With the second outpouring, Katie turned her head and leaned back so that the water poured onto her head, soaking her hair and hopefully smoothing down the fluff. She drank as much as she could as the water dribbled from the spigot. Several little kids pranced around her, sticking their hands into the runoff and playfully flicking their wet fingers at each other.

Shaking her head like a dog, Katie laughed with the children as she sent her share of flicked droplets in their direction. Feeling refreshed, Katie smoothed back her hair and headed for the center of the village. She caught up with a woman who was carrying two pale blue plastic buckets of water while a small toddler tried to keep up with his mother. "Here, let me take those for you." She added some simple hand gestures to indicate to the woman that she was trying to help her, not to rob her of her precious cargo.

The woman gave over both buckets and scooped up her son. Katie thought of the many women she had seen alongside the road during their trip here and the way they had bundles or baskets balanced on their heads. She could see now why it was such a good thing to have both hands free.

Another woman was ahead of them carrying a plastic, gallon-sized jug filled with water. She carried her baby in a fabric sling that was attached in such a way that the baby was on her back, well supported in the sling and sound asleep with his head pressed against the middle of her back, resting between her shoulder blades.

Katie remembered something one of her professors at Rancho Corona often said to the class at the end of his lectures. "Now, go rest between his shoulders." Katie never understood what that meant. She always paraphrased it in her head as "Go be at peace" or "Take it easy and don't stress."

Seeing how peaceful and unstressed the sleeping baby was as he "rested between the shoulders" of his mother, Katie's thoughts were seared with an image of what it meant to trust God and go along for the ride.

Entering the central area of the village, Katie was greeted by her little ladies-in-waiting, who argued about which one of them was going to help to carry the buckets with Katie. They were both too heavy to let the small girls try to manage by themselves, so Katie kept holding them, and the girls trotted along beside her to the hut of the woman she was helping.

"Asante sana," the woman said when Katie lowered the two buckets by her front door. Katie had ridges in both palms from carrying the heavy load all that way. She hoped she remembered this effort the next time she simply turned a faucet in a kitchen or bathroom and the water flowed freely.

The little girls tugged on Katie's hands and led her to where Eli and his parents were giving their farewells to the chief. Even though she didn't understand the words they exchanged, she could see that much respect and love were passing between them.

Eli turned to Katie and motioned for her to meet him over where they had talked the night before. She waited there with her small entourage and watched as Eli came toward her with his head down and taking long strides. He said something to all the little girls, and they scattered.

"What's wrong?" Katie asked.

"I just wanted it to be the two of us."

"Okay. But still, what's wrong? I can tell something's wrong."

He looked up and met her gaze. "I need to make some decisions. Some pretty big decisions. Actually, I've already made the first decision."

Katie felt her stomach do a flop.

"I've decided to go on with the crew."

"Go on where? What are you saying?"

"I'm not going back to Brockhurst today with you and my parents. I've already told them, and they said they understand. Now I'm hoping you'll understand too."

"Okay, what am I supposed to understand?"

"I need to know if going village to village is what I should focus on. I don't think I'll know unless I give it a try. That's why I'm going to the next village with the crew and will be there a few days."

"You're going with the well-digging crew?"

"No, the video crew. They're filming in two more villages before returning to the UK."

Katie felt her stomach flop again. "You're going to spend the next few days with Michael?"

"My dad has the information on where we'll be and when. I'll be back to Brockhurst in a week. Two at the most."

Katie felt as if all the air was being squeezed out of her lungs. In a choked voice, she said, "Why are you doing this?"

"I need to know, Katie. I need to see what it's like going village to village, and this is the perfect opportunity. The film crew is only here for a few more days. When they leave, I'm going to stay on for a while at the last village with the crew that's working on a well dig there. I'll catch a ride back to Brockhurst. We have it all worked out."

"Eli ..."

"I need to do this, Katie. I really hope you'll understand."

She swatted at a fly that seemed intent on using her forehead as a landing strip. No words came to her.

Eli looked over her shoulder and then looked back at her. "Katie, I have to go." He touched the side of her face, gently stroking her cheek with his rough knuckles. "Mpaji ni Mungu."

"Mpaji ni Mungu," she repeated in a hoarse voice. At that moment, though, she was finding it hard to believe that God was going to be her sustainer.

Eli leaned close and brushed her lips with his, a slight kiss that was barely a kiss at all. It was more like their lips were shaking hands.

Katie opened her eyes, and he was already walking away. She watched him go, pressing her lips together as if trying to hold on to his brief kiss and make it sink deep into her memory.

Eli was about twenty yards away when he stopped, turned around, and looked at Katie. He put his fist on his heart and pounded it three times, just as he had done last spring, once in the cafeteria and once at his uncle Jonathan's wedding. The message to Katie was clear. Eli held her in his heart.

Katie put the flattened palm of her right hand over her heart and responded by tapping three times.

I love you, Eli. Do you realize that yet? I love you.

Katie didn't remember much about the first part of the ride back to Brockhurst. Her emotions took her to a deep place, and she managed to pull off a pretty good fake sleep along the bumpy roads. She closed her eyes on the breathtaking African scenery, on Jim and Cheryl, and especially on the vacant space beside her in the car's backseat. Eli would have been sitting beside her if he had come home with them.

For a while, she let herself be angry. Being ignored, abandoned, left out—those were core wounds for Katie from her childhood. Eli's decision to leave the way he had was more painful for her than she was sure he imagined. This was something she needed to get over. She needed to trust God in truer ways. He was the one who would never leave her, never forsake her. She knew that.

In her mind's eye, Katie tried to see again the image of Eli pounding his chest over his heart before he left. He was communicating that he wanted her to be with him. She needed to hold on to that thought.

For a short stretch, when the road was smooth, Katie nearly convinced herself everything was going to be just fine. She was strong, courageous, and capable of weathering this separation. Both Eli and she could handle it. This was only going to work together for good to solidify their relationship. As a matter of fact, this was exactly what they both said they needed to pray for—that their hearts would be strengthened. It was the second part of the verse in 1 Thessalonians 3, and this was how that part of their prayer was being accomplished.

But what if Eli's conclusion at the end of this time is that he's determined to be in the villages, and my conclusion is that I'm determined to help at Brockhurst? How can we go far and build a long-term relationship, and even possibly a marriage one day, if we are living and working in different places? Places where Eli's cell phone won't even work.

No, this wasn't guaranteed to end well.

As Katie continued to fake sleep, she could hear Cheryl and Jim speaking in low tones. She imagined it was difficult for the two of them, in the tiny car, to say everything they wanted to about Eli taking off and going to the villages. Did they know that Katie was on their side, if there were sides in this? Katie wanted Eli to work in the office at Brockhurst too.

If Eli ends up headed for the villages, do I need to be the one to set aside what I'd like to do and follow him wherever he believes God is leading him? Is that how this works? If our relationship is leading to marriage, then marriage is a series of compromises, right?

Katie thought of how odd it was that while attending a Christian college she had heard so many talks in chapel about not lowering your standards and not compromising your goals. Why was that the motto during the season of singleness but not applicable in marriage? It didn't make sense that once you find the person you want to marry, you then give up your own goals and do something that's outside your area of strengths.

Or is that how you determine if you really are meant to be with someone? Do your life goals need to match up perfectly before you know if you're right for each other? This is so frustrating!

Jim and Cheryl were discussing Eli's decision with louder words, and something Katie overheard made her realize that Eli's parents were wondering if Katie had been the one to convince Eli to make this last-minute decision. All her raw emotions flared. She rustled around in the backseat to give them warning that she was "waking up."

It seemed the best way to make things clear to Jim and Cheryl was to dive into the topic of how she wanted to organize the fund-raising effort and set up a desk at the office. As she tossed out some of her ideas to Jim, his enthusiasm rose. Cheryl seemed reserved at first. But then, as Katie went on to explain some of the ways she and Eli had organized the event at Rancho, they both seemed to catch the vision and jumped in with lots more ideas. Cheryl pulled out a notebook to take notes, and Katie felt excited about putting together a plan.

"Did you tell Eli these ideas?" Cheryl asked.

"Yes, I told him last night. I thought he would catch the vision too. I never expected him to take off and go to other villages." Katie felt vindicated after making that statement. At the same time, she felt an ache, knowing that it would be at least a week, and maybe two, before she saw Eli. No amount of being right in his parents' eyes could compensate for that.

"We're having a hard time understanding his decision," Jim said.

"And at the same time, we're trying to be supportive," Cheryl added. "We want him to do what he feels called to do and go where the Lord leads him. We just had other ideas for him, that's all."

Katie felt an unexpected sort of sweet camaraderie with Cheryl. It surprised her how feeling empathy for someone diminished the sense of feeling sorry for herself.

"I guess all of us will have to wait and see what happens," Katie said. More than anything, she wanted to be a clear voice that cheered for Eli, supported him, and believed along with him that God was directing him. Being that unswerving support was a lot harder than she thought it would be.

They arrived back in Nairobi after dark, feeling like weary travelers, eager to eat something before trekking up the hill to Brockhurst. Jim parked the car, and the three of them headed for a modern-looking restaurant called Nairobi Java House. As soon as Katie entered, she thought she was back in college, visiting one of the cafés she and her friends used to frequent.

The three of them slid into a booth, and Katie glanced around, taking in the modern décor with a high ceiling and long, low-hanging lamps. The butter yellow walls were accented by dramatic pieces of art, and the woodwork seemed to glow in the amber lighting.

"What a fun place," Katie said.

"It's our favorite. Do you want to try something local? Or would like something like a turkey sandwich on white bread?"

"They have that here?" Katie opened the menu and ran down the extensive list of offerings. "Do they have ostrich meatballs?"

"No, that's from another favorite place of ours. We'll take you there sometime."

"You know what? How about if you surprise me?" She closed the menu. "I'm going to find the restroom and wash up way more than they probably want me to. I hope they have lots of paper towels."

"I'll join you." Cheryl slipped out and handed Jim her menu. "Could you order my usual?"

"What should I get for Katie?"

"Get her Eli's usual. I think she'll like it."

The two women made their way to the restroom, where Katie looked in a large mirror for the first time in three days. She laughed aloud. Her hair resembled a rag doll's. Even though she had stuck her head under the spigot that morning, some sections retained their crinkle from the braids. She had a streak of mud on her neck, and her eyes were bloodshot.

Pointing to her reflection, Katie said, "And now I know the real reason Eli took off running."

Cheryl smiled at Katie's self-effacing comment but didn't add to it or detract from it. They both looked pretty haggard.

Katie pointed to the modern sink. "Does it freak you out sometimes going to villages and then coming back to civilization? I mean, this feels like such a luxury. Running water, flush toilets, espresso drinks."

"We spent our earlier years in the village, so it doesn't feel unusual to me. I don't go to the villages that often now, but I do love being there. So, no, I don't think it gets to me." Cheryl washed her face and combed back her limp hair with her fingers.

"What is it that you like most about being in a village?"

Cheryl glanced down at her hands and then washed them a second time, trying to remove the dirt from under her fingernails. "There's something elemental about life in the villages that always has appealed to me. The basics are the same around the world no matter where you live, aren't they? Mothers love their babies, children laugh and play, young men pursue young women." Cheryl smiled, catching Katie's eye, as they both looked in the mirror.

"Shouldn't you add that young women who are ready to be pursued are left behind when young men run off to other villages for weeks at a time to catch their dreams?" Katie hoped her sarcasm wasn't coming across too strong.

"Actually, no. That wouldn't happen in a village. Young men would pursue young women, and then those young men would marry those young women."

"And then what would happen?"

"What else?" Cheryl said with a clever twist in her voice. "They give the happy mother grandbabies."

Katie wasn't quite ready to go down that trail. All she wanted to do was figure out what was next for Eli and her.

"Listen." Cheryl put her hand on Katie's shoulder. "It's going to work out, Katie. It will. Everything has a purpose."

"I know." Katie heard the flippant tone in her voice and tried to add a spiritual curlicue for Cheryl's benefit. "God has a plan for us, together or separate. And it's a good plan."

Katie hated that she had just spouted the "right" answer the way she had heard lots of others do when she was at Rancho Corona. It was as if, whenever anything went wrong, their default was set to a robotic-sounding "God is in control," and that would explain the pain or the life complication.

Katie believed that truth with all her heart. But she preferred quietly to believe, trust, and wait to see how God was going to do one of his God-things rather than turn the dial to an automatic response. She never wanted to sound stale or trite. She wanted to sound like a God lover.

It was hard to tell if Cheryl took Katie's answer as sincere. She gave Katie a motherly smile, and the two of them exited the restroom and returned to their booth. When they sat down, Jim pointed to the beverage awaiting Katie. "It's a Malindi macchiato. That's Eli's usual. Let's see what you think of it."

Katie gave an appreciative nod to Jim as she reached for the handle on the glass espresso mug and noticed the design squiggled in chocolate on top of the foam. Before she took a sip of the steaming beverage, Katie thought of how much Rick would like this place. He would want to study their menu and sample the signature dishes. Nicole would take pictures of the chairs, windows, and light fixtures. Together they would devise a way to incorporate some of this place's elements into one of their new restaurants. And they would be happy.

Katie paused, realizing that she had just thought about Rick and Nicole as a couple with no twinges of hurt or regret. She really was happy for them. She did wish them well. That small realization gave Katie an unexpected sense of hope about Eli that she couldn't explain.

"Go ahead. Try it." Jim nodded at the Malindi macchiato.

Katie took the first sip and closed her eyes, letting it slide down her throat slowly. "Oh, that's nice. Very spicy. I can see why Eli likes it. It wakes up your mouth."

The next Eli-inspired offering arrived at the table just then: Masala fries. The three of them shared the plate like an appetizer. The thick-cut french fries had a spicy sauce drizzled over the top that made Katie want to lick her fingers and order a second batch.

Their sandwiches arrived, and Katie's was a toasted bacon, cheese, and tomato, nice and crispy. "This is Eli's favorite? Really?"

Cheryl nodded as she took a bite of her hamburger. Katie was envying Cheryl's meal because it looked like a great burger, and it had been months since Katie had had one. The burger even came on a sesame seed bun with lettuce, tomato, and pickle, just like she ate all the time in California. Next time she came here, Katie would order for herself. She would definitely pick the Masala fries again, but she would go for a burger instead of a toasted cheese sandwich.

Katie saved the last bit of the Malindi macchiato to drink at the very end so that she would have the lovely, spicy taste in her mouth the rest of the way home. She swished the final swig around and remembered how she and Eli playfully had fought over the mocha dregs from their shared drink on her second day at Brockhurst. If he were here now, she probably would let him have the last of her macchiato. That's how much she missed him.

Katie looked around the cozy café one more time before they left. If she and Eli ever did go on a date, which according to him was not what they did, she would like for him to bring her here. They could each order a Malindi macchiato and savor their own dregs.

The fatigue of the journey seemed to catch up with all of them after their stomachs were filled. They strolled slowly to the car, and in the dark of the night, they headed up the hilly road to cooler, less congested Lemuru.

As they drove closer to Brockhurst, Cheryl checked her cell phone and let out a low, "Oh, dear."

"What is it?" Jim asked.

"They found Evan."

Katie leaned forward. "Callie's husband?"

"Yes. He was beaten and left for dead."

Katie held her breath.

"Callie sent the message. She said he's receiving medical attention, and she's gone to be with him. She left the children with Esther at Brockhurst and wants to know if we'll take them when we return."

"Of course," Jim said. "We'll put them in Eli's room."

Katie offered to help with the children or do anything else she could.

Despite being dead tired, Katie felt very happy to open the door to her small room and see all the comforts that had been provided for her there. The first thing she did was take a bath. Not a shower but a bath. It was only the second time she had used the bathtub, because it seemed like a luxury to consume all that water when a five-minute-or-less shower would do the job. Tonight she needed to soak and use the attached shower nozzle to wash her crinkled hair.

When Katie slid into her bed and felt the fresh and fragrant sheets, she considered herself the wealthiest woman in the world. Stretching out in the dark and peacefully cool room, she listened to the frogs croaking away under the bathroom window that was cracked open to let in the calm night breeze. It was open only an inch. Not enough to give way to any monkeys real or imagined.

What would it be like to be married? To go to bed on a night like this and lie beside the man with whom I will spend the rest of my life?

Her blissful thoughts were radically altered when she thought of how different the nights would be going to bed in a mud hut in a village. Katie had always considered herself a no-fuss, low-maintenance kind of gal. She didn't need much to get by. She didn't mind being dirty and roughing it. At a moment like this, though, she certainly did like her bathtub and her bed.

Katie thought back to several months ago when she and Christy had gone to Newport Beach and had to share a large bed at the home of Christy's aunt Marti and uncle Bob. At the time, Katie had been contemplating what it must be like for Christy and Todd to sleep next to each other every night. In the middle of those thoughts about how great Christy and Todd were for each other, Katie had realized that she and Rick weren't knit together at the heart the way Christy and Todd were.

And that was the night Katie decided to break up with Rick.

She let her thoughts float back to the day she broke up with Michael. She hadn't practiced what she was going to say, but she had decided she would tell him in the school parking lot at the end of the day so she could hop into her old car, Baby Hummer, and drive away before she changed her mind. They didn't make it to the parking lot. Michael was waiting for her by her locker, and she blurted her announcement out with heartless precision. "I am breaking up with you, and there is nothing you can say or do to change my mind."

Michael was right. I did owe him an apology.

She hadn't said good-bye to Michael when they left the village, either. At the time, Katie was too numb from Eli's announcement to give Michael a final good-bye. She wished now that she had. In spite of Michael's impetuousness, he deserved better.

Katie thought about Eli being with Michael and the other videographer in a new village tonight. No doubt they were once again stretched out on a tarp under the stars. What did guys talk about on "sleepovers" like that? Would they talk about her? Katie didn't like that possibility. She wondered how Eli would handle Michael's brazen and direct ways.

Closing her eyes and pulling the blankets up over her shoulders, Katie gave herself a final hakuna matata mandate and turned on her side, eager to sleep deep and dream sweet.

She woke when it was still dark. Her eyes opened wide in the shadowed surroundings. Her heart pounded. She had been dreaming of her childhood. Memories of things that had really happened seemed to have inspired a hodgepodge sort of dream in which she was watching herself as a young girl.

Rolling over in bed, she listened to the still sounds of the night: a distant chortle of a frog, the steady ticking of the alarm clock she had picked up at the Sharing Closet. In the comfort and safety of the darkness, she let her thoughts roll back to her childhood, paying attention to the trigger points that had remained with her from the dream.

She recalled a moment when she was no more than four or five and had impulsively burst through the front door of the house and found her parents in a heated argument. Instead of running to her room as usual, Katie had marched into the fray with her hands on her hips and spouted something she had heard the day before on a sitcom.

"You two need to go rent a room!"

She had no idea what it meant, but on TV the actors had laughed.

In real life, her parents stopped fighting and looked at her, and for a moment they seemed to have forgotten what they were angry about. Her dad sort of smiled at her. "Where did you come up with that?"

Delighting in having their attention, Katie imitated another scene she had seen on an old rerun. With a funny little wobble of her head, she said, "I've got a million of 'em."

That's when her mother laughed, and it was the sweetest sound Katie could remember hearing from her mother's lips.

Capping her moment in the spotlight, Katie remembered waving as she had seen funny people do a number of times on shows and saying, "Thank you, thank you. I'll be here all week."

That got both her parents laughing and looking at her with a curious mix of appreciation and wonder. She remembered how their expressions made her feel. She also recalled the directive that seemed to have been written on stone in her heart that day. *To get my parents to love me—or at least to like me—I need to make them laugh.*

Katie sat up in bed and drew in a deep breath. She was so tired. Was her subconscious trying to put together the Eli puzzle for her in her sleep? Had she cut and pasted those childhood beliefs into her life as an adult?

To get Eli to like me—no, to love me—I need to always . . .

She stopped herself before filling in the blank. She didn't want to write any more false truths for herself. That belief system was then. It had been dismantled. This was now. When she boarded that airplane in San Diego and came to Kenya, she did it as an act of faith. In some ways it could be considered an act of obedience.

Katie knew that she didn't want the kind of life in which she rattled off a platitude about God being in control while in her heart she was trying to manipulate the circumstances to ensure the outcome was what she wanted. What was true, genuine, and lasting had to be that she believed God, really believed him, with all her heart, soul, strength, and mind. If she believed he knew what was best and was working everything out for a purpose, then she could live each day with confidence and hope.

"Because my hope is in God," Katie murmured in the darkness. "And he has never abandoned me nor stopped loving me."

With that verbal declaration, Katie hunkered down, pulled up the blankets, and thought about Christy's advice to enjoy the "what ifs" in Katie's unfolding relationship with Eli and to experience the mystery of riding along inside the unknown.

Then Katie cried just a little because her exhausted spirit didn't know what else to do.

The next morning, Katie volunteered to watched Callie and Evan's three youngest children. She took them out into the largest open area of the conference center and had fun making up games for them to play on the grass. They knew some games from the children in the village where they lived, and Katie tried to teach them the game she had learned earlier that week in the village she had visited. After all of them had worked up a thirst, Katie gathered them close and asked who wanted to go to the Lion's Den with her to get something cold to drink.

Three hands shot up. They were such cute kids. So well-behaved. She could easily picture Eli being in a group like this little flock while he was growing up in a village the same way they had. For them, climbing trees and playing games with small rocks and twigs was normal.

On their trot over to the Lion's Den, the littlest chick in Katie's brood said, "Do you know what we got last night, Katie?"

"No, what?"

"Guess."

"Okay, give me a clue."

"It was a treat. A yummy treat."

Her sister said, "You're giving too many hints."

"Try to guess," the little doll asked again.

"Was it a new toy?"

"No."

"A DVD?"

All three children looked at each other as if they weren't sure what that was.

"Do you mean a movie?"

"Yes, a movie," Katie said. "Did you get a new movie?"

"No."

"I give up."

"It was apples! We each had our own apple to eat before we went to bed. Apples are my favorite. I had a whole apple for myself."

The simplicity and sweetness of that little girl's jubilee hit Katie in a profound way. She thought of all the times growing up when her school lunch came with an apple on the tray and she glibly threw it away. It was just an apple. A stupid apple. Not a cookie or an ice cream bar. An apple. Yet to a child who had grown up with very little, having an entire apple was better than a new toy or DVD.

When Katie entered the Lion's Den with her entourage, no one was working behind the counter. "You guys order whatever you want," Katie said. "I'll make it for you." She went behind the counter and washed up as Adam read the menu to his sisters and they decided what they wanted.

"Two orange juices and one milk, coming right up," Katie said after they placed their order. She set them up at one of the tables and pulled her laptop out of her shoulder bag.

"Are you working?" Adam asked.

"Sort of. I'm checking my emails."

"Can we send an email to our dad?" Adam asked.

"I have a better idea," Katie said. "Why don't you guys make pictures for him?"

She remembered seeing a box of colored pencils and some paper in the drawer of a table by the fireplace. Katie scooted off to retrieve the items, and when she returned, she passed them out to the kids and told them she was sure their pictures would make their dad happy.

With the three of them busy drawing, Katie pulled up her emails. The first one she opened was from Nicole. In her sweet way, Nicole gave Katie an overview of how she and Rick arrived at their decision to marry in October. Rick and Nicole were offered the opportunity to renovate a restaurant in New York City. As Nicole described it, since Rick and his brother had already sold their other cafés, the timing was perfect for Rick and Nicole to take on this new endeavor.

Nicole also made it clear that she wanted to tell Katie all this but hadn't been able to connect with her before their good news was announced. The end of Nicole's email read:

When you have a chance, I'm eager to hear all the details about you and Eli. Rick and I both loved the photos you posted of you guys feeding the giraffe. Rick said you looked like you were glowing in the pictures. I thought Eli looked pretty glowy too, the way he was looking at you.

If there's any chance that you and Eli are coming back this way in October, we would love for you to come to our wedding. I wanted to explain that I didn't ask you to be one of my brides-maids because of the distance. I want you to know, Katie, that if you were still here, you would have been the first one I would have asked.

I miss you, Katie. Write me when you can. Rick says hi. Say hi to Eli for us.

Hugs,

Nicole

Katie leaned back and checked on her little artists. They were still busy coloring. She let Nicole's email settle on her. Parts of it felt a little awkward and uncomfortable. That was mostly because Nicole's words pulled up images of her and Rick cuddled up together, so in love, so eager to dream together about their future and move ahead with those dreams. Katie felt as if she and Eli were on pause. She told herself that was okay. That's where they were for the moment. They wouldn't be on pause forever.

I guess it's easy for some couples to figure out what's next and to make the commitment to each other effortlessly, like Rick and Nicole. Eli and I aren't that couple.

Katie couldn't identify exactly what sort of couple they were, but then she decided she didn't need to make any declarations to Nicole, even though she had asked for details. Katie liked keeping Nicole and Rick's impressions as they were — that Eli and she were happy and that coming here was the right decision for her.

Katie tapped out her reply to Nicole, keeping it short and wishing Nicole and Rick all the best that God had dreamed up for them. Her concluding line was simply, *I'll tell Eli you said hi, and I'll keep you updated.*

She left the details of her love life at that. Katie knew that she and Nicole could never be the same midnight whispering girlfriends they had been in college. That season of their friendship was over. It would always be Nicole and Rick from here on out, just as the relationship dynamic with Christy had changed when she and Todd married. Katie and Christy managed to adjust. She hoped she and Nicole would be able to adjust as well.

Katie went through the rest of her emails quickly and found herself smiling when she came to one from Christy. She read the update about how Todd's dad had met a woman he was serious about and how great that was since his parents had split soon after Todd was born. Now Todd's dad was getting a second chance at love.

Christy's email went on to say:

They met in the Canary Islands, and Todd thinks that if they get married, that's where the wedding will be. I checked a map, and the Canary Islands are off the coast of West Africa. So that means if we end up going to the Canary Islands someday in the next, say, year or so for their wedding, then we'll have to fly to Kenya to see you and Eli.

Katie stared out the Lion's Den window. The possibility of Todd and Christy coming to Kenya was a delicious thought, and she savored it a moment until her next thought turned her spirit sour. *Even Todd's dad is about to get married. I don't think I can read any more emails about people who are having easy, breezy times with their relationships. Everything is making me miss Eli even more. This is torture.*

She closed the laptop and said to the kids, "Let's see your fabulous artwork."

The children held up their pictures for her to admire. She tried to make all the right sort of affirming sounds and nods as each of them went into detail explaining what they had drawn and why.

Adam had chosen a box-style car with five round faces. None of the faces had smiles. On the top of the car was a stick figure of a person sitting, and behind the car he had drawn stick figures of people raising their arms.

"They're yelling for us to leave," he explained.

In the bottom right-hand corner, he drew a small bed and another stick figure lying in the bed.

"Is that your dad?" Katie asked.

"Yes. He's getting better now. But he has to stay in bed and rest first."

"And who is that on top of the car?" Katie asked.

All three of the children looked at her as if surprised that she didn't know the answer. "Our guardian angel, of course."

"Of course."

Katie thought about guardian angels again later that week when she was walking to the office after lunch. She had heard that Evan was being released from the hospital that day and would be brought to Brockhurst to convalesce and to be with Callie and their four children. One of the women who was at the table with Katie at lunch had said that God had protected Evan, and his being alive would have a powerful effect on the people in the village where they had been serving.

It seemed to Katie that in Kenya the lines were narrow and the veils were thin. Danger did lurk in the corners of this beautiful country, but the veil between the eternal and the temporal seemed to be made of something much more vaporous than Katie had experienced in California. Maybe her senses were more heightened to those things than before. She wasn't sure. All she knew was that God seemed closer in Africa. His work was being accomplished in ways that seemed more visible and immediate than she was used to seeing.

Watching God at work was having a deep effect on Katie. It was increasing her faith.

She entered the office four days after they had returned from the village and saw that Jim was moving a folding table over to the valentine wall. "Look what I hunted up," he said. "It's not much of a desk for you, but it's a start."

"Nice!" Katie pulled out her laptop and placed it in the center. "Now all I need is a name plaque, and I'll look official."

"We heard from Eli," Jim said.

Katie's heart did a little flutter. "You did? How is he doing? Any idea when he'll be back?"

"He's doing okay. It looks like he'll be catching a ride back to Brockhurst a week from tomorrow."

Katie waited for more details. "Was that it? Did he email you?"

"No. He called about twenty minutes ago. He's with the well-digging crew now, and they were driving through an area that had phone service, so he took the opportunity to call. He said the film crew left yesterday."

With Jim's basic sentences, Katie tried to fill in the blanks. Eli was on his way to another village. He wasn't with Michael anymore. He would be back in eight days.

"A week from tomorrow, huh?"

Jim nodded. "You know, I have to admit something, Katie. I wasn't in favor of Eli taking on this role of being onsite in the villages, but I may have spoken too soon. He's accomplished a lot in only a few days. We needed to negotiate clearance on some land before the team could move forward in the village where Eli was yesterday. Apparently he did it. Single-handedly. I didn't think he had enough of a command of Swahili to do it. I guess Cheryl is right. I may have underestimated my son."

An onslaught of mixed feelings came over Katie. On one hand, what Jim was now expressing was the sort of respect and understanding she had hoped would develop in their father/son relationship. She wanted Jim to see the same leadership abilities she had seen in Eli, and now he did. It was great that Jim and Cheryl were seeing Eli as the capable man Katie knew he was.

What twisted her emotions around was that it sounded as if Eli was finding his place out on the road doing fieldwork. The chance of his being content to settle in at Brockhurst and work with her in the office was narrowing.

To complicate that even more, Katie's enthusiasm for working on the fund-raising hadn't diminished. Her latest idea was to put together a fund-raising packet for potential groups. Cheryl, Jim, and she had gone over the list of needed materials to include in the packet, and Katie was working next to create the master documents. She also had a good running start on compiling a list of potential schools and churches.

Her productive pace slowed on a cloudy morning five days before Eli was supposed to return to Brockhurst. A large group of Christian writers and publishers was holding a conference on the grounds, and this was their last day. Katie had enjoyed the conversations she'd had with many of them over meals.

This morning, however, she skipped breakfast because she wanted to get to the office before anyone else. She had a number of personal emails she wanted to send before the day started to roll along.

The first email went to Christy. The two forever friends had been keeping up a back-and-forth email correspondence ever since Katie wrote Christy after the time in the village and spilled the details about Michael, Eli, the fund-raising position, and how it seemed that Jim and Cheryl had embraced her as one of their team, part of the big Brockhurst family.

Katie even told Christy about the valentine wall and the passionate kiss. Katie added the details about Jim's comment that "you could make a baby with a kiss like that." And then, of course, Katie told Christy about Eli's decision to venture off on a nomadic trip to other villages. That was the latest topic the two of them had been emailing about, which was why Katie didn't want anyone peering over her shoulder in the small office and reading their emails.

This morning Christy's email started with:

Life with you is never dull, Katie. Does Eli realize that? I'm guessing he does by now. Since you asked for my opinion, I'll give it to you.

Do you remember when I broke up with Todd for that stretch of time because he had the opportunity to do what he had always wanted to? Letting go like that was the hardest thing I've ever done.

But think about what happened after that. At the time, Todd and I both thought he was headed to Papua New Guinea, but he ended up in Spain, which is where he met Eli, which is partly why Eli decided to come to Rancho, which is why he was at our wedding, which is where you met him, and which led to your being where you are today. Quite a nice little trail of God's mysterious ways, isn't it?

Katie felt her throat tighten. It was true. She hadn't seen the trail this clearly before. It was like Cheryl had said: everything has a purpose. One step of obedience led to the opportunity for the light to shine on the next step and so on.

Christy's email continued.

I know that God can accomplish his purposes any way he wants. But when I look back over the years and see this chain of

events, I have no doubt that all of this is a beautiful, continu-
ous God-thing that started with something difficult when my
heart surrendered Todd to the Lord. When you follow the trail
of God's faithfulness in your life, Katie, I know he will give you
the courage you need for whatever is going to happen next.

Katie nodded, even though no one was there to see her affirmation. Or maybe there was. God's Spirit felt close. Covering her, guid-
ing her, protecting her like the guardian angel on the top of the Jeep in
Adam's drawing. She looked around the empty room, half expecting
to see a translucent angel feather floating in the air. She was going to
stop and type a response, but there was more to Christy's email.

Katie, do you remember when we were in England doing that
short-term mission project, and we called each other "Mis-
sionary Woman"? We thought we were being so daring and
sacrificial by giving up a week and a half of our lives to stay
in a castle (all right, it was freezing and that was a hardship,
but it was a castle!). What we did then had kingdom value. I
don't doubt that. We thought we were doing so much good, but
really, when I look at where you and I are now, we are so much
more in the flow of God's good kingdom work.

I believe that in what I'm doing right now, partnering with
Todd in working with the teenagers at church, I have become
Missionary Woman 2.0. We're on to the next season, the next
level, you and me. This is good work.

Katie leaned back in the office chair and thought about Christy's
scenario of the helpful, supportive wife of a youth pastor. Yes, she
agreed, things were just right for Christy and Todd.

But we're not them. Eli and I are wired differently. Life isn't like
that here. At all. Eli and I aren't like Todd and Christy. We're not that
couple. We're not like Rick and Nicole. We're us. The thing is, the way
we're headed, will there be an "us" at the end of this short trail?

Katie set to work, typing as fast as she could to answer Christy while everything was fresh in her mind. She was nearly to the end of her email when Cheryl opened the door of the office and entered with a cheery "Jambo."

Katie minimized the screen so the unfinished email wouldn't show and turned to greet Cheryl with an equally cheery "Jambo, *rafiki*."

"Oh, good! You remembered the word for 'friend.' Are you ready for your next Swahili word of the day?"

"Bring it on." Katie enjoyed the lessons both Cheryl and Jim had been giving her during the past week. Katie wanted to surprise Eli when he returned and greet him with at least one complete sentence in Swahili.

"Okay, here it is. *Wapi choo?*"

"Wapi choo," Katie repeated. "So what did I just say?"

"You asked, 'Where's the bathroom?'"

Katie laughed. "I'm sure that will be very helpful at some point, but you do remember that I'm trying to learn something that I can say to Eli when he gets back. I'm thinking that 'Wapi choo' isn't exactly going to make his heart soar with joy over my accomplishment."

Cheryl slid into the chair at her desk. "Okay. You're right. Here's a good line for greeting someone who is special to you: *Napenda kuku-ona mpenzi wangu ni furaha ya moyo mangu.*"

"No, not gonna happen. That sounded really pretty coming from you, but you've noticed what a slow learner I am. Can you give me something in between 'Where's the toilet?' and 'Napa wapa snapa mango'?"

Cheryl laughed. "You do know, Katie, that you should be careful when you try to make up your own Swahili words. One of these days you're going to manage to say something dreadful."

"Okay, so give me another line. Something shorter. But wait. What did that greeting for someone special mean? Maybe we can shorten that."

"It's very sweet. It means, 'I love to see you, my dear. You are the joy of my heart.'"

"Ohh." Katie melted just a little. "That is sweet. But I don't think I could say that to Eli. He would think I was joking. I need something not as sugary, you know? Something that's more true to who I am and what he would know is really coming from me."

"I'll give that some thought," Cheryl said. "By the way, did Mary catch you at breakfast?"

"No, I didn't go to breakfast. What did she want?"

"The group that's staying here this week for the writer's conference is going to Lake Naivasha tomorrow, since it's their final day. She wondered if you could go along as their guide since Eli isn't here."

"Guide? How could I be their guide? I've never been to that lake. I don't know anything about it." She didn't want to be diverted from all she was trying to accomplish in the office and wasn't sure why Mary would think Katie was a natural replacement for Eli on a tour.

"*Guide* is the wrong word," Cheryl said. "Basically, she just needs a representative from Brockhurst to do a head count and to call the office if any problems develop. You would be the point person, that's all. I didn't mean for it to sound as if you had to be a tour guide. Lake Naivasha is beautiful. Last time we were there, we watched the hippos come up from the water at sunset. It was quite a sight."

Katie liked the way this diversion was beginning to sound. "All I'd have to do is ride along and check names off the list as people get on and off the bus? I wouldn't have to give everyone the history and scientific facts of each location the way Eli does?"

"No. You don't have to try to do it Eli's way. You'll also have to settle the bill with the restaurant where they've set up a lunch for the group. It's all been arranged through the Brockhurst main office. As you know, we used to have a tour company—in this office, as a matter of fact. Now that they've moved out, Mary is trying to juggle a few of these promotional tours that were booked before the tour company relocated in Nairobi."

"I can do that," Katie said. "I can ride along, count noses, and hand over a check. I'll go talk to Mary about it." Katie quickly clicked on her screen and ended her email to Christy midsentence with a couple of dashes and a final line that read, *Gotta go see a lady about some hippos.*

She hit Send, closed her email, and scurried out the door. Katie almost felt guilty for feeling so happy about the opportunity to see the hippos. If she was missing Eli dreadfully, as she was, then shouldn't she be so depressed that nothing, not even wild hippopotami, would float her boat like this?

Note to self: *Ask Christy if she thinks it's possible to be falling in love with a place and a person at the same time, and if so, that's not cheating, is it?*

19

Loading up the tour bus with the group of writers and publishers felt familiar to Katie, because it was the same bus and driver that had taken the Texas group to the giraffe reserve almost a month earlier. Katie didn't remember the driver's name, but he remembered her, and when she climbed on board, he greeted her by saying, "Jambo, *Ekundu.*"

Katie had no idea what the "Ekundu" meant, but she hoped it was flattering or at least pleasant. She responded with, "Jambo, rafiki."

The driver seemed to like her calling him "friend."

Remembering how Eli had taken the microphone and welcomed everyone last time, Katie followed suit. "Jambo! How's everyone doing? My name is Katie. I'm your unofficial guide today. So if you have any questions, I can pretty much guarantee that I won't be able to answer them."

She received a sea of blank stares. Katie was aware this was an international group, but she had dined with them all week and knew that English was the common language. So she tried to ramp up the enthusiasm. "Are you guys ready to see the hippos at Lake Naranja?"

"Naivasha," one of the African women in the front seat across from Katie said, quietly correcting her. "We're going to Lake Naivasha."

"Right. Yes. Lake Naivasha. Not Naranja. *Naranja* means orange in Spanish, and I know that because I'm from California, and my friend had a surfboard he named Naranja because it was orange."

221

Katie could tell by the expressions changing before her eyes that she was tottering way off track.

"Okay, but enough about my friends and me. This trip today is all about you and your friends. So please sit back and enjoy the bumpy ride. Although I am happy to say that our rafiki here behind the wheel is known for providing his passengers with a much smoother ride than you'll get in any of those white shuttle buses."

The group seemed to have reconnected with her on that comment, and she guessed that arriving at Brockhurst had been the same sort of experience for them as it had been for Katie and Eli.

"So, if you were hoping that our ride today was going to be just like what you experienced in those vicious, vibrating vehicles, I hate to disappoint you, but there are no free African massages on this bus."

Two of the men from the Philippines let out a cheer from midway back. Katie had met one of them at lunch earlier that week and appreciated his lighthearted spirit and engaging smile.

"Thank you for that affirmation there, Ramon. Keep those cheers coming. I need all the encouragement I can get. In case you hadn't guessed, this is my first day on the job."

Ramon and the guy next to him let out a lively shout of "*Mabuhay!*"

"Whoa!" Katie said a little too loudly into the microphone. "And what does that mean? Because if it means "Please sit down and stop talking, Katie," then you'll just have to be straight-up with me on that, because I don't speak Filipino."

"It means 'long life,'" Ramon called out.

The guy next to him cheered again. "Mabuhay!"

This time everyone in the bus echoed the cheer.

Katie thrust her arm in the air. "All right! We've got us a party bus goin' on here. Woo-hoo! Mabuhay!" She held the microphone out like a lead singer at a rock concert inviting the audience to sing back their favorite lyrics to the song.

The gang complied and cheered, "Mabuhay!" into the microphone.

On the backside of the group cheer, a polished-looking gentleman sitting up admirably straight two rows back filled the air with his cultural version of the cheer and added, *"Viva! Viva!"*

Katie remembered that he was a publisher from France, because when she sat by him at breakfast the first morning the group arrived, she was fascinated with the flowing conversation he was having with some of the West African publishers who spoke French. She didn't understand a single word, but it was beautiful to sit with them and feel as if her ears were tasting a smorgasbord of brand-new sounds.

Her ears were filled once again with the same sort of intercultural buffet of words as everyone on the bus let out a holler in his or her native language. The lovely cacophony brought smiles to everyone's face, as Katie once again held out the microphone to catch their cheers.

All right! Not bad. My work here is done.

Katie took her seat as the lively atmosphere pervaded the bus. She felt pretty good about the way she had helped to bolster the energy level.

Now, what if the UN took that approach to every summit meeting? If people from around the world took the time to laugh together, I can't help but think that world peace would break out.

She took the same seat alone in the front behind the driver as Eli had and pulled out the notes in her folder, the same way she remembered Eli had. The schedule indicated that they should arrive at the Lake Naivasha resort at 11:30. They would have their lunch first and then walk through the wildlife preserve area to the lake. Katie was assigned to herd everyone back to the tour bus by 2:30. Once everyone was on board, they would head for Brockhurst and be back in plenty of time for the evening meal.

Seemed easy enough.

As the bus rumbled down the road that led to Nairobi, Katie realized she recognized some of the turnouts along the way. That realization gave her a surprising sort of happiness. It reminded her of the feeling she had when she moved into the dorms at Rancho, found her way into town to the Dove's Nest Café, and then managed to drive back to campus without getting lost or making a wrong turn. That meant she was home—and that she knew how to find her way back home.

"Katie?" The African woman in the row across from Katie who had corrected her on the pronunciation of Naivasha leaned over. "You're Eli's Katie, aren't you?"

"Eli's Katie?"

The woman extended her hand, as if she had forgotten her manners and should have introduced herself first. "I'm Ngokabi. I've known the Lorenzos for a long time. I heard about you last year." She touched her hand to her straight black hair and pointed to Katie. "I knew it had to be you because of the red hair. Ekundu."

"Is that what the driver called me, Ekundu?"

Ngokabi nodded. She was a lovely young woman with high cheekbones and a narrow chin. She reminded Katie of some of the athletes from Rancho who looked as if their arms and legs were built for running.

"Ekundu means 'red,'" Ngokabi said. "He meant it as a nickname. Do you mind it?"

"No, I like it. Ekundu." Katie pointed at Ngokabi and said, "What does your name mean?"

"It's traditional from my family. It means 'Daughter of the Masai.' It's an honor for me to have this name, because it is the same name as my father's firstborn sister."

Katie wasn't sure why that would be such an honor.

"You see, with the tribes in Kenya, we have a progression for names. I am the third daughter, so the third daughter is named after the father's firstborn sister. If I had been a boy, I would be named for my father's firstborn brother."

"So your name was decided before you were even born."

The woman next to Ngokabi said, "Is that not how it is with all of us who have been called by God? He knew our name and every hair on our head before we took our first breath."

Katie thought about that point as Ngokabi went on to explain that forty-two tribes lived in Kenya, and the woman next to her was from the Kikuyu tribe. Her facial features, a broad forehead and a rounder face, were different from Ngokabi's.

"My namesake was a much-loved woman," Ngokabi said. "She taught a women's Bible study for twelve years, and now the publishing house I work with in Nairobi is producing her material. It's exciting to see her hard work live on even after she is gone."

Their conversation continued the rest of the ride to Lake Naivasha. Even though Katie hadn't intended to return to the opening question of "Are you Eli's Katie?" the subject somehow did a swooping circle, and there it was in front of them once again for Katie to confirm or deny.

She tried to choose her words carefully. "I suppose you could say that. Yes, I'm Eli's Katie. We're going together. But he's in a village now and has been for almost a week and a half. We have a lot to figure out. It seems we have very different career paths." Katie realized her head was bobbing, as if she were trying to convince herself of what she had just said. All of it. Did they have different career paths? Really? That sounded so western when she heard herself say it.

And was she really "Eli's Katie"? Is that how he had referred to her, or was Ngokabi taking something she had heard from Eli and giving it her own spin? Katie wondered if it was okay to say that they were "going together." Was that their own code for their relationship, or was that how Eli had referred to her?

All the uncertainties weighed on her in a disagreeable way. Katie was glad that Ngokabi didn't probe the topic or offer insights. She didn't even seem particularly interested in how Katie was sorting out her relationship with Eli. It seemed as if Ngokabi had just stated a determined fact, the way her name had been chosen for her before she was born.

When the bus driver pulled into the tree-filled area marked with a large sign for Lake Naivasha, Katie felt ready to stretch her legs, grab some lunch, and see those hippos.

"All right, rafikis, we are here. The hippos of Lake Naivasha await us. Let me give you a rundown of the plan for our lovely afternoon, just in case you didn't catch these details earlier. When you disembark, be sure to tell our driver what a great job he did."

Everyone clapped. Ngokabi said something to the driver as he was turning off the motor, and he gave a wave in the large rearview mirror.

"Okay." Katie motioned for everyone to stop clapping and stay in their seats one more moment. "So here's the plan. We're having lunch first. You can meander your way into the restaurant, and you'll find a separate room that has been prepared for our group. My notes say it's a cookout, and you can go through the buffet line as many times as you like."

"Mabuhay!"

"I thought you'd like that, Ramon."

A wave of chuckles and chatter rose.

"Now, wait, let me make sure everyone knows that we must be back to the bus by two thirty at the very latest. We'll eat, walk down to the river, try not to be eaten by the hippos, and then find our way back here by two thirty. Got that?"

A variety of responses resounded as the group rose and made its way past Katie and out the door. She felt like a flight attendant, nodding, smiling, and giving a few playful "Buh-bys" to some in the group.

She gave a little salute to the bus driver and brought up the rear as the meandering group stopped for photos in front of the Lake Naivasha sign and made their way toward the restaurant that was well marked in English. This resort was different from the one she had stopped at with Eli's parents in Aberdare. That one had been traditionally British in its architecture and furnishings. This one was African in style, and Katie loved the carved wood and wild animal print fabric on the chairs.

It took her a little while to remember that she had completed her job when she gave everyone the information and escorted them off the bus. She didn't need to shepherd them around or check in on them. In a way, this felt like summer camp, and she was the camp counselor.

That thought made Katie smile. It was almost as if one of her small, forgotten dreams had come true. In high school she had dearly wanted to be a camp counselor, but her parents had put their foot down, saying she wasn't allowed to keep the commitment she had made to her youth pastor. Christy ended up going in her place, and Katie was befuddled to this day as to why her parents, who showed such little care, concern, or involvement in many areas of her life, had been against her going to camp.

It was one of those inexplicable things about her family that she knew she would never grasp. Another mysterious thing she didn't understand was the way her parents had responded when she called them a few days after she had arrived in Kenya and explained how she planned to stay indefinitely.

Her mother had said, "I can see it."

That was all. Just, "I can see it." Katie hadn't known if she should take that as a jab, as if her mother were saying that their impulsive, odd little child had run off to Africa on the heels of college graduation—no surprise there. It was so opposite of anything anyone in Katie's extended family would have done that it must have seemed like this was something Katie would do.

Her father said he wanted her to send him an elephant tusk. Then he laughed as if he had made a great joke.

Katie knew she should never hope to receive her parents' approval and blessing on something she did. But to her surprise, after she had given her mother her mailing address during the phone call, Katie received a graduation card from her in the mail along with a twenty-dollar bill. The handwritten note was short. "I meant to give this card to you at your graduation, but your father forgot to remind me, and I left it in the car. I don't know if the Africans can cash American money, but maybe you can use it there somehow. Your father and I are proud of you. Please be safe."

The card had arrived early in Katie's stay, when she and Eli were spending lots of time together and everything felt buoyant and new. The card and her mother's handwritten message hadn't meant much to her then.

As she sat in the exotic restaurant at Lake Naivasha at a table with writers from the Czech Republic and Bulgaria who were busy talking about publishing, Katie ate her papaya and pineapple starter salad and thought of how, in essence, she had received the blessing she had longed for. She never told Eli about the card; she wished she could tell him now. Her parents, in the best way they knew how, had told her, "We're proud of you. Be safe." That was huge. How did she miss the significance of that? Katie felt warmed inside in an unexpected way. Getting away from Brockhurst and the Lorenzos for the day was giving her a chance to back up and see other facets of her life.

Joining the others from her table, Katie went outside the main eating area to where the barbecues were smoking like crazy and three chefs in spotless white jackets and tall chef hats stood ready to carve the meat that was roasting on the spit. Katie picked up a plate and followed Sasa, a publisher from Prague, as they scooped up ugali, rice, and mixed vegetables from large serving trays. When they got to the meat, Sasa asked what it was.

The chef replied, but neither Sasa nor Katie was sure of what he said. They both went ahead and motioned for the chef to carve some meat for them and loaded up their plates.

"It smells wonderful," Katie said. "Asante."

Returning to the table, she dug in, enjoying every bite of the firm, well-seasoned meat.

"How do you like it?" Svetlana, the publisher from Bulgaria, asked.

"Delicious."

"I agree. It is the best goat I've ever had," Svetlana said.

Katie felt her last bite stopping halfway down. She swallowed hard and took a long drink from her soda can. "Goat. Hmmm. So that's what it was."

Sasa gave her a "Well, how about that?" sort of look, and the two of them quietly kept on chewing and finished their meal.

Katie knew she had come a long way from scrunching up her nose at ostrich meatballs and turning down the chance to try a flying peanut. This had been a delicious meal, and she had enjoyed every bite. Well, maybe not that last one ...

Some of the group had already made their way down the trail to the lake. Katie lingered at the table, taking dainty, delightful bites of a piece of coconut cake that perfectly topped off the gourmet luncheon. By the time she had finished, she was the last one at the table. And that's when she missed Eli more than she could hardly stand.

Deciding to once again assume the role of Princess Hakuna Matata, Katie lifted her cloth napkin to her mouth and dabbed the edges of her very lonely lips. Then, folding her napkin like a proper princess would do, Katie gracefully backed her chair away from the table and headed out the door for the main attraction.

She was strolling by herself on the trail that led quite a way down to the lake when Ngokabi came up behind her. "Are we the last to leave the restaurant?"

"I think so." Katie was glad for the companionship. "This is beautiful, isn't it?"

To their left, in the grove of slender acacia trees that surrounded both sides of the trail, Katie heard a rustling. She looked over her shoulder and saw a zebra. Then another and another.

"Ngokabi, look! Zebras!"

"Yes?"

It seemed to Katie that Ngokabi's response was about the same as if they had been walking down the sidewalk at Todd and Christy's apartment and Katie had said, "Look, a stray cat."

Katie stayed where she was, awestruck by the zebras, as she counted fourteen of them. She pulled out her phone, set it on zoom, and took several pictures before moving on down the trail with patient Ngokabi, who had waited for her.

Katie grinned. "My first zebra. What can I say?"

Ngokabi's expression remained respectfully attentive. She asked Katie if she had been to the Masai Mara on a safari.

"No. Eli told me a little about it. I'd love to see a lion or cheetah. Or an elephant. That would be amazing. We went to the giraffe reserve, and I fed Daisy out of my hand." Katie was still feeling proud of that.

"Did you? I've been to see Daisy. She can be fickle."

"She liked me."

Without changing her expression much, Ngokabi said kindly, "I can see how she would. You have the Lord's presence in your life. I understand why Eli spoke of you the way he did."

Katie wasn't sure she wanted to press this topic of conversation. She already was missing Eli terribly. He would have understood her amazement over the zebras. Unable to quench her curiosity, she asked, "What exactly did he tell you about me?"

"All good things, of course. He was waiting patiently, very patiently, for you to turn your head his way."

For the first time, it hit Katie how long Eli had waited for her to pay attention to him. For some reason Katie couldn't explain, Eli had set his affections on her the day they had met. He prayed for her and certainly thought of her for a year before Katie turned her head his way and gave him the same attention and consideration he had already focused on her.

Here Katie felt like she was dying because it had been almost two weeks since she had seen Eli and since they had last talked. She thought she was the one who was mastering the art of patiently waiting, yet Eli had waited a year.

"He's amazing," Katie said.

"He feels the same way about you. I'm sure you know that."

Katie nodded, even though at times she had let herself wonder if her attraction for him was a one-sided exercise. It wasn't. She knew it. Deep in her heart she knew it. If only they didn't have this huge obstacle of their opposing goals. Why was it that way for them? Their friends who were couples didn't have that same challenge.

Ngokabi and Katie came to the end of the path where the rest of the group had gathered, standing in small clumps, pointing to the water, and shielding their eyes from the sun with their hands.

Katie was startled to see the vastness of the lake and what a soft, powdery blue shade it was. High above the lake the clouds floated like forgotten wishes blown from tiny pink candles on a child's birthday cake. The ground around them was flat, covered with green marsh grasses. In the distance, a wide and all-encompassing plateau rose at the far end of the lake. That's when Katie realized they were in a deep valley. The Rift Valley. This was where the earth was being slowly pulled apart, revealing fertile soil and cavernous lakes. Eli had stood by her side when they peered down into this immense green valley, and now she was in the valley looking up.

"There's one!" A man in the group who was from India had brought a pair of binoculars. He was the first to spot the bubbles and spouting spray of the emerging hippo.

At first the huge creature rose only high enough to reveal the top of its head; its small, flittering, round ears; and its severe-looking eyes. It was evident that the part hidden below the water was terrifyingly huge. Even though they were far away from the where the hippopotami were reported to come up on shore, it still seemed like they were awfully close. Katie could hear the great beast's snorting sounds and deep groans.

Then, in a series of motions that were magnificent and yet seemed a little silly at the same time, the SUV-sized creature emerged from the muddy water and trotted up on the shore in a way that made him look as if he were prancing around on his thick-as-an-oak-tree legs that seemed way too short for his immense carriage.

The group seemed to draw in their collective breaths when the enormous hippo turned in their direction and gave them a terrible gaze. Katie noticed for the first time that a uniformed game warden was with their group. He was equipped with a pistol and a walking stick.

Fortunately, he didn't need to employ either deterrent, because the hippopotamus trotted in a small circle twice and then plodded his way back to the lake.

"He's just making sure we know who's in charge," the game warden said. "We know. We don't challenge his control over his domain."

They waited and watched another ten minutes or so and tried to count the number of hippos in the water by the raised heads and wiggling ears that looked more like small floating gray mounds. Katie checked her phone for the time and saw that they had about forty minutes before they had to be on the bus. She decided to head back before the rest of the group so that she could settle the bill and be in place to do her nose count as the group boarded.

Katie also noticed that she had a new text message on her phone. It was from Eli. She clicked on it and read, I MISS YOU.

Her heart melted a little, and then she remembered that was the message he had written to her when they were on the bus on the last tour. She recalled how he had been in the seat in front of her, and the two of them had kept a texting conversation going. What she just read had to be the old message. But it wasn't. She scrolled up and back and saw that this new I MISS YOU had been sent twelve minutes ago. That meant Eli was in range of cell service in whatever village he was in.

Katie loved the idea of the possibilities that seemed open to them. They could communicate again!

I MISS YOU TOO, she texted back. I'M AT LAKE NAIVA-SHA. JUST SAW A HIPPO. THINKING OF YOU.

As she walked back to the building, she watched for zebras and checked for a reply message from Eli at the same time. Her eyes went up, her eyes went down. The zebras had moved on. Eli must have moved out of range as well, because he didn't reply. Katie kept checking her phone after settling the bill, visiting the restroom, and collecting her colorful group. They had to wait on the bus for one rather lively member of their bunch named Nicholas, who was from Scotland. He had become "otherwise engaged," as his associate, Graham explained.

That delay set them back only five minutes, and they were on their way. Katie didn't feel the need to provide a stand-up routine, and blessedly none of the lovely people on the bus requested one.

Sitting alone by the window, Katie pulled out her phone, hoping for another text from Eli. They were on the road for more than an hour when her phone beeped, indicating that she had received a new text. It was from Eli, and her lips rose in a smile.

SHOULD I BE OFFENDED? he wrote.

"What?" Katie murmured. She quickly typed, WHY?

The response came back, YOU JUST SAID YOU SAW A HIPPO AND THOUGHT OF ME.

Katie laughed aloud and then drew her shoulders in to ensure privacy as she responded. TWO UNRELATED INCIDENTS. HOW ARE YOU DOING?

Katie waited for his reply, and as she did, something inside her wished he would indicate that he was terrible, miserable, and ready to return to Brockhurst so he could see her. That he couldn't stand the thought of spending another moment without her.

Something like that.

However, nothing prepared Katie for the enthusiasm in his virtual voice as she read his reply. I'M DOING GREAT. EXCELLENT! I'LL BE STAYING ON ANOTHER FEW DAYS. IT'S GOING BETTER THAN HOPED.

Katie didn't text back. She didn't know what to say. Was she glad that things were going so well? Yes, of course, in a general team-effort sort of way. But her heart ached at the thought of "another few days" being added to the separation side of the scale. That side already felt far too weighted to be balanced out with the hope, courage, and patience she kept trying to add to the other side.

After several minutes of gazing out the window and thinking about her choices, Katie decided to take the route that Eli had selected over the course of an entire year as he waited out being overlooked by Katie.

With a grace she could feel growing inside her heart, Katie texted back the words that she knew would mean the most to Eli: I'LL BE PRAYING FOR YOU.

For the next four days, Katie lived out the sort of walk of faith and steps of obedience that she and Christy often talked about as they exchanged emails. Katie had to believe that one step would lead to the next and that a purpose was tucked away in all this. She helped out at the Coffee Bar, watched Callie and Evan's children for an afternoon, and cranked out all the work she needed to do on the fund-raiser packet.

Michael emailed her the name and contact information of his father-in-law as he had promised. He included a note that read:

Since I know you're wondering, I didn't mess with Eli's mind too much the days we were together. I did tell him I thought it was rude of you to leave without telling me good-bye. He said you were upset about him going on without you. Understandable. I told him it always makes the homecoming sweeter. At least that's what my darling wife tells me. Let's keep in touch. Eli has my contact info too. He's a good man. But then, I think you already know that.

All the best,

Michael

Katie appreciated Michael's sending the information, and she appreciated his comment about the homecoming being sweeter. She hoped that would be the case when Eli returned from the village. The nice part about Eli's having off-and-on cell phone service in the location where he was now meant that the two of them had kept a pretty steady stream of conversation going over the past four days.

They had a good rhythm going. Being able to send snapshots of their everyday moments helped too. That evening at dinner, Katie saw that they had banana pudding for dessert. It had been a while since Eli had feasted on double desserts of banana pudding, so Katie took a picture with her phone and sent it to him with the text message, IF YOU WON'T COME BACK FOR ME, WILL YOU CONSIDER COMING BACK FOR THE BANANA PUDDING?

Eli's reply came through when Katie was already in bed. He wrote: YOU'RE CRUEL. WE HAD TWIGS FOR SUPPER. AT LEAST THAT'S WHAT IT TASTED LIKE.

Katie texted back: FOR YOUR HOMECOMING DINNER, I'LL SEE IF I CAN TRACK DOWN AN OSTRICH AND MAKE AN ENTIRE MEATLOAF FOR YOU. HOW DOES THAT SOUND?

QUESTIONABLE, was his prompt reply. IT SEEMS BEST TO LEAVE THE OSTRICH RECIPES IN THE HANDS OF THOSE WHO KNOW HOW TO COOK.

ARE YOU SAYING YOU THINK I DON'T KNOW HOW TO COOK? she typed back.

Eli's reply was short: MICROWAVE POPCORN, SMOOTHIES, GREEN FACE. THAT'S ALL I'M SAYING.

Katie laughed aloud in her bed. She had forgotten about the night that she and Christy had decided to have a girls' night at Todd and Christy's apartment since Todd was at a church event. They smeared their faces with some sort of avocado facial mask, whipped up strawberry smoothies in the blender, and attempted to make microwave popcorn that resulted in the decrepit apartment microwave catching on fire. Katie put out the fire with the smoothies, so the crisis was averted.

The second crisis was when Eli knocked on the door a few moments later because he had smelled the smoke. Katie greeted him nonchalantly with a green face and had the brashness to give him a hard time about carrying a bag of trash to the apartment complex Dumpster.

"Okay, point taken." Katie muttered to herself. It amazed her how many memories she and Eli had made over the past year at school without even trying. She tried to think of what to text back.

Eli beat her to the next topic. DID DAD SHOW YOU THE PHOTOS OF THE MASAI MARA TRIP?

Earlier that day Katie and Eli had banter going on over something that had happened at Eli's uncle's wedding. Katie thought for sure the glitch had occurred at Todd and Christy's wedding. Both weddings had been held on the same meadow on upper campus at Rancho Corona, but they were a year apart.

The end of that string of unnecessary text messages came down to the comment Eli made to cap it off: POINT IS, WESTERN WEDDINGS ARE STRESSFUL. BETTER TO BE OUT ON THE MASAI MARA WITH A FEW CLOSE FRIENDS, A MINISTER FOR AN EXCHANGE OF RINGS AND VOWS. DONE.

She had texted back, WHAT IS IT YOU LOVE SO MUCH ABOUT THE MASAI MARA?

He replied, ASK MY DAD TO SHOW YOU THE PHOTOS.

Katie saw the photos that afternoon on Jim's computer. They were breathtaking and enchanting. A few years ago, Jim and Eli had gone there on a safari. They stayed in a white canvas tent set up on a wooden platform. Inside the large tent were full beds, not just cots, draped with romantic-looking sheer mosquito netting and some luxurious decorator throw pillows. They had a bath house tent that had a claw foot tub and an old-fashioned pedestal sink with towels folded over a bronzed ring towel rack.

Jim had showed her how dinner was served in the evening at sunset with cloth napkins at the tablecloth-covered tables. Directors' chairs were set up around a blazing fire pit, and in the morning, tea and coffee were served in a silver teapot that a server brought to the door of their tent.

During the day the guides drove them around in a fortified Jeep. One photo was of a lion that had come right up to Eli's closed window and placed his mighty paws on the glass pane.

Katie agreed when she saw the photos that it looked like the most amazing, over-the-top sort of safari adventure imaginable. She had no idea such excursions existed. When she saw the final photos of the colorful hot air balloons that rose over the terrain and transported tourists to a bird's-eye view of the wildlife, Katie knew she wanted to go there one day.

When she had asked Jim if he and Eli had ventured up in a hot air balloon, he said, "No. Eli said he wanted to save that for another trip, another time, with ... well, not with me."

Katie was sitting in bed with her phone in her hand when she replied to Eli's texted question and wrote, YES, I SAW YOUR DAD'S PHOTOS. AMAZING!

Eli replied, DID YOU SEE THE TENTS?

YES. ARE THEY NICER THAN WHERE YOU'RE STAYING TONIGHT?

THE STARS ARE MY BLANKET. BTW, I DRAINED DAN'S CAR BATTERY RECHARGING MY PHONE TODAY.

DID AN ANGEL COME TO FIX IT?

NO. USED JUMPER CABLES TO THE DIGGING RIG.

IS THE WELL ALMOST READY?

TOMORROW!

THAT'S GREAT NEWS!

I KNOW. DO YOU WANT AN ENGAGEMENT RING?

Katie stopped short.

She typed WHAT?!?!?! but didn't send the text yet. She scrolled back to reread the stream of conversation to make sure she hadn't missed anything significant. No, she hadn't. Eli had just slipped in that random thought. Although, with the question about the wedding on the Masai Mara that he had tossed in that afternoon, Katie had to admit her thoughts were forming a picture of what it would look like to get married in the wild and for their getaway car to be a hot air balloon.

If Eli was asking what she thought he was asking, then he had arrived at the question-asking stage sooner than Katie thought he would. But then she remembered how he had a head start on their relationship—by a year.

Before Katie could send her reply, Eli sent another text. YOUR SILENCE IS DEAFENING. GUESS WE CAN LEAVE THAT UNANSWERED.

Katie erased the WHAT?!?!? she had typed a few minutes ago and texted back a simple answer: NO.

She waited for Eli's reply. And waited. After twenty minutes she gave up and turned off her light. It was so frustrating not having steady phone service. Or had her reply gotten through just fine, but now he was retracting his thoughts and wishing he hadn't asked the ring question in such an unexpected, random way.

Katie couldn't sleep.

Was he proposing? Preparing to propose? Just making small talk? What? Eli, you're driving me crazy!

Katie couldn't figure out why Eli would throw that line into the conversation. Wasn't the plan for them to sit down and talk things through nice and slow after he returned from the village? Wasn't that how things were done in Kenya—nice and slow?

She picked up her phone and checked it again. Still no message from him.

Letting out an exasperated *grrr!* Katie pulled the blankets up over her head. One growl wasn't good enough, so she let out another.

Somehow she managed to fall asleep and spent the night doing a series of flips and flops. With the morning light she was even more aggravated. She wished she hadn't quickly typed back NO as her answer about wanting an engagement ring. It was a true answer. She didn't want a ring. No diamonds, pearls, emeralds, or rubies. That wasn't her. A wedding band, yes. A rock of any kind, no.

What upset her was that Eli had asked the question in a text. In the middle of a text conversation. He just dropped it in. Such a random question shouldn't have received an immediate answer. She should have made him wait. They really needed to talk through what the future looked like for them. In all their texting, they hadn't once discussed how they were going to figure out how to overlap their interests, or if one of them needed to cancel his or her goals. They needed to come to some sort of reasonable conclusion.

Then, after they had sorted that out, they could talk about their future together. As a couple. Rings and hot air balloons would be open game then. At least that's how Katie had pictured things going. During the two weeks Eli had been gone, her thoughts had been stringently focused on one step following another. Now, apparently Eli was all the way at the end of the path, and Katie hadn't even put on her shoes yet.

She was in such a bungled state of emotions that she pulled out her phone and started the day with a text to Eli that said, PLAY FAIR, OKAY?

His reply came through when she was at breakfast: HUH?

Katie read the message and let out a huff. *Are you playing clueless, or are you really that distracted and disconnected?*

Her text back said, WHEN WILL YOU BE HOME?

His unaffected reply was, SOON.

Katie felt like throwing her phone at the wall. She put it away so she wouldn't be tempted to type about how this was torture and she didn't want to do any more snippet conversations with him. She wanted him here, now, in her life and in her face the way she intended to get in his face about messing with her emotions.

"How are you doing, Katie?"

The question came from Callie, who had taken the seat across from Katie. For the past two weeks, whenever Katie saw Callie, Katie was the one asking her how she was doing. Apparently Katie's countenance communicated that she was under a storm cloud today.

Katie gave a one-word answer, as if she were texting her reply to Callie. "Men!"

Callie smiled. None of her children were with her this morning, which was unusual. Katie thought of how Callie had looked nearly a month ago when she first sat in this dining hall and could neither eat nor drink, as the women of Brockhurst ministered to her and her children.

"I'm guessing your frustration this morning is not with men in general but with one particular man."

"Yes. One particularly particular man."

"How is he doing? Cheryl said he was due back here any day."

"I've heard the same rumors."

"And how are you doing as you wait for those rumors to come true?"

"I'm ... I don't know. I was going to say I'm okay, but to be honest, since that's the way everyone tends to be here at Brockhurst, I'm pretty perturbed with this particularly particular man."

Callie laughed.

"How's your man, by the way?" Katie felt the need to change the topic and shift the focus off herself.

"Evan is doing so much better. Thank you for asking. He's been up and walking the last two days and able to eat quite a bit more. I'm so relieved. I can't tell you what a scare that was."

"I can't imagine how terrifying that must have been."

"Well," Callie leaned closer. Her green eyes looked clear and warm. "Since, as you said, we tend to be honest in our Brockhurst family, I'll tell you the truth about the terror. I learned some things that I would never want to have to learn again this way, but those truths feel like a treasure to me now."

Katie met Callie's gaze with her green eyes and moved her plate aside. "I could use some treasure thoughts this morning."

"I discovered that when God wants to draw us into a place of deeper intimacy in our relationship with him, he undoes everything we previously knew about his ways to show us a different side of himself. When that happens, you end up confused and afraid because you thought you knew God and knew how he worked in your life." Callie smiled softly. "But then you tell the fear to go away."

Katie nodded. She understood that important step to clearing the path on this walk of faith.

"And you lean in closer to the Lord. You listen very closely, and when you don't hear a single word from him, not a sound, you wait. But here's what I learned in all this while we were waiting to hear any news about Evan. You don't wait in silence. During that stretch of time when we didn't know where Evan was, I couldn't sleep, eat, or think. But I could remember. And as I recalled all the things God had done for us in the past, it was like I wasn't alone in the waiting room of my heart any longer. I hung every one of those memories like pictures on the wall, and then I would look at each of them in my mind's eye and say, 'Thank you, God. Thank you.' I started to praise God instead of question him."

Katie said, "I would think that still had to be difficult to do."

"Yes, of course it was. But what happened was that when I started to praise God and to thank him, I broke through the darkness. My heart ended up on the other side of the fear."

Sipping the last of her juice, Katie let Callie's words sink in.

Callie reached across the table and lightly rubbed the top of Katie's arm. "Katie, what are you afraid of?"

"Nothing." The answer popped out so quickly it surprised her. But what surprised Katie the most was that this conversation reminded her of the night before she boarded the plane to fly to Africa. Todd had asked her what she had to lose by going, and she had spouted out the same answer, "Nothing." Now she was afraid that she had everything to lose if she and Eli couldn't reach agreement about what was next for them separately and together.

Katie propped her elbow on the table and rested her head against her open palm. "I don't know, Callie. Maybe I am afraid."

"You're in a waiting room right now with your relationship with Eli. That's okay. Go ahead and cover the walls with memories of pictures of all the things God has done, and then walk through the gallery every day and tell him thank you, thank you. It really is powerful, Katie. It doesn't matter what the obstacles are in front of you two. You keep praising God, and suddenly you'll find that your heart is on the other side of the fear and uncertainty."

Katie nodded, wanting to believe Callie's admonition. "And then what happens after we get to the other side of our big obstacle?"

Callie smiled. "Simple. You follow your heart. And you keep praising God for everything as it comes to you. And I do mean everything. You thank him for the good and the horrible."

Katie drew in a breath and thought about how different this was from the way she wanted to think about her life. She wanted life to be easy and happy and to all fall into place in ways that made sense to her.

It seemed that what she was learning since she had arrived in Kenya was that in the same way that Africa was beautiful and yet untamed and wild, her understanding and growing relationship with almighty God was beautiful and yet just as untamed and wild. Here it seemed that God had turned his neck, and she was seeing another side of him, as Callie had said.

"Tell me," Katie said. "How did you know that Evan was the one for you?"

Callie tilted her head. "I knew Evan was the one for me because I couldn't picture myself doing life with anyone else. He said he couldn't picture himself doing life without me. It was easy to say yes and take the next step."

"What about your position here at Brockhurst? Did you guys have the same goals? Did you have to let go of your dreams to follow him as he pursued his?"

"I don't think it was a matter of having mutual goals or letting go of dreams. We merged our lives and plans and adjusted along the way. I think you've noticed that life here is different than in the States. People don't tend to value their careers or try to hold on to their personal objectives. Everything changes here all the time. What matters is that when God gives you someone like Eli, you say, 'Thank you,

Lord,' and the two of you get on with doing life together. You work things out as you go. Flexibility is the best gift we can give each other. That's how all of us survive and thrive."

To Katie it felt like Callie had filled up this morning conversation at the breakfast table with a whole bath full of great advice, complete with sweet-smelling insights. Katie wanted to just sit in it and soak.

However, she had to hop out of the tub of camaraderie and get herself upstairs, because she was scheduled to work at the Coffee Bar that morning and the next two mornings.

Every one of those mornings, as she made mochas for a lively group of women who were at Brockhurst for an African women's leadership conference, Katie thought about Callie's comment that flexibility was a gift. The more she relaxed about her enthusiastic plans for the fund-raising projects, the more she somehow managed to get done, even though her mornings were now devoted to making coffee.

She also had to be flexible in her texting communications with Eli because he was having phone problems. He sent Katie a text from Dan's phone. Dan was one of the guys on the digging crew, and Eli said in his cryptic way that his phone had died, they had hit some problems with the well, but now they were only a day away from completion. Then he texted, SOON.

That was his last message. Katie hoped it meant he would be back at Brockhurst in a day or two, but no one seemed to know.

Ever since her conversation at breakfast with Callie, Katie had been hanging those memory pictures of what God had done in her life in her mental waiting room. She had fallen in bed at night with whispers of thankfulness on her lips and awaken in the morning with a sweet song of praise echoing in her ears. Somehow, suddenly, just as Callie had described, Katie was on the other side of the obstacles that had seemed so insurmountable with Eli. She was following her heart, and her heart was leading her straight to Eli's arms. The only problem was that she had no idea where Eli's arms—or the rest of him—were at the moment.

The last day of the women's conference, Katie had pulled her hair back in a ponytail and actually found a tube of mascara that she brushed on her lashes. She put on the beads Eli had bought for her at the Rift Valley lookout and kept her phone well charged and at her side all day, hoping Eli would be back today.

His message through Dan's phone the night before had been, ON OUR WAY. Jim said they should arrive before sunset, but there was no guarantee.

She went through her routine, serving in the Coffee Bar, looking toward the door every few minutes, hoping to see that handsome face that had visited her nearly every night in her dreams for two weeks and a day.

One of the women who ordered a white chocolate latte thanked Katie by saying, "May the peace of Christ be on you, sister."

It reminded Katie of the pastor from the Congo who had stood in the same place weeks ago and prayed for Katie when she was awaiting the antibiotics. She remembered how he had said something about her past catching up to her and that she was supposed to remember the peace.

Her past had caught up with her. But her present had overtaken everything that was behind her, including Michael, and now she was fully ready for the future. She did feel at peace.

"Asante sana," Katie said to the woman. "May the peace of Christ be upon you too."

Each time the door opened she looked up, hoping to see the head of windblown brown hair that she missed so much.

She got the feeling that everyone who stopped by kept looking at her with knowing crinkle lines around their eyes. It was as if they knew her little secret. She was in love. Katie was sure it had to be obvious to everyone. It certainly was obvious to her.

All afternoon she sat in the office only half concentrating on the computer screen. Her head turned to look out the open window every time she heard anything that resembled footsteps. By midafternoon her neck was sore from her self-induced whiplash, so she kept her face toward the valentine wall and her eyes on her laptop.

At 4:17 her phone gave a friendly buzz. She grabbed it and eagerly read the text from Eli. The message was from his phone. He must have gone to Nairobi for a new battery. The text read: GREAT NEWS. DAN WANTS TO WORK WITH US FULL-TIME.

Katie's heart sank. No communication in several days, and this was his big news? Not an update on when he would be back or any further communication on the personal topics they had texted about earlier in the week. All he thought to tell Katie was that Dan wanted to work with them. Great.

She texted back, AND WHEN MIGHT I HAVE THE JOY OF SEEING YOU AGAIN?

SOON.

Katie was beginning to hate that answer from Eli.

He texted again. SO NO RING, HUH?

Now Katie was even more surprised. She was the only one in the office at the moment and was glad Eli's mom and dad weren't there to see the exaggerated faces she was giving her phone in response to Eli's texts.

NO, she typed. Then she slapped her phone down and muttered, "I refuse to have this conversation with you in text messages, Eli Lorenzo."

"How about if we talk about it face-to-face then?"

Katie turned around slowly and blinked before she dared to believe her eyes. There he was, in the doorway, filling the frame, as he leaned casually against the side with a sly grin on his face and his phone in his hand.

"Eli!" Katie jumped up and nearly tripped on her way to give him a hug.

"I need a shower," he warned her.

"I don't care." Katie gave him a hug, but then suddenly she did care. She pulled back and said, "I'll catch you on the flip side of that shower. How's that?"

"Good." Eli grinned and took her hand in his. "You look gorgeous, Katie."

"And you look ..." She tried to choose the right words. His adorable, carefree hair had been cut short. It looked uneven, as if he had done it himself with a sharpened stone while he was in the village. The other big difference was that his goatee was back. She went with that rather than the hair when she finished her comment. "You look like the Goatee Guy I've missed like crazy."

"So I'm back to being Goatee Guy, huh?"

Katie reached up and gave his scruffy face a rub with the back of her knuckles.

"Did you want to finish that conversation now? About the ring?" Eli asked.

Katie gave him a hesitant look. "You're not going propose to me right now, are you?"

Eli laughed. "No, I'm not."

"Well, you were so random in your text. One minute we're talking about jumper cables and phone batteries, and then you throw in a rather significant question. How am I supposed to know what you're going to say next?"

Eli pulled Katie over to one of the desk chairs and lowered her into the seat as if she were a delicate princess. He pulled up the other desk chair so that it was facing her, and he leaned back in his very dirty clothes and looked relaxed. Apparently the shower had been downgraded on Eli's agenda.

"Dan is going to work with us full-time."

"So you said. In your text. Cool." Katie knew her sarcasm was obvious, but she didn't care. She kept going. "What other fascinating updates would you like to talk about?"

"I'd like to talk about us. I'd like to talk about this obstacle that seemed to be overwhelming when you and I went opposite directions two weeks ago. And I'd like to talk about what's next."

"Perfect. I have some breakthrough thoughts on that very topic after having several exceptional conversations during your absence."

"So have I," Eli said. "You first."

"Okay, here's what I think. We work it out as we go along. I'm excited to develop the fund-raising project, but that doesn't mean this is my career for the next fifty years. Flexibility is the best gift we can give each other. If we're going to go far, we know we have to go together. The together part of us is at the heart level. So even if we're not in the same place every single day, we're still together."

His confident grin was so strong, so assuring. "That's the same conclusion I came to. Then Dan decided to come on board."

"What is it with this guy, Dan, and his decision to work here?"

"He wants to do the same thing I want to do. We found that we functioned well as a team in the village, and that means we can tag-team our efforts."

"So you wouldn't have to be gone for months at a time."

"Exactly. It's not an either-or decision for you and me anymore. It's a both-and situation. We can both do what we feel called to do, and we can go far together." He paused and set his gaze on her.

Katie blinked, realizing that they really were on the other side of what she had pictured to be such a huge obstacle. Their small steps of faith had led them into a wide, open place brimming with possibilities.

When Eli didn't say anything, Katie said, "Okay."

Eli said, "Okay." He stood and headed toward the door.

As a brash afterthought, Katie threw out one more line. "So you're not going to stick around and propose to me now that we have that all figured out?"

Eli kept heading for the door. He stopped right before exiting. "I'm not in a hurry, are you?"

Katie felt a dip in her spirit at his response. It wasn't as if she expected him to get on his knee or anything. Waiting was realistic. It fit with Eli's way of being on African time. It made sense. She shrugged. "No, I can wait."

"Good." He left and then turned around, came back, and stood in the doorway. "I forgot to tell you. You know the meteor shower we saw in the desert last year?"

"Yes."

"We should be able to see another one tonight. I thought I'd go up to the knoll above the tea fields to watch the show. Do you want to go with me?"

"Of course. Will you have crocodile meatballs for us to enjoy this time as we watch the sky?"

"Nope. I'll see if I can manage to get us some banana pudding though. How's that?"

"Lovely."

"Good. I'll meet you in the dining hall later. I thought I'd better take that shower."

"Excellent idea."

Katie tried to go back to work after he left, but she couldn't. She kept going over their conversation. Their relationship seemed to fall in place as if the pieces had been cut to fit together. Could it be this easy? This calm?

At dinner Katie was aware once again that everyone was looking at her. No one said anything, but they all seemed to be hiding smiles and winks, as if they were in on a secret. She wished Eli were there to eat dinner with her since that's what they all seemed to want to see. Eli didn't show up for dinner. She didn't see Jim or Cheryl either. None of that concerned her. It was just that she felt all eyes were on her.

After clearing her dishes and helping to wipe down the tables, Katie looked up and saw Eli enter the dining hall. He was freshly scrubbed and combed and looking a whole lot better than when he had come by the office.

He walked over to her with his easy gait and slid his arm around her waist, giving her a hug.

"You sure cleaned up nice."

"Took me a while. Are you ready to go see some lights?"

"What about dinner? Are you hungry?"

"No, I'm fine." He took her hand, and on the way out of the dining hall, Eli picked up a hanging lantern to light their path.

The evening sky still held tinges of apricot and bronze as they hiked together holding hands. Eli talked almost the whole way about his time in the village and how he saw things lining up for the next few months. He asked Katie about her trip to Lake Naivasha, and she gave a full report on her tour guide skills. She also went through her list of Swahili words and admitted that she hadn't managed to learn a full phrase yet.

"I have one you can learn," Eli said. *"Japo kidogo chatosha kwa wapendanao."*

"Too long. I'm still at the wapi choo level."

"This is a good one, though," Eli said. "It means 'a little is enough for those in love.' "

"Oh, that is a good one."

Katie was about to say, "So, what do you think? Is that true for us? Are we in love?" But then she knew she didn't need to ask. It was evident in her heart, in his touch, and in their words.

Above them a full moon made a leisurely appearance over the tea fields, touching the elegantly curled leaves and leaving them stained with shimmers of buttery light. As Katie and Eli ascended to the lookout knoll, Katie stared down on the tea fields, soaking up their beauty by moonlight.

"Katie?"

"Yes?"

"Look. Over here on this side."

She turned and looked down on the Brockhurst side of the valley and drew in a gasp. Spread out across the lawn were hundreds of amber lights flickering like fireflies. "It's so beautiful! What is it? Is everyone having a party we weren't invited to?"

"Not exactly," Eli said.

"It looks like letters, doesn't it?" She tried to make out the shapes, certain that it spelled a word in Swahili. "K-W-Y-M-M. What is that? Ka-why-mm? What does it mean?"

"It's not Swahili. But it does mean something."

Katie looked at Eli. "You know what this is?"

"Yes."

"So tell me."

"Figure it out."

Katie tried to remember if anyone she knew was having a birthday or if this was some local custom she had heard about but not yet observed. Nothing was coming to her. The dozens of individual lights continued to flicker in their KWYMM formation. It didn't make sense to her.

"I give up."

"You can't give up," Eli said. "That's not an option."

"Then at least give me a clue. Remember how nice I was to you last year when you were trying to figure things out in California? I gave you helpful clues about cultural customs. So give me a hint or something."

"All right. Here. This is about as obvious a clue as I can give you." In the light of the moon and the glowing lantern, Eli's expression appeared timid and yet resolved. Taking her hand in his, he went down on one knee and looked up at her with a contented grin.

The reality of what was happening rushed at Katie like a wild African breeze. The letters in the valley below spelled out a golden message, and the message was for her. Each letter went into her heart like a javelin.

K = Katie
W = Will
Y = You
M = Marry
M = Me

The spinning earth seemed momentarily to pause for Katie, and she was sure the stars above were leaning closer to see what would happen next.

"Well?" Eli asked patiently from his kneeling position.

Katie caught her breath. "I thought you said this afternoon that you weren't in a hurry."

"What was I supposed to say? You kept asking me if I was going to propose. I had to throw you off track. So? I'm asking now. Are you going to make me ask you again?"

Katie pulled herself together and let what was happening sink in. Eli wasn't messing around. He really was proposing to her. Everyone at Brockhurst was in on the secret. In the same way that a single candle had glowed in the window of his parents' cottage on the night of Eli and Katie's arrival, now hundreds of candles held by staff and guests flickered for them in the valley below, welcoming them into the rest of their lives.

"Okay. Sorry. All right. I'm ready now. Go ahead." Katie adjusted her position and looked into his eyes. "Ask me again."

"Katie?"

"Yes?"

"Will you marry me?"

Drawing in a deep breath that was overflowing with a sure and certain peace, Katie answered, "Yes." Then, as the peace bubbled up into joy, Katie hollered at the top of her lungs. "Yes, yes, yes!"

Eli rose to his feet and wrapped his arms around her, pulling her close and whispering in her ear, "I love you, Katie."

She closed her eyes and let Eli's beautiful, life-giving words melt into her soul. "I know. I know you do. And I love you, Eli. I love you so much."

He pulled back and looked at her. In the glow of the lantern, she could see tears glistening in his eyes.

"And you're sure?" he asked.

"Yes, very sure. As sure as I've ever been about anything. I will marry you, Elisha James Lorenzo, and I will live with you and visit villages with you and have babies with you, and I will cook ugali for you and cut your hair and—"

"Cut my hair?"

"Yeah, I was going to tell you that whoever cut it for you in the village really butchered it. I think you should let me cut it next time. I'll do a much better job."

"Okay, I can agree to that. Any other negotiating points before we settle the deal?"

"I was thinking about our kids the other day. I'd like at least two. Maybe four. No more than four though. We never talked about that. I don't want only one child, if we can help it. I mean, I know it's ultimately up to God."

"Agreed. Anything else to haggle over?"

"Nope. I'm good. Oh, wait. I don't want to live with your parents. I mean, I love them and everything, but . . ."

"Already worked that one out. As a matter of fact, I'm moving into Upper Nine this week."

Katie raised her eyebrows. "Really? What else did you work out?"

"This." Eli reached into his backpack and pulled out a flare gun. He pointed it toward the canopy of celestial observers and shot the single burst of flaming light into the night sky.

In the distance, like a faint rumble, Katie thought she heard a cheer. "Is that from everybody at Brockhurst? Your candle crew?"

"Yup. They're cheering for us. I told them I'd send up a flare if you said yes."

"*If* I said yes? Did you have any doubt?"

"No."

"But what if I did say no? Then what would you have done?"

"I had another signal ready for them to release the wild monkeys."

Katie laughed, her chin up, her hand tucked into Eli's rugged grip. When she looked at him, Eli was staring at her. His intense gaze no longer unnerved her.

Katie met his deep stare with an equally focused look from an unveiled heart. A slow grin rose on his face.

"You're going to kiss me now, aren't you?" Katie asked.

"Yes, I am."

She leaned closer, murmuring under her breath, "Finally."

Their lips met, and for one exceptional, lingering moment they expressed to each other their fervent affection and reverent hope for what was yet to come.

Drawing back slowly, Eli spoke a benediction over them as the African stars leaned low, the ancient moon sighed, and the meteor shower sent off its fireworks. It was the word Katie had long waited to hear, and as Eli spoke it, she knew then that their hearts were knit together.

"Forever."

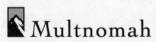

Talk It Up!

Want free books?
First looks at the best new fiction?
Awesome exclusive merchandise?

We want to hear from you!

Give us your opinions on titles, covers, and stories.
Join the Z Street Team.

Visit zstreetteam.zondervan.com/joinnow
to sign up today!

Also—Friend us on Facebook!

www.facebook.com/goodteenreads

- Video Trailers
- Connect with your favorite authors
- Sneak peeks at new releases
- Giveaways
- Fun discussions
- And much more!

ZONDERVAN®
.com